LIVE AND LET WITCH

E.B. LOROW

Live and Let Witch

E.B. Lorow

This book is a work of fiction. Names, characters, places, and incidents are either products of the author's imagination or are used fictitiously. Any resemblance to actual events, locales, or persons is entirely coincidental.

Cover design by C. K. Gregory

Foreground photography by Motortion

Background photography by Caitlin Jones

Published by Imagination Unlimited

Edited by Cedar Trees Publishers

Contact info, http://eblorow.com/contact

Newsletter sign-up, https://landing.mailerlite.com/webforms/landing/k4k4w4

ACKNOWLEDGMENTS

I owe big thank you hugs to my editor Ana E. Ross. She's a NY Times bestseller, herself, and she did a fantastic job helping me polish this story. As a women of color, she was able to act as my sensitivity readers in addition to being a grammar nerd.

And just in case I didn't get the biracial part right, I consulted Ana's daughter, Nikoya Borelia. She gave me a lesson in how to care for black and brown curly hair. Who knew there were so many steps and it was so much more complicated!

I'd also like to thank my husband for noticing my laptops battery was bulging *before* it decided to explode. I lost a couple days while waiting for a replacement, but we were having a hurricane, so the power was out anyway. See how I always find the silver lining in things?

DEDICATION

About a year ago, my husband and I were coming out of a movie and decided to stop at the restrooms before we left the theatre. As I exited the stall I heard a loud commotion by the ladies' room door. A woman was screaming the foulest obscenities at her daughter for telling her to 'shut up.'

The mom was out of control. She kept yelling, "You're fourteen. You don't get to tell me to shut-up! You are a &%^()_)_ ^%##^&( )^%... I don't want to repeat the terrible things she said, and in public! Can you imagine? The girl's self-esteem was shattered.

A few brave women by the door managed to separate them, taking the mother out to the lobby while the girl stayed inside the relative safety of a bathroom with strangers. Collapsed against the wall, she looked as if she wished it would open up and swallow her.

It was none of my business, but I couldn't leave her like that. I engulfed her in a protective hug and said nothing for quite a while. I just let her cry and hug me back.

Nobody deserves that. This girl looked like a sweet young lady and if the worst thing she'd ever done was to tell her loudmouth mom to shut-up, well... I give her credit!

I truly wish there were some kind of formal parental training, which might prevent this kind of heartache from happening.

When I eventually let go of this poor girl, I searched my heart for something to say. Something helpful. I had nothing. All I did was say, "Only four years. You only have to endure for four years, then you can get out and do what you want." Probably horrible advice.

Anyway, this book is dedicated to that girl. I wish I could tell you I got her name, or slipped her my business card and I know she's doing well, but I didn't. Every now and then I think of her and picture her standing up straight and proud in a bubble of white, healing light.

If any kid who reads this can identify with her or Jenika, the heroine of this book, just know that nothing lasts forever. Stay as safe as you can. Protect your self-esteem by blocking negative messages from those who are gifted with your care, but who fail you. They're wrong about you. You're a worthwhile human being who deserves to be treated respectfully.

Act with integrity despite having a poor role model. Then be proud not only of who you are, but what you managed to overcome. Positive, happy lives are possible, and you deserve one.

CHAPTER 1

"WHAT DO YOU WANT?"

"I want what every kid here wants. I want my freedom and I want my powers back!"

"Well, that's not going to happen. What else do you want?"

I let out a deep sigh. "I guess I'll have a chocolate pudding."

The cafeteria woman retreated to the back of the kitchen and returned with a tiny plastic container of the requested pudding. *'Please sir, I want some more...'* The famous line from Oliver Twist ran through my mind as I took the tiny dessert.

"Here you go Jenniker."

My name is Jenika. Jen-EE-ka. For some damn reason, people insist on mispronouncing it to sound like Jennifer with a K and a Boston accent. As a result, I wound up accidentally giving myself a nickname. "It's just Jen."

"Okay, Just Jen."

Oh, yeah. That never gets old.

"Some prize," I muttered as I dropped the pudding cup on my tray. I probably wouldn't be recommended for 'student of the month' again. Not that my stepfather would proudly display a bumper sticker on his car that says: *My juvenile delinquent was named inmate of the month at the Haven School for Wayward Witches!*

Yes, they have the nerve to call us students here. We're inmates. Incarcerated in a juvenile detention center for magicals. That's what they call witches. It's as if someone said, "Let's get rid of all the negative connotations, so they don't know they're in witch kid jail. And while we're at it, let's have a real good laugh and call it Haven."

I dropped my tray with a clang on one of the tables. A long metal picnic-size table bolted to the floor with two cold benches attached on either side. Everything here is either nailed down, too heavy, or too awkward to lift. Goddess forbid some understandable frustration results in impulsive acting out and injury since we're unable to use our powers—even to protect ourselves.

I hadn't quite sat down when fellow inmate Francine, also known as Alien, ran up to me and grabbed my hand.

"Come with me," she hissed.

"What?"

"Come on! I have to show you something."

Normally I'd be a little scared if any of these kids zeroed in on me and tried to drag me off, but I could probably take the willowy blonde in a one-on-one fight. She was some kind of pampered princess from Connecticut, and I was from the mean streets of Detroit. 'Nuff said.

I groaned when I thought about what kind of spit might wind up in my lunch if I left it untouched. "Can I eat first?"

"No. The surprise might disappear, and trust me, you don't want to miss this!"

"Damn," I muttered, grabbing my roll, which was the only thing I could eat without a spork—the combo plastic spoon and fork with tines, too short to stab any vital organs.

I let her drag me out of the cafeteria and down the white, cinder-block corridor to the front entrance of the building. "Look!" she said, when we reached the glass paneled door.

I peered through the wire reinforced double paned glass. *What the...*A huge stone vat stood across the curved gravel driveway, topped with a naked boy made of green copper, peeing a stream of water. The water ran over a scalloped edge pan, down the rocks, and pooled into the bottom receptacle. "Is that a fountain?"

"Yes. And it wasn't there yesterday, was it?"

"Not that I remember."

"Do you know what that means?"

"Not really. No."

"Somebody in here still has their magic! We know the staff would never put that there. Right?"

"Yeah, I doubt it. Goddess forbid we drown ourselves."

"More like drowning our sorrows!" She almost jumped up and down. Then she glanced around and when she was sure we were alone, she whispered, "It's filled with vodka!"

I was momentarily speechless with so many questions vying to come out of my mouth at once. "How the heck did that happen? And how do you know it's vodka?"

"I tasted it." She glanced behind her at the corridor and waited a moment to be sure no one was coming. Opening the door, which was usually locked, she whispered "Come on!"

The gravel crunched as we tried to quietly make our way across the driveway to the fountain. I was sure we were going to get in trouble, but for what? Investigating a strange fountain? And what could they do? Take away my pudding? Big whoop.

Francine was already leaning over the rock wall, slurping up the contents. For a moment I wondered if I was being punked—set-up to be the butt of some joke.

But with no one around to witness the humiliation, it wouldn't be a very well-thought-out prank.

I leaned over and took a sniff. Anyone who thinks drinking vodka won't give them away because it doesn't have a smell is delusional. Every weekend, half my old neighborhood smelled like vodka. The other half smelled like pot.

But just to be sure… I leaned over and touched my tongue to the liquid. Nothing terrible happened. I don't know what I expected. It's not like my tongue had the power to ignite a fountain of vodka and spread flames everywhere—although, I accidentally shot lightning out of my hands once, and that's how I ended up in Haven. But like I said, we don't have our powers in here. The first thing they do to us when we arrive, is suppress the powers we had.

The liquid tasted like 'escape from strict rules with a side of naughtiness'. Just like Francine, I began taking bigger and bigger gulps and swallowing the straight alcohol, even though it tasted gross.

"Nice view," someone said from behind us.

We both whipped around to see a boy about our age, bending to one side, as if admiring our ass-etts.

"Who are you?" Francine demanded.

"My name is Patrick. Do you like my gift?" He pointed to the fountain.

"You put this here?" I asked, relieved that it wasn't

some kind of test created by our teachers. If so, we would have failed miserably.

"Uh huh. It looks like I'll be joining the general population tomorrow, and I thought I'd make a few friends before I got here."

"What makes you think you can buy our friendship?" Francine asked, almost angrily.

I put my hand on her arm and muttered, "Down, Alien. He's just looking for allies. Can't say I blame him."

I called her Alien, because she made the mistake of telling some inmates that she alienated people. I just used her old nickname to remind her of that fact.

I straightened up and faced him. "So, you put this here now, knowing they're going to suppress your powers tomorrow?"

"Yeah. I was told a little bit about this place. My cousin was here for a while. I guess they only give your powers back when you demonstrate you can handle them. But how do they know you can use them responsibly, if you have no powers?"

I laughed. "That's what our classes are for. We only get our powers back one at a time, and only for a few minutes. If you don't use spells correctly to accomplish whatever assignment you're given, you might not get another chance for weeks. It's a good thing you got this out of your system now."

"Great," he said, sarcastically. "Well, after you've

drunk your fill, or filled up and gotten drunk, tell your fellow inmates about my gift. You might as well have a little fun before I get here. After that, we'll find more creative ways to have fun." He raised his eyebrows a couple times.

"Ugh. I threw up in my mouth a little bit."

"I wouldn't count on that, Patrick," Francine gurgled.

Then he disappeared. Which was weird, because this place was warded up the wazoo against intruders.

"How do you think he got in?" I asked Francine.

"I don't know. Maybe because he's already been sentenced, he technically belongs here?"

"I guess that makes as much sense as anything else. So, should we pass the word, like he said to?"

"In a minute." She whirled back around and practically stuck her whole face into the fountain, gulping down enough Vodka to get a grown man hammered. She was tall and might weigh 110 pounds, soaking wet —which she was now. I was shorter, but weighed about the same.

"Careful. You're going to feel that tomorrow," I warned.

She pulled her mouth out of the liquid just long enough to say, "Yeah, or I could die tomorrow. Meanwhile, I'll be feeling no pain today."

I didn't quite know what to do. We'd be in trouble the minute one of our teachers smelled us. I might still be able to get away with it, if I changed my shirt and brushed my teeth quickly.

"Okay, I'm going in. I'll try to send out a couple of the boys, since he wants friends."

Francine gave me a thumbs-up, without even lifting her head.

⁕⸺⁕

Just as I was hurrying down the corridor to my basic cell, which they call a room simply because it has walls and a door, a teacher caught my eye.

"Oh, Jenika! Jenika Jones? Come here, please."

Oh crap. I didn't know if she could smell me from this distance, or if she had something else to talk to me about. Either way, it was too late to pretend I didn't hear her. I stopped where I was, leaving about twenty feet between us. "I was about to go to my room for a minute. Do you need to talk to me right now?"

She smiled. Not something most teachers do a lot around here. "It's important."

I sighed. I didn't have much choice, but to obey. I walked over to her slowly, keeping as much distance as I could between us as I tried to figure out which way the breeze was blowing from the air conditioning vents so I could stand downwind.

"It's all right, Jenika. I'm not going to hurt you."

"I, um... I didn't think you would."

"Why don't we go to my office? We can talk more privately there."

She still had that smile on her face. Was it creepy or nice? Who could tell in here? Some teachers were a little bit of both.

I followed her to a door with a shiny new nameplate screwed into it. It said Ms. Broome. That's weird. A witch named Broome. Well, that's not as weird as some names I'd heard. Any football team's jerseys can supply an impressive amount of names explaining why those guys had to become so tough.

She opened her door, magically, I'm sure. No key was involved and yet she wouldn't have left it unlocked. Other teachers had keys that were concealed somewhere, or they just used magic.

"Come in, and sit down." She gestured to one of the two turquoise, upholstered chrome chairs on the other side of her chrome and glass desk. By the look of her empty desk, it didn't seem like she had a lot of work going on at the moment.

"I've been assigned to you, and I was hoping we could get to know each other."

"Assigned? One-on-one? I didn't know we had teachers assigned to us for anything. Don't we have guidance counselors and social workers already?"

"Some of the social workers and guidance counselors could use an extra hand. I volunteered to take on a few kids."

"You're new here, aren't you?"

"Yes, I am. I just got here last week."

I smirked. "I knew it the minute you said you volunteered. You won't volunteer much after this."

She leaned back and crossed her arms. "Oh, no? Why do you say that? Are you going to give me a hard time?"

I sat up straight. "Oh, no. No. That's not what I meant. Believe me, I'm trying to be as trouble-free as I can. I mean, I'm not a troublemaker. I mean, I don't want any trouble, and I won't cause any, either."

She must have understood because the smile slowly faded and she leaned forward, clasping her hands on the top of her desk. "I understand that you're one of the easier students here. However, easy isn't always a good thing. There are concerns."

"Concerns? How could you possibly have concerns, if I'm behaving appropriately?" *Ninety-nine percent of the time.* "I have nobody interfering from the outside. No visitors to screen. No packages to search. I get no letters to be redacted. I keep my room clean and free of contraband... What are you talking about?"

She let out a low breath and said, "Exactly that. You have no outside contacts. We tried to get in touch with your stepfather, but he never responded. I understand your mother was killed a few years ago..."

"Yes. She was in the wrong place at the wrong time."

"That's all you have to say about it?"

"It's not like anyone murdered her on purpose. It was just a drive-by."

"*Just* a drive-by?"

I knew I had kind of stepped in it. She was staring at me without the expected pity—or any other expression on her face. But I'm an empath, and I can read people's faces better than anyone I know—even without my powers. Right now, she's trying *not to* show her emotion and if she did, it would be pure pity.

"Okay. So, it wasn't *just* a drive-by. It was a really horrific incident. It changed my life forever. I'm not making light of it. I've just learned to live with it."

She waited a few beats and then nodded. "I understand that, and I commend you on making a difficult adjustment, but there's been more, hasn't there?"

I sighed deeply. "Yes. What else would you like to know about?"

She leaned back in her chair and opened her hands. Even though I didn't have my magical abilities to confirm I was reading her right, I knew body language. She was open to my side of the story.

"Why don't you tell me whatever might still be affecting you."

I was confused again. "I don't know what you mean. I really don't. What's affecting me here? I'd say not a whole heck of a lot. This place is pretty tame compared to my old high school."

A tiny ghost of a smile appeared again. "That could

be what's affecting you here. Not necessarily in a bad way. Relief is an effect. You seem fairly comfortable here. Maybe too comfortable. Are you more comfortable here than you were in your old high school?"

I had to think about that for a minute. Here I was ensconced with magicals, like myself, but none of us had our powers. Here we were just commonplace thieves, vandals or more nefarious problem children.

I was here because I'd electrocuted someone. That's terrible. But it hadn't been intentional. The guy had come up behind me and covered my eyes. Before he'd had the chance to say, "Guess who?" I'd whirled around and defended myself from a perceived attacker. I hadn't even known I had the power to shoot 220 volts out of my fingers. It had been a knee-jerk reaction, and I'd already been on edge. I truly wish I had just thrusted my knee into his groin.

I shrugged. "It's really about the same."

"Except for the school shooting, I imagine."

I sighed again. "Yeah. There was that."

A long pregnant pause followed. Finally, she said, "I understand if you're reluctant to go through it all again. I know a little bit about you, but I'd like to hear the story from you."

I groaned. "Do I have to?"

She shook her head. "No. You don't have to tell me anything, but it would help both of us. I'll be checking in with you periodically. I can ask you about the same things over and over again, hoping you'll open up to me in time, if you would rather do it that way."

It was all I could do not to groan again. I really, *really* didn't want to go through the whole story again. I had talked to police officers, detectives, guidance counselors… Maybe I could think of some way to abbreviate the trauma and give it to her in one quick summary. Stupidly I said the first thing that came to mind. "I think I have PTSD."

Her smile lit up her whole face. I thought that by diagnosing myself we could move on. Her body language said we were just getting started. *Damn.*

"I have to get to class. Can we talk later?"

"Yes, but we need to address your past as soon as possible. You're scheduled to leave here in a month. I want you to have the best chance at succeeding out there."

"Uh huh. I really have to go now."

She rose, strolled to the door, and opened it for me. As I walked past her, she said, "I don't think changing your clothes and brushing your teeth will help. I can smell vodka all over you."

I clamped my lips shut as I exited her office, waved goodbye, and ran to my room.

In class, Francine was so drunk, she was practically falling out of her chair. She giggled at nothing, and I had to turn around to shush her.

She slapped a limp hand over her mouth, as if telling herself to shut-up. Yeah, she wasn't drawing attention to herself at all... *Idiot.*

I don't know whether it was the conversation with Ms. Broome, or the fact that I'd consumed a lesser amount of alcohol, but I was a lot more sober than Francine. I kind of wish I had escaped reality like she had, but what good would that do me? Ms. Broome had nailed it. Reality here wasn't nearly as bad as the reality I came from. My stepfather had threatened to give me up to a foster home that already had six other kids, all assholes. He hates me.

I think I was still reeling from the small bit of insight Ms. Broome had brought out in me. Unfortunately, my partner in crime was putting her head down on her desk, snickering. She poked me in my back and whispered loudly, "Aren't you feeling anything? I feel high as a kite. Was there more than vodka in that fountain?"

I whispered, over my shoulder, trying to be a lot quieter than she was, "Will you shut up? It doesn't take much to set off these teachers' psychic alarms. I don't think this is the teacher to test. She's a hard-ass."

"Yeah, she really has a broomstick up her butt."

As if conjuring her, our buttoned-up teacher strode

into the room and placed a book she had been holding on her desk. She gazed out at the dozen faces in our class and zeroed in on Alien and me. Alien is what I'm calling her now, because this side of Francine is certainly alien to the stuck-up, rich bitch routine she's usually known for. She acts superior, as if I'm lucky to be her so-called friend.

I don't have any friends here at the moment, but I used to. Genevieve Howe was my only real friend and she finished her sentence early. I miss her. I didn't have many friends where I came from either. Those of us who didn't want to go home after school hung out in groups, but it was for self-preservation, not because we actually liked each other. Usually, we hung out in parks and made up rap lyrics to pass the time. I know. Shocking to think that kids from Motown might be into music.

Back home when I had my powers, I could control certain things, but I had to be sure nobody knew I was a witch, or they'd be taking advantage of me, every chance they got. 'Do my homework with a snap of your fingers,' or 'Conjure some blow for me, will ya?' Whatever I could *humanly* do was all the power I pretended to have. Here, without my powers, I might as well be an actual fuggle. That's what inmates call non-magicals.

Our teacher, Mrs. Stick-up-her-butt... (Okay, that's not her real name, but looking at her ramrod-straight posture, that's the only name I could come up with).

Her real name was Mrs. Stickton. Anyway, Mrs. Stickton folded her arms and slowly made her way down our aisle, stopping in front of Francine and me. She looked back and forth between us, until her gaze landed squarely on Alien. "Miss Costa."

Francine looked up at her and drew out the word, "Yeeesss?"

Mrs. Stickton strolled around the desks, which were, of course, bolted to the floor. We couldn't toss them into her way to slow her down as we ran—and where would we go?

Then Francine started giggling again, and just had to poke me, as if I should be giggling too. *"For God sakes, Alien, shut the hell up, and leave me out of this."* I tried to telepathically communicate the words, but she obviously wasn't reading me. I didn't expect her to, but I was willing to try anything at this point.

Mrs. Stickton stepped back a foot and pointed to a spot on the floor right in front of her. "Francine, stand up."

Francine may have finally realized that she was in trouble. She let out a great sigh, and then heaved herself out of the chair to wobble on the spot indicated.

While Francine swayed back and forth. Mrs. Stickton just stared at her. I was holding my breath even though I had just brushed my teeth. I didn't reek of alcohol the way Francine did, but I was a little worried about guilt by association.

"Miss Jones?"

I folded my hands on the top of my desk, and with as little emotion as possible, answered, "Yes, ma'am?"

"I would like you and Francine to stand in front of the class and do a role-play exercise for me. For *us.*" She swept her hand in an arc to indicate the whole class.

Oh dear Goddess in Avalon. What is she going to have us do? And is there any way we can do it without royally screwing up? I doubted it.

Francine tried to straighten up and cleared her throat. "I don't think that's a good idea, Ms. Stickton."

"And why is that?" she asked, all syrupy sweet.

"Well, you see.… I'm not feeling too well. I might barf."

The rest of the class broke out in snickers and giggles.

Mrs. Stickton turned on her heel and marched to the front of the room, then she waved us down in front of her desk. "I'm sure you can handle a simple exercise with your magical powers restored, temporarily."

Oh, dear. I wasn't sure of that, at all, unless Francine's first spell was a *sober up spell,* which I doubted she would even do. She was enjoying her high too much.

Francine swerved her way down the aisle to the teacher's desk and turned around. She snapped at me, impatiently, "Aren't you coming?"

I let out a deep sigh of resignation and followed her down to the front of the room.

Mrs. Stickton said, "I'm going to lift the suppression of your powers for one minute. In that time, I want you to pick up something in the room—something small, and make it levitate to the other person until they can grasp it."

Francine let out a snort. "Easy. I'll go first," she said.

Mrs. Stickton placed her palms up on either side of Francine's shoulders and lifted her hands toward the ceiling, removing the suppression of Francine's powers and said, "All right. Go ahead."

Francine magically lifted the book from the desk where Mrs. Stickton had placed it a few moments before. She didn't exactly bobble the ancient-looking tome, but instead of sending it to me, she brought it to herself. She opened the book and apparently was going to read from it, but then got this evil look on her face. I guess she thought she would have a little more fun and suddenly the book shrank into a small paperback, and turned into a racy romance novel.

"Her chest heaved as she bit back an angry retort," Alien narrated loudly. "How could this gentleman be so infuriating? He was a Duke, after all, and he was supposed to be her guardian! How could she be so attracted to his ice blue eyes and strong jaw-line?"

The class burst out laughing, and Francine did too.

Mrs. Stickton's face turned bright red, but Francine

couldn't see that because she was looking away, laughing with the rest of the class.

Mrs. Stick-up-her-butt quickly turned her hands over and forced them down much faster than teachers usually do when they shut down our powers, which caused Francine to drop the book. On its way down, it turned back into the ancient manuscript, spilling pages all over the floor.

Mrs. Stickton gasped. I took a step back.

Francine was in soooo much trouble, but apparently, she didn't realize it quite yet because she was still giggling. I grabbed her arm as she was bending over to pick up the pages. "Don't touch anything," I ground out between clenched teeth. "Let me do it."

I bent over and gently picked up the pages, keeping them as close to their proper order as the scattered papers would allow. There were a few so far separated from the rest it was impossible to tell where they should go. Mrs. Stickton stood ramrod straight, waiting for me to hand her the book and missing pages. Then she waved her hand and the loose pages sorted themselves. She gently placed the tome back on her desk. I imagined she would have to repair it later.

"Miss Jones, Miss Costa, you are both to report to Mrs. Whitehall's office, immediately. I will summon a guard to escort you."

At last, Francine realized how much trouble we

were in and groaned aloud. "Nooo. We were just having a little fun. We'll be good. Won't we Jenika?"

"Leave me out of this."

Mrs. Stickton folded her arms. "I think it's too late to be left out of anything, Miss Jones. I'll let Mrs. Whitehall sort out what happened to your right minds, and what to do with both of you. I have a class to teach."

She made a hand gesture like she was brushing us out of her way, and a wind blew up behind our backs, gently pushing us toward the door. A guard waited for us in the hall, and that was that. We were marched down to the principal, or if you prefer the more accurate description, the warden.

CHAPTER 2

Just outside Mrs. Whitehall's office, Francine and I sat on chairs that looked like they came in a box from Sweden. Some kids call our administrator Mrs. Blackhole, because that's where our grievances would go—into a big black hole. Her office was tucked away behind the secretaries' area, which probably looked like every other school office in the country.

Our row of six chairs, bolted together, lined up across from the secretary's counter, presumably for people to wait for their turn at the guillotine. Okay, I'm being overly dramatic. As far as I know there has never been a beheading here. Let's hope Francine's and mine won't be the first and second.

Mrs. Whitehall opened her office door and standing right behind her was Ms. Broome. Oh, no. I wonder what they were talking about. My paranoia said it was me. Or is it paranoia when you're probably right?

Ms. Broome gave me a sad smile that conveyed, *I'm sorry you got caught, but karma's a bitch.* Or something like that. Without my empathic powers, it's difficult to narrate someone else's inner monologue.

She shook hands with Mrs. Whitehall and left quickly without even acknowledging me. Mrs. Whitehall strode to the secretary and whispered something to the woman. The secretary handed her a note and nodded at the two of us. Mrs. Whitehall read it and scowled. That didn't bode well for us.

"Come in, girls," she said and marched back into her office without checking to see if we were following. There was no need to really. When kids are sent to the principal, aka warden, they do what they're told, otherwise everything just becomes worse for them. 'Resistance is futile,' as my funny uncle used to say before he died in a car accident.

I went in first and Francine slunk in behind me, as if she could hide her five-foot-eight body behind my five-foot-four frame.

Mrs. Whitehall sat behind her big wooden desk and gestured to the two chairs facing her on the opposite side. "Sit."

Like obedient dogs, we sat. We didn't have the option of being outraged by the way we were spoken to.

She leaned back in her chair and steepled her

fingers. "I understand the two of you were inebriated in class just now."

Was that a question? I didn't hear a question. So I just sat there quietly, waiting for her to elaborate. She sat there waiting for *us* to elaborate. Finally it became so uncomfortable I had to speak up.

"I'm sorry, Mrs. Whitehall. This wasn't planned. A fountain appeared out front, and we probably shouldn't have even tried drinking from it, but we did."

Francine sent me a look that might as well have had daggers shooting out of her eyeballs. I shrugged in her direction. As if to say, *"What? Did you think she would be stupid enough to believe a denial"*?

Mrs. Whitehall rose and paced with her hands behind her back. "I know about the fountain. It was brought to my attention, and has been taken care of."

Whew. So, I didn't tell her anything she didn't already know.

"How did you to learn about it?" she asked.

This time I wasn't going to answer. If I did, I'd wind up throwing Francine under the bus, so I just stared at her. She refused to make eye contact with me. She fidgeted. She looked at the ceiling, the floor, the bookcase, anything and anywhere, except at Mrs. Whitehall or me.

"Is there something you want to tell me, Miss Costa?"

"No," Francine answered quickly.

Mrs. Whitehall strode over and stood in front of Francine. She folded her arms and just stared at her. The room became so emotionally charged and uncomfortable, if Francine's powers were available, some kind of weather event would probably be going on—maybe a tornado. She'd had the ability to affect the weather before all her powers were suppressed.

"Okay, okay! I found the fountain first. I looked outside and saw it. Not knowing if the door would open or not, I tried it, and it did! So, of course I went out to look at the thing, since it hadn't been there yesterday, or early this morning, or at any other period of time since I've been here," she babbled, then clammed up.

Mrs. Whitehall nodded and returned to her chair behind her desk. When she was seated, she clasped her hands on the top of her desk and encouraged her to go on.

Francine then looked at me, and I shrugged. She rolled her eyes and finally continued with her confession. "Okay, I looked at it. I sniffed it. I tasted it, and I was pretty surprised to realize it was a vodka fountain. Like 100 proof or something."

I don't know if she knew what a hundred proof was, but I had to agree it was pretty potent.

"So, when I realized that, I had to tell somebody. It's not Jenika's fault that I chose her. We're not good friends, but if not for her, I'd have no friends here at all, so she was the only one I felt even halfway comfortable talking to about it."

"What did she say to you?" Mrs. Whitehall asked me.

I glanced at Francine and realized there was really nothing I could say to help or hurt her. All I could do was reiterate what happened from my point of view. "I was just about to sit down and eat lunch when Francine came into the cafeteria and told me she had to show me something. I didn't know what it was, but she seemed pretty excited, so I left my tray where it was and followed her to the front door. I was surprised when she opened the front door easily, and then I saw the fountain. Yeah, it hadn't been there before, so I was pretty curious about it too. When she said it was vodka, I looked down at it, sniffed it, and then took a little taste."

"A little taste?"

"Um, maybe a couple of shot glasses full?"

Mrs. Whitehall leaned back in her chair. "What if it wasn't vodka? What if it was strychnine? Arsenic? Chloroform?"

"Well… I guess we'd be poisoned and unconscious, lying on the ground," I said.

From her severe frown I gathered that wasn't the correct answer, even though it was probably the truth.

"You do understand that I'm unable to overlook this as a little prank, right? I need to know exactly where the fountain came from, who put it there, and anything else you can tell me. This could have been disastrous. The fact that it was *only vodka*," she emphasized, "is immaterial. Somebody put an item on our grounds that was tempting and could have been lethal."

Okay, I hadn't quite thought of it like that. Yeah, a vodka fountain is kinda wrong, but I never thought it could be 'disastrous' or 'lethal' or any of those other words, she was using.

I glanced over at Francine and hoped she would take the lead, but she didn't. I finally had to fill in the rest. I was saving my own skin, but I owed no loyalty to a kid I didn't even know.

"Some guy named Patrick appeared behind us. I don't know where he came from, but he said he was sentenced here and would be coming tomorrow. He said the fountain was a gift to make friends before he got here, and he wanted us to go tell the other kids about it. I guess he thought they would like him more when he arrived tomorrow." I shrugged.

"And did you tell any of the others?"

"No, ma'am," I said. Francine just shook her head.

Mrs. Whitehall didn't give much away, except that she scratched her head. In body language that usually means contemplation or confusion. So, I just let her be confused, because I had no more information.

"Is that what you remember too, Miss Costa?"

"Um… Yeah. I guess."

"Let me put it this way, do you have anything to add to that?"

Francine shook her head. "No, Mrs. Black— I mean Whitehall."

Oh, crap. She almost called her Black-hole. I didn't know if the warden had ever heard her nickname, but she'd probably figure it out now. I don't think our teachers are allowed to read our minds, if they're able, but I doubt they are. They'd probably have quit by now, if they could hear the awful stuff kids thought about them.

Mrs. Whitehall rose and went to her door. Opening it, she said, "You're dismissed. Stay in your rooms and sober up. I will speak to you later about your punishment. Understood?"

"Yes, ma'am." We both said at once and exited quickly.

She slammed her door as we rushed off. "I can't believe we only got grounded in our rooms," Francine said. "I thought we'd be dragged off to solitary for sure."

"It would've been worse, if we'd tried to lie to her. I'm pretty sure the teachers have seriously accurate, bullshit detectors."

"Yeah, you really sang like a canary, didn't you?"

My jaw dropped in shock. "What did you expect me to do? We don't know who that kid is. Not really. What would you have done if I'd stayed quiet? Just sat there and let her stare at you from now until next week?"

Francine shook her head. "Never mind. Let's just forget it. My buzz is wearing off. Seriously, I know what they mean by *buzz-kill* now."

"Yeah, but I'd hate to be you tomorrow," I said as a parting shot. I probably should've kept my mouth shut.

She gave me a look that said, "If I could kill you and get away with it, I would."

⸺ ✶ ⸺

Patrick showed up the following day. We didn't see him until we were sitting in the cafeteria with our lunches. Francine and I sat together. Kids who sat alone tended to be picked on, so there we sat, frenemies, facing each other in the last row of metal tables.

Francine insisted on facing the whole room with her back to the nearest wall. Mafia-style. Her last name was Costa and she was from some town considered to be a suburb of New York. Not that any of that means anything. Her dad could own a shoe store for all I knew—but according to her, he was the head of some kind of crime family and had some high-powered lawyers who tried to get her out and couldn't. Wow, was she mad the day she got that news!

We watched surreptitiously from bowed heads as Patrick went through the food line with his tray.

"Do you think he saw us?" I asked.

"Not yet."

The unasked and more important question was, *does he know we told the admin that he's the one who gifted us with the Vodka fountain?*

When he reached the end of the line, he scanned the room. We kept our heads down, but it didn't help. Francine's bleached blonde hair was growing out, so her dark roots made her look like a reverse skunk. Light blond on the sides, dark in the middle. I'm betting that was the giveaway. My own hair was always unruly, so I tied it back and bobby pinned the sides. I know it's not the most fashionable look, but I'm not trying to impress anyone here.

"Shit. He's coming this way," Francine said. "Don't tell him we snitched."

You think? I kept my words to myself. I never know what to say around her. She's so volatile and sarcastic she'd probably find fault with anything I said.

"Ladies!" he said with a grin. "How are you this fine day?"

Francine groaned. "Put it this way, if you can't lower your voice, just shut-up."

He chuckled and set down his tray. "So, where are my new friends?" he whispered. Still standing, but leaning on the table, he glanced around the room.

"Damned if I know," she said.

I was staying out of this conversation altogether

unless I had to answer a direct question. And then I planned to lie through my teeth.

He finally slid in beside me. It was uncomfortable, because I didn't know him, and I had to scoot over to keep him from touching me. Francine probably expected me to lie about implicating him, if she didn't beat me to it. I hoped she would, but volunteering information didn't seem to be her style.

"I don't understand," he said. "Didn't you tell the others about the fountain?"

Francine and I stared at each other, until finally I caved. "We didn't get a chance. Thanks to you, we got in a lot of trouble after it was discovered, and removed."

"You just let it be discovered by chance?" He raised his voice as he continued, "You didn't go find other inmates and tell them about it?"

Francine put her hands over her ears and actually growled. "Keep your voice down. And as far as telling anybody, no. We didn't. We had to go to class, and that's when we got in trouble, because we were drunk off our asses."

Patrick laughed, long and loud. Francine pushed her tray aside, rested her forehead on the cool table, and covered her ears, trying to shut out his laughter altogether. By the time he finally stopped chuckling, a lot of the kids around us were glancing over to see what was so funny.

I couldn't stay silent any longer. "Look, I don't think you understand what goes on here. If you wind up making a friend or two, you're lucky. We watch each other's' backs, but basically we have to look out for ourselves."

Francine frowned. "Most of us don't like each other, but if we did, it wouldn't be because we were buying anyone's friendship. Everyone here is savvy enough to see right through a bribe. As it is, you aren't welcome to sit with the two of us at this table, because we *did* get in trouble."

"Our punishment could have been worse, but Francine might feel differently. She's experiencing her own punishment as well as our loss of TV privileges."

He leaned back and crossed his arms. "So, in other words, you're telling me that you two are my only friends."

Is he kidding me? "I didn't say that at all."

He unwrapped his spork and stabbed his dry pork chop while saying, "That's what I just heard."

I shook my head. "Whatever gets you through the day…"

"Hey, you want to hear a joke?"

"No," we both said.

"What do you call a pig who knows karate? A pork chop!"

Francine bolted upright, slammed her fist on the table, making us both jump. She leaned toward his face.

"I don't know where you came from or why you think you're so special, but everyone here is in the same damn boat. We're not friends, but we don't get each other in trouble. You just have to do your time and hope nothing bad happens until you get out of here."

He didn't look upset at all. In fact, he seemed really blasé. "Well, that's a shame. I like to make friends wherever I go. Friends enjoy each other. They entertain each other. Life is more fun with friends."

His life is fun? I couldn't help wondering what he'd done to get sentenced here. It must have been something extra 'fun.' I couldn't remember a lot of fun after my mother died. Before that, sure, we had some fun times. My grandfather liked to play cards and board games with me, but after he died and my mother got shot in front of the funeral parlor, it was just my stepdad and me. He didn't know how to have fun. He didn't like his job at the post office, and with his temper, I guess it was just lucky he hadn't 'gone postal', as they say.

He didn't know about my being a witch. My mother insisted I never tell him. He just thought I was strange. We never got close, even though I think we tried. We wanted to get along for my mother's sake, but after she was gone we wound up avoiding each other whenever we could.

Eventually he came right out and told me he didn't want a kid at all, and if my mother hadn't already come with one, we wouldn't be living in the same house. Before my mom died, he moved us to the suburbs at her request.

I tried not to hang around the house too often. I just went there to sleep. Finally he gave up pretending to care and moved us back to the city, which got rid of his commute. Without my witch powers, I might have gotten into more trouble than I did.

Luckily, I had those powers in my back pocket. In the city, it's harder to avoid people. If I couldn't talk someone out of doing something I didn't like or want, I could protect myself. Yet, like here, most of the people I hung around with were just worrying about themselves.

It was harder to make friends in the burbs, because I was shy and often the only black kid in my classes. Weird, I know. But there are still places that might as well be segregated, even in the 2020s.

In Haven, the races didn't seem to matter as much. Yeah, it was the opposite of what you see on TV. Some of us could serve our time, then move on with our lives, *if* we behaved ourselves. So, we didn't form rival gangs and all that crap. If we didn't behave in juvie, the adult magical lock-up we'd graduate to was nicknamed Hell. We didn't need to be told why.

I couldn't wait to get out of here and actually become an adult, able to make my own choices and decisions. I didn't know where I would live, but I could find a cheap room and get a job as a waitress some-where. I didn't need my witch powers to survive. I had plenty of street-smarts for that.

Francine grabbed her tray. "I don't feel well. I'm going back to my room to throw up." She rose, giving Patrick her *dagger stare,* as if daring him to laugh, and then she stormed off.

His eyes followed her until she disappeared from sight, and then he returned his gaze to me. "What? I was just trying to be nice."

I chuckled, *not* because I thought it was funny, more because it was so ironic. "In the future. Don't try to be nice to us."

He shrugged. "Okay. I guess it's true what they say; No good deed goes unpunished."

"Yeah, only we got punished for your deed."

"So, what did you do to get here?" he asked, after a few silent moments of chewing the tasteless rubbery pork.

"None of your damn business."

"Whoa!" He leaned away from me with his hands up in surrender. "Don't shoot. I'll tell you what I did."

"You can if you want. I still won't tell you anything."

"Fine. I have nothing to hide, but if you do..." He shrugged.

"Still not telling you what you want to know."

He smiled slowly. *Arrogant jerk.*

"I'm a thief," he said, matter-of-factly.

"Good for you." I was about done with this conversation, but I wasn't through with my lunch yet, and I wasn't going to walk away from it, two days in a row.

"I see you have bobby-pins in your hair. I can teach you how to pick a lock."

I snorted. "I don't need to pick any locks."

"Hey, you never know when it might come in handy. You don't have your powers here, right? What if you were trapped? How would you get out?"

I had no answer.

"Let me show you, just for fun."

"Don't bother. I don't like your idea of fun."

"Okay, then how about for your edification."

"My what?"

"Enlightenment. Learning something new. Picking a lock is a simple trick if you have a couple bobby pins on you."

I scratched my head and caught myself. Confused or contemplating? Maybe both. At least he was cute to look at while he prattled on. He resembled one of the Jonas Brothers—the hot one.

"Fine. Show me."

He held out his hand for a bobby pin. I removed one and handed it to him.

"The first thing we have to do is remove the rounded tip from the straight side of the bobby pin." He stripped it off with his teeth.

"Hey! I was going to use that again."

"I'll buy you another one."

"I'll let you." I didn't want to tell him no one was putting money into my commissary account.

"Once the rubber end is off, we can begin making our bends. Start by pulling the bobby pin apart, and then roughly straightening it out. Here. You try." He plucked the other bobby pin from my hair and handed it to me.

"Now you owe me two bobby pins."

"I'll buy you a whole package of them."

I rolled my eyes, but followed his lead, stripping off one end with my teeth and straightening the metal into one long piece.

"Next, pretend you're sticking about one third of the straight end into the keyhole and apply enough pressure to bend the end into a hook, like this."

I watched, but I was in danger of getting bored if this took too long.

"Now that we have our right sized lock pick, let's move on to forging our tension wrench."

"Foraging what?"

He laughed. "I'll explain… The tension wrench has an L-shape, and this makes forming it as simple as one bend. Start by placing the closed end of the bobby pin about an inch into your lock's keyhole and firmly apply pressure downward until you bend the pin 90 degrees. That's all there is to it. We now have a usable set of lock picking tools, but before we can attempt to pick any locks, it's important to understand how a pin and tumbler locking mechanism works."

I groaned. "I'm afraid this is getting complicated. I'd rather just say, Abracadabra open!"

"Oh, c'mon. You're almost there. And what if your abracadabra doesn't help you? Now that we have our picks and tension wrench, we can get down to business."

"Great," I said, deadpan.

"Before we get to play with our new toys, you need to learn how to properly use the bobby pin tension wrench. As I mentioned earlier, this little ol' tool is used to accomplish two things. First, it gives us the leverage we need to apply rotational tension, similar to that of a key. Secondly, it's this little-bent piece of metal that helps us keep the pins at the shear line."

"The what now?"

"The binding pin. We apply rotational tension on the plug, to stop it from rotating. While the pin is bound, we push the pin to the shear line, using our pick. Now everything comes together."

"Finally. Thank the Goddess."

"Hang in. There's more."

"Crap..."

"As the first binding pin reaches the shear line, the plug will turn ever so slightly. Because the plug slightly rotates, the pin we forced up will settle on top of the plug and so long as you maintain the correct amount of tension, it will stay there. This is what we, in the lock picking trade, call 'setting a pin.'"

"Fascinating," I said, without enthusiasm.

"Relax. Now that we know what our goal is *inside* the lock, we can finally get it working."

"Oh, joy. Do you recognize sarcasm?"

"Just one thing… If we apply too much pressure, we stand a chance of binding more than the first pin, making it difficult to set the remaining pins. However, if we apply too little force, the pin won't set, and it will fall back into the plug."

"*Really* bored now."

He ignored me and just kept on talking as if I were still listening—which I wasn't. I glanced around the rapidly emptying cafeteria and finished my meal.

"The trick is to start light, then increase the tension. Developing a feel for using the tension wrench is what separates the novice from the master."

"I guess I'll be a novice forever since I have no desire to practice, and I won't remember this if I ever get locked in somewhere and have to pick my way out."

"I was locked in a basement and had to pick my way out once. You just never know."

"Oh," was all I could think of to say.

Patrick tucked his 'key' into the pocket of my jean jacket. "Okay, so changing the subject, I hear you have to rhyme spells. I'm not good at rhyming. Is there an app for that?"

I gave him a sly smile and rapped out a little something off the top of my head, "A girl who likes rap don't need no app. She thinks in rhyme all the time."

Patrick sat up straighter and applauded. "Nice job. Maybe you can help me with the rhymes. I suck at that."

I rolled my eyes. I didn't want to help this troublemaker in any way, shape or form. "Look, I don't know you. I don't even think I like you. I hope you'll find other people to hang around with. No offense."

"Some taken."

"Fine. I don't really care. I just want to finish my time and get out of here."

Patrick smirked. "Can I tell you another joke?"

"Please don't."

"Why do rappers need umbrellas?"

"Oh, Lord and Lady. Go ahead, tell me. Why do rappers need umbrellas?"

"Fo' drizzle."

"That's it. I'm not listening to you anymore…"

"Okay, okay. I get it. Maybe Francine will be more open to my friendship."

"I'd wait until she's feeling better, and even then, you shouldn't expect much. She barely tolerates most of us and openly dislikes the rest. Maybe you can find some of the boys to hang out with."

Patrick gazed around the room. Most of the guys here looked tough. They wore all black, and had lots of piercings and tattoos. Not at all friendly. There were small groups of *tentative* friends among them. There was no such thing as unconditional acceptance of a newcomer in a place like this.

"Yeah, I don't see anyone who looks like they would welcome my friendship."

"Oh? Why? Just because you're a basic, clean-cut, good looking Canadian who's well-dressed and obviously doesn't fit in here."

Patrick crossed his arms. "I'm not basic or Canadian, but the rest of your description is accurate."

Egotist.

"But to be honest," he continued, "I get along with just about everyone. I'm a friendly guy."

"Good. I'm sure you'll have no problem finding other kids to bother."

"Ouch. Fine. I'll go." He lifted his tray, moved to another table, and sat down with a small group of guys. They glared at him.

I just shook my head. "He won't last a day," I muttered under my breath.

CHAPTER 3

Ms. Broome entered the cafeteria about that time. She glanced around and finally spotted me. "Jenika, can you join me outside for a walk?"

"I guess I could." I had study hall after lunch, and the thought of going outside on a beautiful day was appealing…but what did she want?

"Such enthusiasm." She gave me a wry smile.

I rose and took my tray to the front of the room and placed it on what we called the "poof-deck." Simply set your tray, leftovers and all, on the shiny surface, and *poof* it magically disappeared. There were a few fun items like that, just to remind us who we used to be and what we were missing.

As soon as we reached the outer door, Ms. Broome waved a hand in front of the locking mechanism and it opened. Neat. I doubted it was the type of lock Patrick's lesson would help me with anyway. Truth is, I *was* paying attention, but I didn't know where I'd go if I exited the building. It's not like my powers would return without help. I think…

As Ms. Broome and I strolled along a worn-down grassy path, the Florida sunshine warmed me. I lifted my face and closed my eyes to drink it in when all of a sudden I bumped into something solid. Startled, I opened my eyes, jumped back, and let out a girly, "Eep!"

"Oh! Sorry," she said. "I don't know where the invisible barriers are yet. Still new here."

Was she really sorry? Or was she warning or testing me somehow? "It's okay. I'm fine, but we should probably move back onto the path."

"Sure thing," she said, and we resumed our walk. "I'm guessing you didn't have invisible fences in your old school yard."

I chuckled. "No. Nothing like that. We didn't even have a yard."

"Tell me about your old school."

Ah, nice segue. I thought I could outsmart her by asking, "Which one?"

"All of them."

Damn. When will I learn not to give her more ammunition than she already has? I took a deep breath and mentally ran down the list. "Okay, I spent first grade in two schools. I was an Army brat, but you probably already knew that."

"Talk to me as if I don't know a thing about you."

I groaned out loud. "All right. For what it's worth, I was born in Nebraska. My father was stationed there until I was halfway through preschool. Then he got transferred to Japan and we lived off base. I went to an International school for the next couple years. My mother didn't like living there. She said she missed the alphabet."

"Did you like it there?"

"I don't remember."

She gave me *the look.* You know the one. I think all teachers have had to learn it as part of their teaching degree. It's the one that says, 'I don't really believe you, but I won't call you a liar.' I tried to ignore it, but the silence grew uncomfortable.

"What were we talking about?"

"Japan. Did you like it there?"

Damn. She remembered. "We didn't stay long. Not more than a couple of years, I think. Like I said, my mom didn't like it there, so she and I moved back home to Detroit to live with my grandfather."

"And your father?"

"He stayed in Japan,"

"Uh huh…"

Great. The ball was back in my court again. "In case you were wondering, they didn't get divorced right away."

"Okay. Tell me about your life during that time."

"What time?"

"The time you were living with your grandfather."

"Oh. It was okay. I missed my dad, but my grandfather was a pretty good substitute. I went to fourth grade in Detroit. I assume that's what you wanted to know since we were talking about the schools I went to."

She nodded. "That's part of it. Did you like living with your grandparents?"

"Grandfather. My grandmother had already died of cancer."

"Oh, I'm sorry."

I shrugged. "I don't really remember her. Army brat in Japan and everything. It was way too far to visit." By now I was feeling a little more comfortable, so I figured I'd volunteer a little information. "I loved my grandfather. He was funny as hell."

She smiled.

"I didn't know he was covering up an illness with his sense of humor."

"What kind of illness did he have?"

"Sickle Cell Anemia."

"Oh, dear. That's quite serious, isn't it?"

"Yeah. My mom was going to nursing school, and I think she wanted to know how to take care of her dad."

"That's commendable. Was your grandfather taking care of you while she was in school?"

"Sometimes. Most of the time I went to an after-school program. I remember that being an okay place, but in school I was being teased. Not about anything specific. I think just because I was shy, I was an easy target. Not long after that, my parents got divorced."

"I'm sorry."

"Quit being sorry, will you? It's not like you had anything to do with it." I didn't mean for that to come out sounding angry.

"I wasn't apologizing. I was sympathizing."

"Oh. Sorry." Sheepishly, I added, "That was apologizing." I smiled and so did she. I guessed we were back on okay footing.

"How long did you stay at the Detroit school?"

"I was in sixth grade. My mom was worried about my going to middle school in the city, and by that time she had remarried. They only knew each other a few months, but said it was love at first sight. Anyway, she quit nursing school, and we moved to the suburbs."

"She didn't make it through nursing school?"

"She said it was really hard on both of us, since she had to study every minute she wasn't working or at school, and there were other jobs she could do at night, so she could take care of me during the day."

"And I guess your grandfather wasn't able to babysit anymore."

"Yeah. I was sad to leave my grandfather, but he convinced us I'd be better off in a new town."

"And were you?"

"Maybe, but he wasn't. My grandpa got worse, and he didn't tell us." I let out a deep sigh without even realizing it. We had reached the end of the yard, so I hoped that was the end of the conversation.

"Go around again?" she asked.

"Ugh. Do we have to?"

"No. We can continue talking inside."

"Are those my only options?"

"What is it you don't want to talk about, Jenika?"

I sent her a glare. "Like you don't know."

She stood straighter. "I'm not sure what you're reacting to. Can you tell me what that is?"

I looked at the sky and prayed to the Goddess to open the earth and swallow me, if I cried. I hated crying, especially in front of other people. There were other kids out here.

Ms. Broome waited. I felt trapped, and there seemed no way out other than through, so I took a deep breath and plowed on. "My grandfather died of SCA during a bone marrow transplant."

"Oh, no. That must have been awful for you."

"Yeah. Can we stop now? I've had enough psycho-analysis for one day."

She nodded. "We'll pick up where you left off later."

I wanted to hit my head against the brick building. "Fine," I snapped. "Let's get it all out now. My grandpa died. The funeral was in the church that he and all his friends attended in the city. My mother was shot in a drive-by in front of the church right after the service. I lost the two people I loved most in the same week."

"Oh no!" She looked genuinely shocked. I guess that little detail never made it into my file.

Before she said she was sorry again, I finished the story. "My step-father said he never wanted me. I just came with the deal, and without my mother, he had no one to take care of me. So he threatened to send me into the foster system. My uncle talked him out of it."

"Where was your biological father?"

"He did a tour in the Middle East, then got out of the service and disappeared. At one point I heard he was doing civilian work, but it was some kind of top secret stuff."

I was so going to cry. Instead I took off running. When I reached the front door, it was locked. *Shoot!*

Ms. Broome met me at the door and without another word, she waved her hand, opened it, and let me inside. I glanced up at her and said, "I'm going to my room now."

She nodded. I rushed to my room, threw myself on my bed, and pulled my pillow over my face. I tried not to make any sound as I wept.

A few minutes later, I pulled myself together and marched down to Ms. Broome's office. There was something she might be able to help me with, and I needed to ask about it while she was in a sympathetic mood.

At my knock, she stopped writing in a chart—probably mine—and looked up. Seeing me through the glass door, she waved me in.

"May I talk to you about something? I can come back later if you're busy."

"Come in." She gestured to one of the two chairs in front of her. "Have a seat."

I closed the door behind me, not wanting anyone to overhear what I was about to ask, then I took the seat she'd indicated.

"How can I help you?"

"As you know, I only have a month left here."

"Yes. I'm aware."

"I'd like to know how to become an emancipated minor."

Her eyes widened. "An emancipated minor?"

I knew she heard me correctly. Was she stalling? It was time to look pathetic. I hung my head. "Maybe I shouldn't have asked."

"If you're considering it, we should talk. Becoming an emancipated minor is nothing to be taken lightly. There are several legal and financial steps. From petitioning the courts, to having a job, getting insurance, making a budget, basically gathering everything you need before setting out on your own. I can help you research the process, but the most important thing is having a job to support yourself. Do you have a job you can go back to?"

"I can get a job with a snap of my fingers." I gave her a sly smile.

"But that's just it, you can't. You should know by now how important it is not to manipulate other people with magic. You should never make someone give you a job you couldn't get on your own merit. How would you know if somebody else needs that job to support a family? Or if you'd be unsuited for it, and wind up getting fired?"

I winced. "I guess… But there has to be a job I can take that nobody else wants."

"Oh, yes. There are plenty of jobs like that. Most of them won't pay you well enough to make it without a second job. If you find a place to live, which you will have to do, you'll need to guarantee that you'll have enough money to pay rent, buy your food, pay for clothing and still have quarters for the laundromat."

I threw my hands in the air. "I get it. I get it, but I still want to do it. Can you help me?"

Ms. Broome tipped her head and studied me for a moment. "What's so bad about living at home when you leave here?"

"I told you. My stepfather doesn't want me. I'm just going to be a burden, and I'd rather take care of myself than have someone mad at me all the time, just for living. And don't tell me he doesn't really feel that way. I'm an empath, so *I know* he does."

Ms. Broome let out a deep sigh. "That I can understand, but it might be difficult to prove to a judge. And I don't need to tell you how wrong it would be to manipulate a judge."

"Do they know if they're being manipulated?"

"They know about us. They have to. They need to know where to send magicals, versus the common criminal—someone who would go to a regular jail or juvie. If they're ready to make a decision they know is wrong, they'll assume they're being manipulated. They'll get a magical intermediary involved and it will not go well for the petitioner after that."

"Okay, I guess that makes sense. Let's say I can get a job, I can find a cheap room to rent, and I can live on my own while paying for all those other things. Can I legally, and without manipulation, get those things taken care of before I leave here? What does it really take, how does it work?"

"Being emancipated means your parent or guardian is no longer responsible for providing you with food, clothing, and shelter. It also means you can get a work permit, earn money, and decide what to do with your earnings. You can also legally live on your own, rent an apartment, and sign legal contracts without parental consent."

That sounded pretty good to me. "You know I'm

one of the more responsible kids here. I can do this. I know I can. I just need a chance."

After a long pause she nodded slowly. "We can try to start the process. I can't guarantee anything, especially if your stepfather hasn't physically hurt you or neglected you. Has he? Has he provided food, clothing and shelter for you? Is there anything you needed that he didn't provide?"

"Other than a hug, you mean?"

Ms. Broome gave me that smile I hate—the one laced with pity. "I'm sorry if he never hugged you. But no, that doesn't count in court. A lot of kids have grown up without much in the way of affection. That can be a handicap as far as mature relationships are concerned, but it's not a crime. Having to start your life without a loving 'got your back' kind of relationship, which helps with self-confidence, is hard, but of course it can be done."

"Like I said, all I want is a chance. What do I need to do? What are the steps I need to take?"

Ms. Broome opened her laptop, tapped her computer keyboard and paused to read for a few seconds, then she leaned back and shrugged. "The process seems relatively simple. First you have to file a petition for emancipation with the courts, which include the reasons why you want to be emancipated as well as proof that you can support yourself financially.

"Next your parents or guardians will be notified of

the petition, and a hearing is scheduled. The judge will hear your case for emancipation, then the court will make a ruling based on the information presented. *If you are granted emancipation, you get a declaration of emancipation.* You have to keep that on hand and have copies available, so you can provide them instead of parental consent in the future.

"It says here you can also become an emancipated minor by joining the military or getting married. However, you're only fifteen, and in some states you'll need parental consent to get married before age eighteen." Her eyes narrowed. "I don't recommend that at all. I don't think I have to tell you why."

"Because I don't have anyone willing to marry me at the moment?"

She chuckled, then shook her head. "No. You need a role model to demonstrate healthy mature relationships, and I don't know if you got enough of that as you were growing up. That's certainly not something you can get here."

"What about you? Do you have a loving relationship?"

She smiled, but didn't look like she was going to share the details. Instead, she just moved on. "Joining the military requires a high school diploma or GED to enlist so you'll probably be seventeen before you could be emancipated anyway."

I blew out a deep breath of frustration. "I can't wait

two or three years. I also don't feel like going into the military, because of what it did to my dad. I'm not just talking about the possibility of getting killed. The separation ruined his relationship with my mom—since we're talking about relationships…"

With her elbow resting on the desk, and chin in her hand, Ms. Broome stared at me for what seemed like a long time. Finally, she let out a deep sigh and sat up straight. "If I help you, we're going to do this right."

I wanted to cheer. She was going to help me! Doing it right seemed like a good idea too. "What do we need to do first?"

"Call your stepfather."

"What?" I must have heard her wrong. "You said the courts would notify him."

"I don't believe in blindsiding people. Your stepdad deserves to hear it from you. From us, if you'd like me to be in on the call."

I crossed my arms and pouted like a two-year old. "I don't want to talk to him."

Ms. Broome closed the lid on her laptop. "All right then. I guess my involvement ends here."

I held it together—barely. "Let me think about it." I had learned that phrase from other teachers. It's code for "I'll say no later." Then I left her office.

Patrick sat down next to me at dinner. For some reason, he wouldn't leave me alone. Francine had a visitor show up with food, so she was having dinner in the visitation room with whomever that was.

"Why are you so glum?" Patrick asked.

"I'm not dumb!"

He laughed. "I didn't say dumb, I said glum."

"Who uses the word glum?"

"Okay. Down? Blue? Depressed? Pick one and tell me why you look that way."

I hadn't realized I looked depressed, even though I felt worse than that. Sad and mad mixed together wasn't pretty, I'm sure. "How do you know I'm glum?"

He shrugged. "You have an expressive face. You're never *Yippee skippy!* but you're more serious than usual. Let me tell you another joke."

"Do you have to?"

"Yes. What did the man say when he walked into a bar?"

"I give up."

"Ouch."

That time I couldn't keep the smile off my face.

"See I got you to smile. Now, why don't you tell me what's wrong."

What the heck? I wanted to talk to someone and, well, Patrick was someone. "Okay, there's this thing I want my teacher to help me with and she said she would, and then she made it conditional on something that I don't want to do."

"Huh? That's all a little vague, don't you think?"

"It's about a specific as I feel like getting at the moment."

"Don't you trust me?"

I burst out laughing.

"Well, I'm glad I could put another smile on your face. Now, why don't you tell me what's really bothering you? I promise I won't tell anyone else. Honest. I won't say a word."

That was probably true since he didn't hang out with anyone else, just yet. I still hoped he would find a group of boys to entertain himself with. He seemed to need some kind of entertainment, and I wasn't in the mood to be his stand-up comic or rapper, or whatever…

"I guess I could try trusting you a little bit. Okay… I want to become an emancipated minor."

"Whoa! Can you do that? You're kinda young, aren't you?"

"I'm fifteen and I don't think I could stand another three years like this. I asked the only teacher who seems to give a damn about me if she could help. She looked up the rules, and it seemed like something I could do, but then she said I had to talk to my stepfather first. If I let the court do it for me, she won't help.

Talking to that angry prick is exactly what I don't want to do."

Patrick sat quietly and nodded. I don't know why I expected him to have some input. What could he offer? He probably never had to look into that possibility, although I didn't know his story at all.

"I know a kid who did that once. I think he was being abused or something."

"Look, I don't want to get into the details. It really isn't something you could help me with anyway, unless you know a way around the rules."

He grinned. "Now you're speaking my language. I love getting around the rules!"

I snorted. *Why didn't I see that coming?* "Look, forget I said anything. It's not your problem and I'll figure something out eventually."

He nodded. "I get it. If my situation hadn't practically emancipate me already, I might want to go that route."

Suddenly I was popped out of my own problem and wanted to know about his. "So you had to take care of yourself? Did you steal food or something?"

"It was more like 'something' or a lot of 'somethings'."

"Oh. But you did it to survive?"

He shrugged. "Sure. It helped pay credit card bills that my mother could barely afford the interest on. Besides, some people just have too much stuff, you know? I'm doing them a favor by paring down their excess."

I laughed out loud. "Seriously? You think theft is giving rich people a helping hand? I guess that's one way of looking at it."

"Yeah, but that's not the way the judge looked at it. No one could figure out how I was getting into these places. People had expensive alarms, guards, sometimes attack dogs. But I was able to walk right in. The bigger the challenge, the better I liked it. Then I helped them downsize."

"I think walking into a stranger's home, uninvited, is called burglary, whether you take anything or not."

His face lit up. "You're right! Most people think burglary means stealing. But even if you just open an unlocked window and reach inside, if it's not your house, you've already committed burglary."

"Why do you sound proud of it?"

"Hey, it's something I'm good at. It's not like I picked easy targets. I'd never find an old couple and rob them in a home invasion. I'm not an asshole."

"No, just a juvenile delinquent."

"Yeah, well…"

I rolled my eyes.

After a few more bites of congealed meatloaf and instant mashed potatoes, which had long since gone cold, I asked about his parents. Probably not my business, but I was curious.

"My dad died of an overdose. That's why I'll never touch drugs. I watched him zone out for the last time. I'd rather experience life's excitement."

"And stealing stuff is exciting?"

"You bet." He lifted his eyebrows like just thinking about it got him excited.

"Don't you have any guilt at all?"

He looked thoughtful for a moment. "I guess there may have been some sentimental value to the stuff I stole, but I stayed away from obvious heirlooms and never took anything people needed."

"So, what did you steal?"

"Cash, jewelry, a mink coat once. I made sure the lady had other warm coats in her humongous closet first."

"Nice of you. How about paintings? Nobody needs a painting, but some are very valuable. Aren't those hard to walk around with? Unless you had a buyer waiting out front."

"Having a car waiting would be way easier for a kid without a driver's license. But you'd be surprised how fast I can pedal my bike even with something big over my shoulder, under my arm, or even balanced on my head."

I burst out laughing. I couldn't help it. I pictured him balancing a giant frame or sculpture on his head while riding a bike down the street.

"So, I guess you must have been caught, eventually."

"Yeah. Those damn cameras. They're everywhere now. I always look for them first, but I missed one."

"What did the camera show?"

"It was a nanny cam. As soon as I realized I was in a kid's room I left, but that teddy bear got a real good look at me, damn it."

I snickered. "Brought down by a teddy bear. Now, that's embarrassing." I leaned back and crossed my arms. "You know, everybody in here gets a nickname. I think I have one for you."

"Do you now?" he said in a cocky voice that just made my decisions even more perfect.

"Yeah. I think we'll call you Teddy Bear."

He looked like he'd sucked a lemon, then one side of his mouth turned up and he began laughing at himself. "I'm glad I didn't tell you about stealing a former Miss America's crown."

I think it was at that moment, I decided I might not hate him after all.

CHAPTER 4

I decided that trying it Ms. Broome's way might be worth an uncomfortable phone call. If he loses his cool, and I kind of hope he does, I'll have a teacher as a witness. My case might hold more weight with the court, *if* she's willing to back up my story.

I didn't exactly know what my claim was. Like I said, I was unwanted. I knew that. There must be a word for it. Emotional rejection? Negative reactions, causing damage to my self-esteem? Harsh internal verbal abuse? I didn't know if I could phrase it appropriately since his opinions were sometimes subtle, and at other times, barely restrained.

Basically, he'd get riled up at the slightest thing and *in his head*, and he'd go off on me. How do you tell a judge the things he wants to say to an empath are as harmful to me as if he said them aloud?

So, here I am, sitting outside Mrs. Whitehall's

office, waiting until she and Ms. Broome figure out what to do with me. *Me,* the student that doesn't cause anyone any trouble, sitting outside the warden/principal's office for the second time in a week.

Mrs. Whitehall's office door finally opened—of its own volition. "Come in, Jenika," she called out.

When I entered the office, she was sitting behind her big oak desk and Ms. Broome was seated in one of the two chairs opposite it. I took the empty chair.

"We've been discussing your case, Jenika, and I'm in agreement with Ms. Broome. We will present your concerns together to your step-father. When do you think he'll be at home?"

"Uh, he works at the post office. His hours are 7 AM to 3 PM." I checked the analog clock on the wall behind Mrs. Whitehall. It said 3:30.

"Does he have a long commute? Do you think he'll be home now?"

"He used to have a long commute when we lived in the suburbs, but he got sick of it and moved us right to the outskirts of the city. It takes him about fifteen minutes to get home. If he has an errand or something, it will take a little longer."

The adults stared at each other, as if some kind of telepathic communication were taking place. Maybe it was. At last Mrs. Whitehall pushed her intercom button and when the secretary answered, she said, "Please try Jenika Jones' home phone number.

Connect us with her stepfather when it goes through."

Hmmm... *When* it goes through. Not *if* it goes through. The teachers and administrators were pretty tight-lipped about their powers, so we had to guess what they were good at, based on little clues or slips of the tongue. I guess if we didn't know what they could do, we also wouldn't know what they couldn't.

As we waited, Mrs. Whitehall gave me a rare smile and said, "I hear you've been doing well in your classes."

"Yes, ma'am." Was I supposed to say something else? Elaborate on how much I enjoyed having my powers back for five seconds? I wondered for the hundredth time how my friend Genevieve was doing. She was recently released, but before that she was my best friend in here, and I missed her badly. Was she using her powers all the time? Or was she still hiding what she could do, knowing it might freak out unsuspecting fuggles?

What would Patrick do when he got out of here? Go back to his criminal ways? What would Francine do? Flood the Midwest again? All of that musing took about ten seconds and then the intercom beeped.

"Mrs. Whitehall? Mr. Ford is on the phone for you."

"Who?"

"Jenika Jones' stepfather. That's who you wanted me to call, correct?"

"Oh, yes. I didn't recognize the name. Put him though. Thank you."

Her phone rang a moment later and she pushed a button without picking up the receiver.

"Mr. Ford?"

"Yeah. What is this about? Did my stepdaughter do something stupid?"

Both adults looked at me. I guess they were expecting a reaction, so I let my shoulders slump and stared at my lap, giving them a peek at what he did to my self-esteem.

"This is about your step-daughter, but she hasn't done anything to warrant the word, 'stupid'. By the way, you're on speakerphone. I have Jenika and one of her teachers with me."

"Oh. She heard that, huh?"

Mrs. Whitehall looked at me, but she didn't respond. I guess it was my turn.

"Hi Phil."

"Hello, Jenika. Um… How have you been?"

If the women in the room wanted to see my maturity level, I had to stuff my sarcasm down deep. "I'm well. And you?"

He hesitated, as if he didn't recognize my voice. "I, uh… I'm okay, I guess. What is this about? Do you need money or something?"

"No, Phil. I want a divorce."

Stunned silence followed for several beats. Ms.

Broome covered her mouth with her hand, but I could see her cheeks rise, meaning she was trying to hide a smile.

"Am I being PUNKED?" he shouted. "Did you manage to get a phone just so you could screw with me? Is that one of your friends who's pretending to be the administrator?"

Mrs. Whitehall jumped in. "This *is* Administrator Whitehall, and you are *not* being punked. Your stepchild is looking into the possibility of becoming an emancipated minor. We felt notifying you first and getting your feelings on that would be the right thing to do."

"Yeah? Well this is how I feel…"

A dial-tone followed.

Mrs. Whitehall's brows shot up. "Did we just get disconnected or did he purposely hang up?" I don't think she was asking anyone in particular, but I knew the answer, so I provided it.

"He hung up on you."

"Hmph. That's no way to deal with a problem. Although you could have given him a more tactful explanation for the call."

I held in my giggle. I certainly could have approached the subject in another way, but I got the response I needed.

Ms. Broome, who had been quiet up to now, sighed. "Is that how you two interact most of the time?"

"What do you mean?"

"Do you try to provoke him? And does he usually respond to it like that?"

"No. I don't have to. He's permanently provoked."

She shook her head. "I'm not sure what we can do to repair the situation, Jenika. Is he apt to call back after he cools down?"

"No."

The two adults stared at each other for a moment, then Mrs. Whitehall said, "You're dismissed, Jenika."

I stepped out of her office, but before I left, I put my ear to the door. Thankfully the secretary had her back to me.

"I hate to do it, but I think we're going to have to put her into our high-risk category," Mrs. Whitehall said.

"I understand. With no magicals in her life and very little support that we know of, she'll bear watching."

The secretary turned around at that point and I pretended to be looking in my jacket's breast pocket for something. "Ah! Here it is…" I pulled out one of the bobby pins and scurried away before she could question me.

I swooped into my class and plopped into my chair. I was only five minutes late.

Ms. Fine didn't even pause in her lecture. "You all know the responsible use of magic is paramount and only to be used in extreme emergencies. Can you tell me why that is?"

Nobody raised their hands.

It didn't seem like the subject matter was very deep, so I doubt I missed much during the five minutes I wasn't there, and I could fake it, if she called on me.

"Miss Jones, what do you think?"

Yup. The late girl gets the question. "Well, I believe that non-magicals might be jealous of our powers, and that could lead to some negative consequences."

Ms. Fine paced and nodded slowly, as if waiting for more. I had nothin'.

Francine turned halfway around and started to whisper to me, but Ms. Fine called on her before I got the gist.

"Ms. Costa, do you have anything to add to that?"

"What?"

"I know you heard Jenika's answer. She's sitting right behind you. So I would like you to elaborate on her answer."

Francine turned back toward the front of the room, and took a deep breath before speaking. "If fug— I mean non-magicals knew we had powers, they'd probably feel threatened and want to experiment on us. The government would find a way to drain our powers, use them for the military, kill us, and tell our parents we ran away."

Ms. Fine stopped her pacing and gazed at Francine with her perfect brows raised. "I'm not sure we need to go that far down the road. Are there any other possibilities you can think of, class?"

Patrick raised his hand and glanced over at Francine since he was sitting next to her. "I think I can elaborate on Jenika's response."

Ms. Fine nodded at him. "Go ahead, Mr. Hightower."

"To elaborate on the comment about people feeling threatened, I believe we would all suffer from their fear. Some humans—I mean non-magicals, might be able to tolerate us, but there will be many who won't. We'd be at risk of experiencing all the negative effects of prejudice that happen to many minority groups."

Ms. Fine nodded and resumed pacing. "Very good. And how do we prevent that from happening, class?"

The entire class recited as one, "Never reveal your powers in front of non-magicals."

"Correct. I cannot emphasize that enough. It may not only result in your harm, but it could harm many around you. Some families have one *or more* magicals. Sometimes a magical will appear in a family, as if from nowhere, yet the whole family might be treated with suspicion. A recessive gene could be involved. Nobody knows, because we have avoided examination up to this point."

Francine turned halfway around and whispered loudly enough for me to hear. "I told you they'd experiment on us."

As if to make a point, Ms. Fine stopped pacing, again. "Since everyone in this room is magical, we can discuss it openly." She resumed pacing with her hands clasped behind her back. "And what would happen if you were speaking about magic with a magical and a non-magical entered the room at that moment?"

Patrick raised his hand. I could tell from the smirk on his face that he had a smart-ass answer.

"Mr. Hightower?"

"We'd immediately stop talking, and if they wanted to know what we were talking about, we'd say we were talking about *them*."

The rest of the class chuckled.

Surprisingly, she smiled. "The first half of that answer was correct. If a non-magical were to enter the room, we would immediately stop. We might even pretend we have no idea what they'd overheard, or we might come up with an alternative subject to deflect the conversation."

She faced the class and continued. "I want each of you to think of a situation outside of Haven...back at home or wherever you will be going to after this, and try to come up with a scenario in which you could be *understandably tempted* to use magic to save yourself or someone else. Now when you have your hypothetical situation in mind, try to puzzle out how you could help *without* revealing your powers."

All I could think of was the school shooting, but that was a truthful situation, not hypothetical. Yet, I was curious to know if I had handled it correctly or if I could have done things differently, without magic. The shooter might suspect I have magic now, but he's in prison, and I doubt anyone would believe him anyway.

"Miss Jones, you look like you have a scenario in mind…"

Oh no. My face must have given me away somehow. "Yes, I can think of one. Let's say there's a school shooter, and I was locked out of the safe room because I was late to class."

"Well, that's believable," mumbled Francine.

I ignored her and continued with my story. "So, it's just me and the gunmen. Let's just say it's a senior student who's been expelled. Do we call him the gunman? The gun-kid?"

"That's a great example. Let's not worry about semantics right now, and just call him the shooter." Ms. Fine said.

"Okay, so it's just me and the shooter in the hall and he points the gun right at me." I hesitated, not entirely sure if I should go on or not. Before I could, Ms. Fine asked a question.

"Has he demonstrated that the gun is loaded or are you sure you're in mortal danger?"

"Yes. He stormed the corridor shooting at the ceiling and I'm an empath, so I know he's bent on murder."

She nodded. "All right. What would you think, say, or do, in that instance?"

"So, I used some opposing magnetic power to push the gun sideways so he would miss. I mean, I *would* use that…"

"Is the gun still pointed at the ceiling?" she asked.

"Um, no. It was pointed toward me, and I pushed it just a little to the left. I mean—it might be. And when I rush him, I'd kick him in the kneecap and he'd fall down, letting go of the gun."

Ms. Fine looked at me intently. Maybe I was too specific. Maybe she suspected it was a real situation. At least I didn't come right out and say I broke his kneecap, which I did.

"What do you think, class? Did Jenika handle that correctly?"

There was a bit of a hesitation, but it seemed most of the mumbles were affirmative.

"I'd say you did well under the circumstances. If you didn't speak a spell aloud or make an obvious gesture to point the gun away, he might not even realize why he missed. She gave me a nod of approval before she moved on.

"Class, this brings up the idea that subtlety is necessary, even in life and death situations. It can be very tricky to know when and how to use your magic. Your best bet is not to use it at all, unless you're in that kind of mortal danger. Thank you for your excellent example, Miss Jones."

I breathed a sigh of relief, and it seemed I had done the right thing at the right time. It wouldn't have helped anyone if I'd let him shoot me. And by breaking his kneecap and disarming him, well… I did the police a favor. Or at least I think I did. He had to go to the hospital first, but at least he couldn't run.

⸺⸺⸺

As soon as class was dismissed I bolted for the door, but Patrick caught up with me in the hall.

"That was some scenario you painted back there. It almost sounded like you actually lived through it."

I walked on for a little while, not answering, then he stopped me with a hand on my arm, and I flinched.

"I thought so."

I squinted at him. "You thought what?"

"You have a touch of PTSD. I knew you weren't making that up. It sounded too real. I know you were trying to backpedal and make it sound like you didn't really know what would happen if you used magic, but you did. Didn't you?"

I resumed walking and wondered what difference it would make, if I told him. Probably not much. I shrugged one shoulder and said, "Okay, yeah. It happened. But I'm here, so obviously I didn't get killed. Thankfully, no one else did either."

"Wow. So you saved your school?"

It was a relief to hear somebody say it that way. "Yeah, not that anyone gave me credit. In fact, it was the opposite. When the kids were piecing the story together, it seemed as if people couldn't believe that I'd disarmed him. He was a lot bigger than me. They speculated that I had something to do with it and was covering my own ass with the story. But it happened just as I described. *This* class would have believed me, because they know I had magic on my side."

Ms. Broome's thoughts came back to me. Maybe she was right, and I was more comfortable here than in my old school.

Patrick nodded. "Yeah, I get it. Kids can be stupid, or mean. Or mean *and* stupid. You saved their lives, and they tried to make it sound like you were in on a conspiracy or something."

"Exactly."

"Assholes." He shook his head in sympathy.

It felt good to have my feelings validated. There were so many things I didn't like about the idea of returning to that school. I kinda hoped I could stay here until I was eighteen, but I knew that wasn't going to happen unless I screwed up on purpose, and they'd figure that out eventually, anyway.

"So, changing the subject," he said, "you told me you'd help me with rhymes..."

I stopped and stared at him. "When did I say that?"

"You know, when you told me you like to rap."

"I didn't say I was going to teach you to do it. You should probably just concentrate on spells that are easy."

He looked like he was going to say something, but wisely didn't. As we were turning the corner toward the study hall he said, "Just give me a chance to try one."

I heaved a big sigh, as if it were a lot of trouble, even though it wasn't. "Sure, give it a try."

He thought for a minute, then rapped, "I'm seventeen and you know what I need, so Goddess, please, listen and heed."

"Okay, and..."

"That's it."

One side of my mouth turned up. "You're right, you're really bad at this."

He let out a breath in a whoosh. "I know, right?"

We were just about to enter study hall when a vending machine suddenly appeared before us. I almost walked into it.

"What the heck? Did you do that?"

"I don't think so. I mean, my powers are still suppressed. Aren't yours?"

"Yeah, I'm pretty sure…" I tried to push the vending machine aside with magic and it didn't budge. "Yup, mine are suppressed too."

He looked excited. "Let's see… I said I was seventeen and the Goddess would know what I need. This must be what I need. A snack. Seventeen-year-old boys always need snacks, right?"

I folded my arms. "I wouldn't know. I'm not a seventeen-year-old boy."

He looked at the machine's offerings, picked the one he wanted and pushed the right combination of number and letter. The machine started to whir, but instead of the snack he wanted, something else fell down into the slot. He stuck in his hand and fished around, then pulled out a condom in a shiny gold package.

I burst out laughing.

His face turned red.

Suddenly a whole slew of condoms fell into that slot and overflowed onto the floor. I doubled over, laughing hard until my sides hurt.

"I guess the Goddess thinks you need protection," I said when I could speak coherently again. "But I don't, so I'll leave you to gather up all this crap. I'm going to study hall."

Shortly after I opened my algebra book, he arrived

in study hall too and sat down beside me. I glanced up and said, "What are you doing here? Shouldn't you be sitting with that pretty blonde that you like?"

He turned around and looked for the snootiest girl there. She was an even bigger snob than Francine. I didn't know if he had talked to her yet or not.

"No, because she didn't see what just happened. You did. What the hell was that?"

I couldn't help giggling. "Apparently it's what every seventeen-year-old boy needs."

"Okay, okay. But where did it come from? You don't have your powers and I don't have my powers, so what are you thinking?"

"I'm thinking that's just the kind of practical joke my grandfather would've played on my uncle. You know, when they were alive."

Patrick sat up straight. "You mean, maybe someone from the spirit world heard us and decided to play a practical joke on us?"

That sounded like as good an explanation as any. I had no idea how it happened, but it really was a joke my grandfather would make as a prank on my uncle, who was seventeen when we moved in with them. Those two were always riffing off each other.

It might have been exactly what one of them would've done, *if* they'd had powers and didn't mind playing around with them, jokingly. But I don't think they did or would, considering the warnings I'd received against using magic. They both had a wicked sense of humor, and that would have been something my Grandfather would love to do. He might pretend he was going to pull a quarter from behind my uncle's ear, and then… *Wait a minute.*

"Do you think maybe some spirit could do that? Since we're all magicals here, would the spirits have to worry about getting one of us in trouble with the fuggles?"

"Fuggles?"

"Oh, you haven't heard that yet? It's a nickname for non-magicals. A contraction. Don't use it in front of teachers, though."

"Fuggles with an F?" Then he snapped his fingers. "I get it." He laughed. "So, you think maybe your grandfather had magic and he's using it to tease us?"

I shrugged. "I don't doubt he would if he could."

"Maybe he can. Maybe he can hear us right now. Wait, you said you're an empath, right?"

"Yeah…"

"I've heard that empaths attract spirits, even if they don't mean to. Their channels are always open or something."

"Really? I never heard that." I was trying to be cool, but a little part of me was jumping up and down inside. I would love for my grandfather to hear us, or at least hear *me*. It would be awesome to talk to him again…and my mom! I missed them so badly.

Suddenly tears threatened to surface. I hastily gathered my stuff.

"You know what, I'm going back to my cell. I don't have the right book to study."

When I got to my room, I thought about what Patrick had said. If I, an empath, have the tendency to attract spirits, well, maybe I'm walking around with spirits following me everywhere.

That made me feel a little squeamish, but then I thought about some of my loved ones on the other side. My grandpa, my uncle, my mom… I wish I could talk to them, and if my grandpa or my uncle were actually here a few minutes ago, maybe I could still reach them.

I had never tried mediumship before, but why not? Some people are very good at it and I would assume that empaths might be some of those people.

Well, here goes nothing.

"Spirits, if you can hear me, give me a sign."

I waited and waited, but nothing happened. Damn. Nothing *could* happen in a room like this. Everything was either bolted to the floor or to the wall, so there wasn't even a painting that could tilt or fall. I had a poster of a sunrise, but that was stuck to the wall over my bed with tape.

"Hello, young lady."

Oh my Goddess! I didn't know what to say or who I was talking to. Well, maybe that would be the best place to start. "Grandpa?"

"What is it you're looking for, my dear?"

"I – I don't know. I'm new at this."

The spirit chuckled, then said, *"You called me, so you must've wanted something."*

I sank down on my bed. "I was hoping to talk to my grandpa, but you don't sound like him. If only I could tell him everything I need... It would start with me needing him back."

"Back on earth?" The voice sounded excited, but it was definitely not my grandfather's voice. I thought family members or close friends usually showed up when a medium was channeling. Maybe it was actually my uncle. But my uncle never called me young lady, unless he was being sarcastic. "So, who am I talking to?"

"Who do you want to be talking to?" I held my breath.

"Come on, Uncle Donnie, is that you?"

He chuckled and said, "You got me."

"Oh, Uncle Donnie! It's good to hear from you. I miss you all."

"We miss you too, sugar."

"What's with the *'sugar'* and *'young lady'*? You never used to call me endearments like that."

"I know. I have a different perspective now. I'll never call you 'brat' or anything negative. All of us learn to do better here."

"Oh. That makes sense, I guess. Where are you? Summerland?"

"That's one name for it."

"Yeah, I know. There are lots of names for the place where souls go after we die. Some Wiccans call it Summerland. Some call it Avalon. Most Christians say Heaven or Hell. But Wiccans only believe in one place and then reincarnation after that. Hey, I never asked you during your lifetime, but are you Wiccan?"

"More like wicked." He laughed.

"Ha ha. You're still a kidder, even in the afterlife, I see."

"Yup. So, I still don't know why you called me..."

"Oh, sorry. Yeah..." I stood and paced, not really knowing how to answer that, but not willing to give up the connection I had established either. "I—um... Well, I'm not happy at home. My stepfather... I don't know if you knew him real well..."

"Not well, no."

"Be glad of that. He's... I guess it depends on the day, but most days he's hard to like."

"So, what are you going to do to him?"

"Do? No. I don't know. I'm just a kid, but I've heard of something I'd like to try."

"What is it?"

"It's called emancipation. I'd like to be an emancipated minor."

"I see. And do you need my help with that?"

At first, I didn't know if he was kidding. How could he help me from Summerland? Then I remembered that spirits do sometimes have the ability to influence certain things, like manipulate electricity and stuff like that, but could they actually arrange something to happen here? Only one way to know.

"Uncle Donnie? Would you be able to help me with that? From there?"

He chuckled. *"Not from here...not really. However, there is a way."*

A way? That sounded interesting. "And what would that be?"

"Well, a soul can leave this place and return to earth if another soul is willing to take its place temporarily."

I stopped pacing and landed on my bed like I had been knocked on my butt. "Are you serious?"

"Yes, you don't have to die or anything. If I can get down there, I can arrange it for you."

"No way."

"Really, I can. When you get to Summerland you learn secrets."

"What kind of secrets?"

"All the secrets of the Universe. What you didn't learn on Earth, you learn here."

I grasped my shirt over my heart. Could that be

true? I had heard that a soul spends about a hundred years in Summerland and reviews their past lives. But why would that take a hundred years? I'll bet learning *all* the secrets of the Universe would take a lot longer. Now it made sense.

"And I wouldn't have to die to take your place?"

"You would be as you are now, just holding my soul's place."

"Wait. Would you have your body here?"

He laughed out loud. "No. My body is gone and I won't be taking yours."

"How in the world can that happen?"

"There's a spell. You don't know it. They don't teach it to Earthbound people. It's one of those things you don't learn until you reach the other side. And then you forget it along with everything else when your soul begins its next life."

"If that's true, why don't all of you make the trip back to help arrange stuff for your loved ones?"

He let out a deep sigh. *There are a couple of reasons. First it would scare people if dead relatives showed up and asked to switch places. But because you're a witch, you know spirits exist and can make appearances in various ways.*

"You mean ghosts?"

"Sometimes, yes. Here's the other reason we don't return… This is going to sound terrible, but once a soul gets to Summerland, all interest in their Earthly life slips away. Most souls just don't care anymore. We're discouraged from interfering and many feel that's just as well."

"Then why do you care what happens to me?"

I heard him chuckle. *"Since when did I ever do what I was told?"*

That certainly sounded like my Uncle Donnie, though I couldn't remember his actual voice. I didn't seen my uncle very often after he got a job in Ann Arbor and moved there. He was about eighteen, I think. I was about seven. He died in a car accident a year later.

"So you're saying there's a way for me to get to Summerland without dying? And then your spirit can come to earth? And you'd somehow arrange for me to become an emancipated minor with no hassle?"

"Yes."

"How?"

"Computers! I can get into the local court's computer system. Sometimes hackers are blamed for things that ghosts actually do."

"Wow." I'd never thought of that. "So, you'd create an approved record of my emancipation, even though I haven't applied yet?"

"I can create the application and approve it. Since it's on a computer, I can access an exact copy, or use an existing one and change the names. Nobody would be able to tell the difference."

"But from what I understand I'd need a paper copy

of my approved emancipation to sign a rental contract or any legal document."

"No problem. Just say you lost it and they'll issue you another one."

"I don't know… I mean, I guess it would be cool to visit Summerland and see what it's like before I have to stay there…" I needed to give his plan some thought.

"You'll love it."

"If it's so great, why would you want to leave?"

"To help you, of course. If you don't want my help, that's fine. Just forget it."

"No! It's nice of you to offer to help me, and I really don't know how I could make it happen without you."

I wish I could talk to Ms. Broome. I didn't think she would approve. No, this is not something she would approve of at all.

"So. Do you want the spell?"

"Can I write it down and think about it?"

"Of course, but don't tell anyone else about this. Promise me, or I won't give you the words."

"Okay, I promise. Let me get a piece of paper and pencil to write the spell down. I don't want to get it wrong."

"Don't worry, I won't let you get it wrong."

I went to my desk and opened the middle drawer where I kept a pencil and pad of paper and took them out. "Okay, I'm ready. Tell me the words so I can write them down and then I'll think it over."

"Of course. You can take all the time you need. Just repeat the words back to make sure you get them exactly right. Okay?"

"Okay."

"Ready?"

"Go."

"Goddess of All, blessed be."

I wrote and repeated, "Goddess of All, blessed be."

Very good. Now say, "Body to mind, soul to soul…"

"Body to mind, soul to soul…"

"The good of all is our only goal."

"The good of all is our only goal."

"Exchange our places, and keep us whole."

"Exchange our places, and keep us whole."

"From Summerland the switch is free."

"From Summerland, the switch is free."

"So mote it be."

"So mote it beeeee…!"

My body hurtled into space.

CHAPTER 5

Was I dying?

I didn't feel any pain. I couldn't see anything except occasional flashing lights, as if I were flying past stars, and then darkness the rest of the time. I couldn't tell whether I was hot or cold, breathing or not breathing... Is this what it's like to die? What on earth had I done?

On earth... "I don't think I'm on Earth anymore," I said out loud. I heard my voice outside my head, even though I know there's no sound in space. I was slowing for a while and finally came upon what looked like a green planet. I know Earth is blue and Mars is Red, but whatever this place is, it's probably not in our solar system. I didn't remember learning about a green planet.

Floating down to the surface, I gazed into the distance as far as I could see, then swiveled in every direction. The most vivid colors and beautiful scenery met my eyes, but there were no people. No sign of civilization at all. Maybe there were animals that would come out later.

That thought scared me. Some wild animals could be bigger than me. Maybe they had eaten all the people? I touched down on the surface of the planet very gently and then straightened up. Gravity felt the same as on Earth. My feet seemed steady and sure, but was I ready to explore? My insides were quivering.

On Earth, I'd expect blue sky, green grass, flowers of every color, and brown tree trunks. Other than the colors being much brighter and more varied, things looked roughly the same—just more beautiful. I seemed to have landed in a high meadow. I saw snow-capped mountains way off in the distance.

Trees surrounded the meadow, partially obscuring the view—trees of every imaginable type. I didn't know a lot about trees, but I recognized what *shouldn't* be around me. A few maples—the ones with red leaves in the fall, stood among tall pines, as well as palm trees! Maybe I was still in Florida. But mountains? No way. There were no snowcapped mountains in Florida. I was pretty darn sure of that.

The air, which was mostly scented by pine trees smelled so fresh. There must be water somewhere. When I quieted my mind and concentrated, I heard some kind of babbling brook or river. If I followed that sound, maybe I'd find some nomadic people, or animals.

Lions and tigers and bears, oh my!

There goes my imagination again. Stop it, Jenika! You're safe. Uncle Donnie wouldn't bring you to a scary place.

The sound of water would lead me into the woods, if I chose to follow it. I might need water. I wasn't feeling thirsty, but maybe later. At a loss, I took a deep breath and wondered what to do.

"Well, standing here won't help me," I chided and ventured into the woods. I created my own path. I looked for footprints or any type of disturbance of the ground, not that I knew a tracker's secrets, but I was hoping for clues that suggested I might not be alone.

I just got here, but it already felt like a mistake. Maybe if I found some people, they'd know how to help me find my way home. But so far, it looked as if my own footprints were the only signs of life since nothing else marred the virgin ground.

I continued picking my way through the fragrant forest. As the babbling sound grew a little louder, I realized that there was indeed a brook in the distance. Finally, I spotted a wide gap between trees and a river came into view. I wondered if the water was safe to drink. As I drew closer, it looked clear and even seemed to be sparkling.

In the distance, a short waterfall created a rushing

sound. Walking toward it, I finally saw another life-form—fish jumping into the falling water, in an effort to reach the river's higher level. Maybe they were Salmon. I remembered hearing about Salmon jumping against the current to get where they had to lay their eggs.

Okay, so I wouldn't go hungry, if I could manage to catch some fish. I had never been fishing in my life, but if my stomach started to rumble, I'd find a way to grab one. So far, I wasn't hungry at all.

Gazing up and down the riverbanks, I still couldn't spot any people. Maybe if I followed the shore, I'd come to a larger river or even an ocean where people might be trading items brought by boats from faraway places. *I* was from a faraway place. I was pretty sure of that.

I remembered enough geography to know that most rivers flow toward the ocean. So, I turned to face the direction in which the water was flowing and walked along the riverbank that way, toward... who knows what?

There's nobody here, I heard myself thinking. Or maybe that was somebody else putting words into my brain with my voice. I didn't know anything about anything here! If this was Summerland, it certainly was beautiful, even if oddly mysterious.

So, how does one learn the secrets of the universe if there's nobody around to teach? Maybe this is just the first stop—the place to reflect on past lives. So far, the only life I could recall was my current one. Hopefully, it wasn't 'a past life' now.

Shaking off fear, I followed the bank of the stream and must've walked about a mile or so when the width enlarged slightly. That continued for maybe another mile or two, the water getting gradually darker and the banks further apart.

I didn't usually walk two or three miles anywhere, but, strangely, I wasn't tired. My school was about five blocks from my Grandpa's house and stores were about four or five blocks beyond that. When we lived in the suburbs, I took a bus to school and my mom drove me to the mall. I didn't play sports, so I didn't get a whole lot of exercise.

Glancing up and shading my eyes, I looked for the position of the sun. It was pretty much overhead, and if this place was like Earth, and east was where the sun rose and west was where the sun set, than I was... *Goddess knows where.*

I let out a heavy sigh and kept walking. I still hadn't come upon a person or structure. Nothing to suggest any kind of human industry was happening here. "Where the heck am I?" I called out to nobody in particular.

Suddenly an opening appeared not far in front of me—maybe twenty feet away, and oddly enough, it was the air itself that was separating. I didn't think it was the hole in the ozone layer. If I'm still on Earth— and that's a big if— I don't think I'm high enough to be anywhere near the ozone layer, so this was definitely weird.

I heard voices… And were those the tops of people's heads inside the rip in the air?

People!

I watched and listened for a while, not knowing if I'd fall in or get swallowed up in this hole. Creeping a little closer, I did see the tops of people's heads bobbing up and down, as if they were running…and then I heard screaming and sounds of panic!

Maybe this is what they talk about when they say the veil between the worlds is thinnest on Samhain. Most people call it Halloween. On earth, it's still mid-October as far as I know, but I'm not sure when the veil starts to thin. I crept closer still to this hole or window, trying to see exactly what was going on.

I was now standing about four feet from the opening when I noticed that the veil hadn't moved. Guessing that I was safe from being swallowed up, I breathed a sigh of relief. I could see people who were about my height, and some who were taller rushing by. But could they see me?

As I paid closer attention, I recognized some of the

faces and realized that I was looking into the corridors at Haven! I called out, but nobody stopped or even looked around. Apparently they couldn't see or hear me. This hole must be some kind of one-way mirror in the veil.

A banging sound caught my attention and I shifted my focus. Two of the guards seemed to be wrestling with something invisible. One guard was thrown against a wall, and the other was tossed against the opposite wall with such force he looked as if he'd been knocked unconscious.

Then it occurred to me… If I'm in Summerland and the spirit I channeled is in Haven—that means they're probably wrestling with *him!* We'd switched places.

But that's not Uncle Donnie. He would never hurt anyone!

The banging continued and from the jiggling front doors it was obvious the spirit was pushing against them.

A crowd of frightened looking students gathered in the corridor.

Ms. Broome hurried toward the group. She looked frantic. "Students! Go to your rooms, immediately."

Needing no further persuasion, they charged off in the direction of the cells. As soon as the last student disappeared around the corner, Ms. Broome demanded, "Who are you? What did you do with Jenika?"

Mrs. Whitehall along with two more guards joined forces with Ms. Broome.

"What's the meaning of this?" Mrs. Whitehall yelled at the conscious guard over the din.

"Someone—or some*thing* is intent on getting out of here. Should we unlock the doors?"

"NO!" Mrs. Whitehall and Ms. Broome yelled at the same time.

Mrs. Whitehall waved her hand toward the door and shouted, "Reveal yourself!"

Nothing happened. She repeated the action and practically growled the words out from behind her teeth. Taking a step back, she looked genuinely baffled when again, nothing changed.

"Should we get the non-magical guards out of harm's way?" Ms. Broome asked.

"Yes, we'll have to."

Wow, whatever was freaking her out must be serious. They always handled belligerent students with magic as a last resort, and this didn't look like it was getting handled at all.

When Mrs. Whitehall saw her secretary running down the corridor toward them, she turned toward her and yelled, "Go back to the office, Marjory. Make an emergency announcement that all students must go to their rooms at once, close their doors, and all guards are to stand watch in the corridors. Teachers are to meet at the library, immediately."

The secretary turned and ran off in the direction of the office.

"Why won't our magic work on him?" Ms. Broome whispered.

"I can think of only one reason. He's a poltergeist!"

I felt stupid and terrified at the same time. I was so desperate for my freedom that I let a poltergeist—the asshat whose place I'm currently taking, and *not* my uncle Donnie—escape to Haven.

I sat down beside a tree and covered my face with my hands. This couldn't be happening. I had been completely fooled. I just wanted it to be my Uncle Donnie so badly that I assumed it was him.

I tried to replay the trickster's conversation in my brain and wondered if I could reverse the spell that had brought me here. I didn't have anything to write with, so I decided to scratch what I could remember into the dirt. I found a twig and brushed the pine needles aside to make a smooth surface to write on. Then I concentrated and tried to recall the words of the spell.

I didn't know if it would help, but I had to try. I didn't belong here. And why had he wanted to change places with me? *Why would he want to leave? It's a beautiful place, and so far it seems peaceful.* Could just plain loneliness make someone that desperate? Or maybe he had a score to settle. I shuddered to think of what that might mean.

I hadn't seen everything, but this place seemed serene and safe. It smelled nice, like fresh air. I wondered if maybe nighttime wasn't as pleasant as the day. That made me nervous. I might need some shelter for the night, but I wasn't a builder and I had no tools.

Wait... Are my powers still suppressed? I hadn't even tried to use them yet.

"Goddess, I'm frightened and alone. I need protection and a home. So mote it be."

The hole in the air closed and a log cabin appeared.

Yay! I have my powers back!

Oh shoot. I can't see what's going on in Haven anymore.

⁕⁕

The following day, I was pleasantly surprised that no lions or tigers or bears had shown up during the night. As I lay there in a comfortable double bed, I took a better look around and noticed that it was equipped with a kitchenette, a full-sized refrigerator, a coffeepot, and a few cabinets that might house dishware. I wasn't much of a coffee drinker, even before incarceration, but the idea of a nice hot cup of tea with honey sounded good.

Prying myself up, I swung my feet onto the floor and glanced down at my clothing. I was wearing pajamas! Where had those come from? It's true I was pretty tired last night. Maybe I'd conjured sleepwear without knowing it.

Before falling asleep, I had been thinking hard about why I'd wanted to come to Summerland in the first place. Yes, it was because I thought my uncle Donnie could arrange the emancipation documents for me, and I trusted his word, but I had completely ignored the possibility of something like this happening. Plus, I really truly wanted to see what Summerland was like. Who wouldn't? I'm sure that contributed to my mistake too.

I'd wrestled with so many regrets as I'd laid there last night, second-guessing everything for a long time. Finally, I'd fallen into a fitful sleep, but this morning I'd awakened weirdly refreshed. I pattered to the kitchen and found a mug in a cabinet. I decided I'd try to brew a cup of tea the easy way and test my powers at the same time.

Remembering old Star Trek reruns, I said, "Earl Gray, hot." For some reason, I even said it with an English accent. My cup was suddenly full and warmed my hand. A little thrill rippled through me. "Oh! And honey, please."

A jar of honey appeared on the butcher block counter. I found a spoon in a drawer, stirred a generous dollop of honey into my hot tea and decided to brave the outdoors as I enjoyed my morning caffeine.

I opened the door and stood there in the doorway, neither inside nor outside. There were no remnants of sunrise, but since I'm not someone who sleeps until noon, I figured it was sometime in the midmorning.

As I took a sip of tea, I wondered how I could possibly get somebody's attention on the other side of the veil. That one-way mirror was a problem. And yet, there was always the hope of being able to communicate on Samhain, when the veil is at its thinnest. Possibly they could see me then.

I'd mark the days, so I wouldn't miss the thinning. That reminded me in an ironic way of how prisoners marked the days of incarceration on their cell walls. We weren't supposed to do that at Haven, but some of the more hardcore vandals did it anyway. They would wind up repainting their rooms, and spending a couple days in solitary, but I guess that, along with writing a little profanity for the guards to see, was worth it to the inmates.

Even though I only had that one-way mirror, I hoped I could get some insight into how it worked. Maybe if I tried to open the veil this morning, I could. I hadn't even tried to open it yesterday. It just appeared all by itself. I'd have to think about how to word a spell so I could do it purposely—and without some kind of horrible misunderstanding leading to a tear in the fabric of the universe or something.

Leaving my doorway, I stepped outside of my little cabin and glanced around to make sure I wasn't surrounded by wild animals, poisonous snakes, or huge spiders. Good Lord and Lady, my imagination is really too much sometimes.

The landscape was as stunning as ever. The sparkling river flowed gently. The sun warmed my shoulders and scalp. The air smelled of fresh pine and flowers. I hadn't even noticed the little purple flowers on the riverbank yesterday. Did they spring up overnight? Who knew what was possible here?

I walked to the spot I had cleared yesterday to use as a rudimentary blackboard. The words my trickster had used remained intact there, so no rain or wind had destroyed them during the night. I decided to make sure anything I wrote would stay intact, so as soon as I wiped a larger area to make a new "slate" to write on, I held my hands above it and said, "Goddess of all protect my plight, keep these words within my sight, any time I look at this patch, make it as legible as when I first scratch."

Well, that was about the worst spell I've ever come up with, but I had done it on the fly. In school when we worded spells, we'd had to write down the exact words, with correct spelling and punctuation, and think about anything that might be unclear or misunderstood. I should have considered doing that here too. It's not as if I were pressed for time. Whatever… It was done now.

At the top of the new patch, I made a calendar and I scratched an X over the date when I left Haven. It was October 23rd. So, I made boxes for the 24th, 25th, 26th, 27th, 28th, 29th, 30th, and 31st. I would be here eight days, and that's only *if* I could get help on Samhain. In other words, I had one week to figure a way to communicate with Earthly witches.

Without my even wording a spell, the hole in the air opened up again. I don't know if it mattered, but it seemed to open up in front of whatever I was facing—this time the river's edge. I stood up quickly and without even having to move closer to it, I could clearly see and hear what was happening at Haven.

I observed Ms. Broome in Mrs. Whitehall's office, both sitting in the upholstered chairs next to each other. With no one behind the desk, they appeared as equals, and seemed to be in quiet conversation.

"Ms. Broome! Mrs. Whitehall!" I yelled. Neither one showed even a flicker of reaction. I hung my head and let out a deep sigh of resignation.

"We've searched every inch of this place. She's not here," Mrs. Whitehall said.

Ms. Broome frowned. "I was afraid of that. Do you have any idea where she could be?"

Mrs. Whitehall hesitated, but eventually stared at

Ms. Broome, intently. "What I tell you next must not go anywhere outside this room."

Ms. Broome nodded. "I can be trusted to keep secrets to myself."

"Good. I have an idea about where she could be, but not how to reach her. Several months ago one of our inmates went missing. When he finally returned, I had a long talk with him. He told me he had been to Summerland."

Ms. Broome straightened her posture and her eyes widened. "Summerland? He was… dead?"

"No, not dead. Apparently he found a way to temporarily visit the place. He hadn't planned on staying, although he was willing to take that risk. He felt the fate that awaited him here would be worse than death."

"In Haven? What fate is that?"

"Adult magical prison. Since our name is Haven, the kids have nicknamed the adult facility Hell."

"But witches don't believe in Hell."

Mrs. Whitehall shrugged. "I'm sure it's just a name they use to scare each other. You know how dramatic teens can be. Anyway, he had hoped his mother's spirit, on the other side, could help him return to a different location outside of Haven. In other words, to escape permanently."

"And I guess that didn't happen since you spoke to

him after that." Ms. Broome scratched her head. "Does anyone else know about this?"

"You're the first one I've told, and I think the only other people who knew about it were his girlfriend and her family. I told him not to tell anyone else, and he said no one would believe him anyway."

"How did he get there?"

"He used a spell from an ancient text that he found in our off-limits library. Don't ask how he got in there… that's a whole different story. Regardless, I've searched the library looking for the text he described, but I haven't found it yet."

Ms. Broome looked excited. "If it's in there, maybe we can get all the teachers to search for it."

"Absolutely not. As much as I hate to say it, I'm not sure I can trust every single teacher. Shortly before you arrived here I had to fire a tenured teacher and eventually testify against her in magical court."

"Oh!" Ms. Broome was quiet for a moment. "I'm her replacement, aren't I?"

"Correct. Believe me, I vetted you thoroughly before you were hired."

Ms. Broome nodded. "As you should. But getting back to finding Jenika, there must be a way to re-create that spell. Can you get in touch with that boy?"

Mrs. Whitehall snapped her fingers. She walked behind her desk and picked up her phone. When the secretary answered, she put her on speaker.

"What do you need Mrs. Whitehall?"

"Get Mr. Holderness on the phone, please. I would like to speak to his son Logan. He was an inmate here a few months ago."

"Yes, I remember him. I'll connect you as soon as I can."

"Thank you." She hung up, and the two women looked at each other for a long moment, before Mrs. Whitehall broke the silence.

"I probably don't have to say this, but I will anyway... You, as Jenika's counselor, and I as Haven's administrator, are the only ones who need to know what's happening now. We will keep any information we find on a need-to-know basis. Agreed?"

"Agreed."

The phone rang and Mrs. Whitehall grabbed it up. "Hello."

"Mrs. Whitehall? This is Mark Holderness."

"Ah, Mr. Holderness. Thank you for speaking with me."

"Of course. I understand you want to speak to my son, Logan. I'm afraid that's not going to be easy."

"Why not?"

"He's backpacking across the country right now. Sometimes he finds a place to charge his phone, and sometimes he doesn't. I wish he had some kind of magical battery spell." He chuckled.

Mrs. Whitehall let out a deep sigh. "I'm afraid this is

urgent. Is there any way you can let him know to call me as soon as he can? You must be able to leave him a voicemail that he'll get when his phone is charged."

"Yes, certainly. I'll do that. Should I give him your office phone number?"

"You can give him my personal phone number." She rattled it off, and I made a quick note of it on my dirt slate.

"You say he's backpacking across the country?" Mrs. Whitehall asked.

"Well, almost across the country. He's planning to wind up in Arizona and visit his girlfriend, Genevieve."

"Genevieve Howe?"

"The one and only."

Mrs. Whitehall laughed. "Why am I not surprised? They're all told not to fraternize with former inmates, but they do. I knew those two would see each other again."

"I'm just happy he's taking some time for exploration. He's only eighteen and should travel—see a bit more of the world before he settles down"

"Oh, I think he's seen a lot already."

Mr. Holderness was quiet for a few moments. I couldn't tell if that meant he knew about his son going to Summerland, or not. That may have been Mrs. Whitehall's subtle way of trying to learn if he'd told his father about his off-world visit.

"Yes, well, I think being well-traveled is a good

thing for a young man."

Still noncommittal... Mrs. Whitehall looked over at Ms. Broome and shrugged. "Well, it was nice to talk to you again, Mr. Holderness. I look forward to hearing from your son as soon as possible."

"Yes, same here. And call me Mark."

"All right, Mark. Thank you. Have a good day."

"You, too."

Mrs. Whitehall disconnected the call and hung up.

Ms. Broome seemed a little less frustrated. "I guess we just have to wait now. Would you mind if I spent some time in the library? I might find that book. Did Logan give you a description of it?"

Mrs. Whitehall nodded. "He said it was very old, and had a brown leather cover with no title. I already looked, but you're welcome to try too."

The opening began to narrow.

"Ms. Broome! Mrs. Whitehall! Wait! It's Jenika! I'm here! I'm in Summerland!"

As the hole narrowed I tried to stop it from closing, grabbing onto air, but it slipped right though my fingers. I didn't really expect to succeed anyway. And what had happened to the Poltergeist? Since I'm still here, did that mean he was still there? If so, how could they be so relaxed?

Evidently, I could only see into the earthly realm for a limited amount of time. I was probably lucky the Goddess had allowed me that much of a peek. I leaned back on my elbows and mumbled to myself. "At least I have a picturesque place to sit and wait for Logan to return her call. Now I just have to hope he remembers that spell and how he got back."

⸺ ✦ ⸺

I had nothing to do except explore this whole new world and think, so I picked up where I'd left off yesterday, deciding to take another long stroll down by the river. Maybe I'd come up with some brilliant idea as I let my mind wander.

So far, this place wasn't bad. I had my powers back and there was nobody telling me what to do every minute. That's what I had wanted, right? My freedom and my powers back? Yeah, but I hadn't counted on the loneliness. Why was I completely alone? Was it because I was the only one with a body up here? Maybe I was surrounded by spirits... I hadn't sensed any, but that didn't mean they weren't around.

I stopped walking and thought about how to word a spell that might reveal the presence of others in my immediate vicinity. Barring that, I would settle for a way to communicate with magicals either here in Summerland or at Haven... or anywhere!

"Goddess, great mother of all, I'm sending out an important call. Please let it reach friendly ears, I beseech you to allay my fears."

I waited, but nothing happened.

"Damn. I was hoping for some kind of sign…"

Suddenly a sign popped up in front of me that read, *Go this way...* with an arrow pointing back into the woods.

I hesitated and pondered out loud, "I'd rather not walk back into the dense trees, darkening the forest, thank you very much."

Then I continued the debate in my head. *Wait... I asked for friendly, so whichever spirit or magical being who sent the sign must be friendly, right?*

On the other hand, I'd thought the stupid poltergeist was a friend too.

I stood there, frozen to the spot while I argued with myself. Finally deciding that I'd rather stay out in the open, I resumed strolling along the river.

"Hey! Where are you going?" a female voice called out.

She sounded familiar… I swiveled all around, looking for the source of the voice.

"Up here!" she shouted.

Up in the trees sat a certain giggling best friend—Genevieve Howe.

"Genevieve! Are you real? And are you really here?"

She swung down from the tree branches and dropped onto the ground. Then she rushed toward me with open arms.

I don't think I've ever hugged anyone so hard in my

life.

"Let. Me. Breathe, or I might end up in Summerland permanently!"

I released her quickly, but held onto her arms. "I'm so relieved to see you! I have to tell you something… Something awful I did, and I don't know how to reverse it."

"I figured that when I heard a distress call. I just didn't expect it to be *you* who needed my help. You're the least screwed-up inmate in Haven."

"Gee, thanks."

Genevieve laughed. "I know, that's kind of a back-handed compliment, right? But listen, I have something to tell you too. Something about Haven."

"I think I know what it is. There's a poltergeist there, and it's *my* fault!"

She gasped. "A poltergeist? Um, no, that wasn't what I was going to tell you. Maybe you should go first." Genevieve took my hand and we strolled along the river in the direction I had been going. I guess walking and talking was a good way of accomplishing two things at once. I still wanted to explore this incredible place before I left.

"Tell me everything," Genevieve said.

I heaved a huge sigh. I felt so stupid, but this was Genevieve, my friend who would still be my friend, no matter what. "Okay, here's the whole stupid truth. I was fooled into thinking the spirit I had channeled with my very first attempt at mediumship was my Uncle Donnie." I waited for that to sink in a bit. She just nodded, and we kept walking.

"So, he told me he could arrange to help me with a situation on earth, but I had to trade places with him to hold his spot in Summerland."

"Okay… I'm with you so far. I don't think it works that way, but, hey, nobody knows *everything*, right?"

"Right." Now I was questioning that whole 'secrets of the universe' stuff the poltergeist fed me. "So… I told my fake Uncle Donnie I would save his place here, if he would help me become an emancipated minor."

Genevieve's eyebrows raised, but she quickly schooled her features.

"So, it turns out, the spirit wasn't my Uncle Donnie. It was this poltergeist thing that I accidentally unleashed on Haven when he took my place."

"How do you know this? Did he tell you he was at Haven?"

"No, some sort of rift in the air opened and I was able to see the other side."

Genevieve stopped in her tracks and stared at me for a moment. "Cool! That never happened to me when I was here visiting Logan."

"You were here? Never mind. Of course you were. You just told me you were."

"But I never saw a hole in the veil. It didn't even occur to me to try to see through it."

"Me neither. This opening just appeared in front of me and I saw everyone rushing around like mad. When I crept closer I was able to see better and recognized teachers, students and guards at Haven."

"Wow, that's pretty cool, and it kind of goes with what I was going to tell you."

Relieved to have the onus taken off me for a minute, I said, "Please, it's your turn to talk."

"Yeah, so you know that Haven is only one of two facilities in the country. Haven East and Haven West. Right?"

I just nodded and let her go on as we resumed walking.

"Well, it turns out that we're there, not only because we screw up do crazy, dangerous or illegal things, but also we're actually more powerful than the ordinary witch. Maybe that's why you were able to look into the veil and see the other side, not to mention also channeling a freakin' poltergeist!"

"More powerful?" That was news to me. Yet, that would explain lightning shooting out of my fingertips. Not many witches can do that. Also it explains Alien being able to control the weather, like raining on top of one person or flooding the entire Midwest. That's certainly unique. "Wow. That makes sense now. I was wondering why there weren't more places like Haven. There must be other witches who have broken the law."

"Yeah, but none quite like us."

"Where do regular delinquent witches go?"

"Regular Juvie."

"Yikes."

She held up one finger, as if adding a thought. "And don't underestimate Haven's teachers. They're also packing more power than ordinary adult witches."

I stopped, grabbed her other hand and turned her so we faced each other. "I'm so glad you're here. Goddess, I need your help."

She laughed. I didn't know what in the world she found funny about that.

"So, is everyone at Haven okay?" I asked. "I couldn't tell the last time I was able to see in."

"I don't know. Why don't you call on the veil to open? Personally, I can't wait to see that."

"I don't know what I said or did to open it the first time. Or the second for that matter. It just kind of appeared."

"Sometimes when I need something really badly, it happens without my saying a word."

"Get out. Really?" I couldn't help my shocked reaction. Maybe I'd never really needed anything until the school shooter aimed his rifle at me.

Genevieve slung an arm around my shoulder and said, "Welcome to the super witches."

I burst out laughing. "Is that what we're calling ourselves? Super-witches? Do we get capes?"

She smirked. "Well, my aunt Hilary doesn't like

calling us minor goddesses. She thinks that sounds pretentious."

I halted. "Is that what we are? Are we minor goddesses?"

Genevieve shrugged. "Who knows? We're in uncharted territory, but it seems like a few of us, the ones that wind up in Haven, have extra strong powers, and we don't always know how to control them. And stuff that we really need sometimes just happens. Or in my case, it wasn't even stuff I needed. I sure didn't need to slap my teacher in the face with a fish, but I was thinking how she resembled a fish with her new collagen infused lips. I must have been thinking too loud."

I burst out laughing again. "I always wondered how the heck you did that. You're kind of a legend around Haven. It's hard to forget your nickname, Fish Face."

Genevieve rolled her eyes. "I know. That was about the worst nickname I could've had. Are there other kids with crazy nicknames there now?"

"Well Alien isn't fond of hers, but she's smart enough to just ignore anybody who uses it. It loses its force that way. When the jerks don't get the reaction there hoping for, they kind of forget about it."

"Yeah, I remember you telling me that I should just ignore the idiots who called me Fish Face, and you were right. You didn't seem to be bothered by Just Jen."

"Why should it bother me? It could have been so

much worse." I gave her a knowing smile.

"That's true. Lake Pirate wanted to call you Lightning Bug."

"Ugh. It might have been shortened to just bug. There's a new guy I'm calling Teddy Bear, because he was caught stealing on a nanny cam stuffed inside a child's teddy bear."

She laughed, and gave my shoulder a squeeze. "So, let's get back to this veil that we'd like to open…"

And just like that the weird hole in the air widened with plenty of room for both of us to see inside.

Genevieve's eyebrows rose. "Cool! I can see the cafeteria… and there goes that snotty blonde, walking in like she owns the place."

The next moment, the door flew open again, and the blonde came running out, screaming.

"I guess we know where the poltergeist is."

"Wow, is there any way we can look into the cafeteria itself, or do we have to follow somebody in there to see what's happening?"

"I don't know. I never tried to open a rift in this new place, but I was able to follow Ms. Broome down the corridor. Let's just hang out and wait. Someone else is bound to go in there soon."

"Hey! There's Alien." Genevieve pointed to Francine Costa who looked like she was headed to the cafeteria.

"Okay, let's follow her in," Genevieve said. "Now, how do we do that?"

"I'm not sure. When I wanted to follow Ms. Broome, I just sort of focused my attention on her back."

So, we focused our attention on Alien's back and our vision followed, almost like we were looking through a movie camera hovering a little above her. As soon as she opened the door, we were gazing into the cafeteria. She took a couple of steps inside and then halted. All the metal furniture had been bent, or broken, or turned upside down. And this was the indestructible stuff that had been bolted to the floor!

"Holy sh…ugar," Genevieve said.

"Really? You're watching your language around me?"

"I promised my Aunt Hilary I'd try to watch my language around the spa guests. It's just easier not to slip, if I never curse at all."

"Got it. I wonder why Alien isn't running and screaming too. It's obvious the poltergeist was there recently."

We watched as Francine shrugged, strode past the destruction to the kitchen, opened the door a crack, and peeked inside. A moment later she walked in. We followed closely behind her and watched as she opened the large freezer and helped herself to a half-gallon ice cream container. Then she glanced around, spotted a squeeze bottle of chocolate sauce, and grabbed that too.

"Good 'ol Alien." Genevieve chuckled. "That girl isn't afraid of anything."

"Nope. After she gave up trying to get her father's lawyers to spring her, she adapted pretty quickly."

"Okay, so I'm not really interested in watching Alien devour a ton of ice cream and chocolate sauce, and then get sick. Where do we go from here?"

I shrugged.

The hole began to close.

"Wait! Don't go yet!" Genevieve yelled.

But it was too late. The hole vanished and the serene Summerland scenery filled the space.

"Damn…I mean, *dang!* That was incredible!" Genevieve said.

"I know, right? The thing is, we must have been able to see what's happening at Haven for a reason. I feel like I need to fix the problem I created. I just don't know how. Do you?"

"Let me ask my aunt. I'll be back—"

"Wait! Should I stay here? How will you know where to find me again?"

"I'm tethered to you," her disembodied voice called. "It's a whole thing… I'll have to explain later." Her voice trailed off until all I could hear was the sound of the babbling brook and birds singing and chirping around me.

"Okaaayyy…" I sat cross-legged on the riverbank and enjoyed the scent of the pretty purple flowers.

CHAPTER 6

I had only inhaled a few breaths when Genevieve and her aunt Hilary appeared. I wasn't exactly sure it was Hilary, because she was doubled over laughing. Her long brown hair was obscuring her face completely. When she finally managed to pull herself together and stand up straight, her hair fell back off her face and I could see it was indeed Genevieve's bohemian-looking aunt, with glowing red cheeks and tears twinkling in her eyes.

Why was she laughing?

"Hey, Jenika. I hear you're in a bit of trouble." Hilary said, then started laughing again.

I looked at Genevieve for a clue. "What's so funny?" I whispered.

She just shrugged. "I think she did a joy spell."

"I'm sorry," Hilary said, waving away the giggles from her face. "Genevieve told me what happened and um, I think the 'joy in place of sorrow spell' I had been working on backfired. Hang on..."

Hilary closed her eyes, mumbled some words under her breath, and made a hand gesture as if pulling down a shade in front of her face. When she opened her eyes, she appeared perfectly normal.

"Oh, my goodness. That was... unexpected." Hilary said. "Have you ever laughed at something completely inappropriately?"

"Yeah. I think so. It relieves the tension."

She nodded. "It was like I couldn't help myself. I have been trying to maintain my positive attitude even when some of the spa guests around me are sad." She cleared her throat. "Clearly that spell needs refinement. I apologize."

"I guess sometimes the best of us have spells backfire," I said.

"Thank you for understanding. Now, about your situation, I'm intrigued... You were able to pull a switch with a... a poltergeist?"

"I'm not sure what I did. I just repeated what he said as I wrote the words down."

"What words?"

"He told me to say... Shoot, now I can't quite remember."

"You wrote the words down?"

"Yes."

"Let's see them." Hilary held out her hand as if I could give her a piece of invisible paper.

"It's on a slate back near the cabin where I stayed last night."

"A slate?"

"Well, not an actual slate. It's a patch of dirt I cleared with a stick."

Hilary cocked her head and stared at me curiously. "Why didn't you just conjure a piece of paper and pen?"

"Well, for one thing, I'm not at the *pen* stage yet. I still need a pencil and eraser, because wording spells correctly isn't automatic, but to be honest I didn't even know what I could do. It took me a while to realize I had my powers back."

"Oh! Did they have you brainwashed thinking your powers would be suppressed until they lifted them? Or that they wouldn't return outside Haven on their own?"

"Um, yeah. Are you telling me that's not true?"

"Well, not completely. Yes, the staff at Haven are pretty powerful and can suppress your powers for a while, but then they count on your not using them until they tell you that you can."

"You mean I could have left Haven any time I wanted to?"

"Probably not. They have an actual invisible fence in addition to their wards. It would give you enough of a jolt to make you think you had run onto a dangerous barrier."

"Are you kidding me? So, a lot of Haven is just smoke and mirrors?"

"And a poltergeist, apparently. Let's focus on that for now."

"Oh, yeah. I think we're about a mile from the cabin. I took a long walk this morning, but I can probably just get us back there with a spell, right?"

Hilary reached out with both hands. One clasped mine and the other, Genevieve's "Just think about where you want us to be and infuse it with the intention of taking us there. If you need words, you don't even have to rhyme. Just say, 'Take us to my cabin.'"

I didn't have a chance to say anything because the next thing I knew we were standing outside *somebody's* cabin, but it wasn't mine. Hilary took a couple of steps back and swore. Gazing at the sky she shook her fist. "Not *my* cabin, Goddess. Jenika's cabin!"

The air changed from hot and arid, to temperate with a gentle spring breeze that ruffled my hair.

Hilary picked at her long skirt, nervously. "I'm having a little trouble with my powers."

Genevieve put an arm around her aunt's shoulder. "It's okay. We've all been there."

"Not really. The more powerful the witch, the more outrageous the results can be when a spell goes wonky."

"Yeah, Fish Face wouldn't know anything about that…" I said, sticking up for my friend.

Fortunately, Hilary laughed. Then she looked over at my little home and smiled appreciatively. "Cute! I love the rustic look from the outside. Is it just as basic on the inside?"

"Go on in and see. That was the first spell I tried when I got here. I was afraid there might be some wild animals that could eat me during the night, so I cast a spell for shelter."

"Nah. You were safe," Hilary said. "I've learned a little more about Summerland recently. There are stages you go through. The first is self-examination. You know how some people say they see their whole life flash before their eyes when they think they're about to die?"

"Yeah."

"Well, that's just a preview. Spirits are given safe, secluded spots to review their lives, their lessons, what they might have done differently, and what they still need to learn."

"Oh, so the poltergeist was here, reviewing his former life?"

"Probably. Only a spirit that angry might not ever learn his lesson… He could simply keep focusing on revenge."

"And that's what he's trying to do? Get revenge?"

"I imagine he would have, except the staff at Haven

has him trapped there. Who knows what havoc he would otherwise cause out in the world?"

Genevieve opened the cabin door and stood in the opening, gazing around the simple room. "Nice. You have everything you need, but no more than that."

"Let me see." Hilary strolled up next to her niece. "Bed, kitchen, a table and a place to sit. Yep, only what you need and not what you don't. Very efficient. So where is the slate you wrote on? I need that, plus the location of the veil between the worlds that Genevieve told me about."

I stared at Genevieve. "How did you have time to tell her about that? You were only gone two seconds."

"We can manipulate time a little bit. Not much more than an hour or so, but your two seconds was more like twenty minutes to us."

"Wow. I'm learning so much about what we can do. Or is that just a *you* thing?"

"If you mean, 'is that something any witch can do?' then no," Genevieve answered. "But since some powerful super-witches can, you could call it a '*we* thing.'"

Hilary smiled at me. "You can do a lot more than you realize, but it takes training, or it will just get you into trouble."

"Like Haven."

"Exactly."

"So you're training Genevieve?"

"Yes. Okay, now… Let's go through this together." Hilary placed her hands on her hips. "I need to know as much as you can tell me about what words you used to channel the poltergeist and everything else you can think of. All the details."

I led them to the little patch I had cleared for my dirt slate and pointed to it. "There, that's what he told me to write and repeat as I wrote it."

Hilary and Genevieve looked at it, but didn't make the mistake of repeating it out loud, thank the Goddess.

Hilary stretched out a hand, and a moment later she was holding a piece of paper and pen. She jotted down the words.

"I don't know. This doesn't seem remarkable enough to do what you did. I would have expected Latin or some kind of poetry with a double meaning."

"Wait," Genevieve said, "There might be something… Could he have manipulated her hand or pen enough to close this letter, there? Do you see it?" she asked, pointing at the paper.

Hilary nodded. "I think I know what you mean." Then she focused on me again. "Jenika, this is just what you remembered, right? Where is the original copy of what you wrote?"

I shrugged. "Back in my room at Haven, I think. Unless Mrs. Whitehall has it by now. She probably does."

"Perfect," Hilary said. "I'm going to visit Mrs. Whitehall. You two stay here."

"How—"

I didn't even have a chance to finish. Hilary snapped her fingers and a bright flash of light temporarily blinded me. In her place was the hole in the veil.

"What just happened?" I asked.

Genevieve and I rushed to the opening and it started to close. We both stepped back and it reopened a little. Just enough so we could see through it, but we couldn't participate.

Hilary seemed to have arrived in Haven.

Genevieve called out, "Aunt Hilary? Can you hear us?"

We could see and follow her as she marched toward the office, her long hair and full skirt billowing out behind her, but she didn't appear to hear or see us. When she arrived at the office, she opened the door a little forcefully, causing it to bounce off the opposite wall. The secretary looked up at Hilary, who stood in the doorway and said, "I need to see Mrs. Whitehall, now."

The secretary rose and with a haughty tone of voice asked, "And you are?"

Hilary looked a little contrite. "I'm sorry. I'm Hilary

Howe. I met with your boss a few times after she recommended me for elder status. I thought you might recall my face from that time or from when my niece Genevieve was here."

I looked over at Genevieve and mouthed the word, *elder?*

She nodded and shrugged, like it was no big deal.

The secretary shook her head. "No, I don't remember you. But if you'd like to make an appointment…"

"Is Mrs. Whitehall here or not? She's going to want to see me since I might be able to help you with your poltergeist problem."

The secretary's brows shot up and she grabbed her phone. Before she could push a button, Mrs. Whitehall's office door flew open and she strode out to embrace Genevieve's aunt.

"Hilary! It's good to see you. How did you hear about our little problem when none of your charges are here? Did you change your mind about becoming an elder?"

"No. I still have my hands full with my nieces, but I would like to help, Jenika."

Mrs. Whitehall grabbed Hilary by the shoulders and said, "Jenika Jones? Do you know where she is?"

"Yes, but I think we should speak privately." She glanced over at the secretary.

Mrs. Whitehall escorted her into her office. "Of course. Come in."

When the door to the office closed, the secretary simply shook her head, and then we lost our view as the hole in the air quickly contracted. I sat back on my heels. "Dammit. I wanted to hear what they were going to say about me."

"Maybe the Goddess would rather you didn't," Genevieve said.

I thought about that for a moment and wasn't very happy about it. "So, what we do now?"

Genevieve shrugged. "Aunt Hilary told us to wait here. So, we wait here."

"Well, look at you, Ms. Rule-follower."

Genevieve chuckled. "My twin sister and I have been learning about things like rules recently. It seems that some rules were made to be followed."

"That's right. You found your twin. How are things working out with her?"

Genevieve smiled. "She's catching on quickly."

"Good. She hasn't replaced me as your best friend, has she?"

"Never." Genevieve threw her arms around me and her reassuring hug told me I had nothing to worry about. We were still BFFs.

Only a few minutes later, Hilary reappeared. She had the spell I had originally written in her hand, and showed it to me.

"Is this the spell you wrote and repeated?"

I took it and nodded. "Yup. This is it."

I was about to hand it back to her when she pointed to one part of it and said, "Take another look. Did you close that S to make it look like a figure 8?"

I lifted the paper closer to my eyes and took a good look at the spot she pointed to. Where it was supposed to say 'switch' now was 'eight witch.' I don't think I wrote the number eight. He said switch and I'm pretty sure that's what I wrote."

"I'm sure that's what you meant to write, but he may have been able to manipulate your hand or pen slightly for the ink to close those openings on the S."

Genevieve looked over my shoulder at it. "Isn't a figure 8 the same thing as the symbol for eternity?"

"Hilary smiled at her niece. "Exactly. So instead of saying *switch*. This could say *eternal witch*. And if someone were stuck in Summerland for eternity, that wording might point to that particular witch."

I took a step back. "Oh, crap. I get it now. If I wrote *Eternal witch* is free from Summerland, like it says, I probably freed him. And instead of going back as a regular spirit he went back as a poltergeist? Is that what an eternal witch is?"

"Perhaps. We don't know all the details and mysteries of Summerland, but I suspect there may be a few stubborn souls, who don't want to review their lives, or refuse to learn from the past and don't reincarnate."

"How did Mrs. Whitehall deal with the poltergeist? I heard her saying she'd get some supplies for an exorcism and meet the teachers at the library. Is he still wreaking havoc?" I asked, woefully.

"They didn't want to try an exorcism in case you'd be affected. They have him trapped in one of the solitary confinement cells. He's not happy about it, that's for sure."

"What happens now? Can we use this to reverse the spell?" Genevieve pointed to the paper I still held.

Hilary took it from me and glanced at it. "I think so."

"Will I wind up in Haven's solitary cell, and will he wind up back here?"

"That's what Mrs. Whitehall and I were talking about. We don't really know exactly what's going to happen to him, but we think we can get you back to Haven."

"What if I wind up in the same cell with him? You said he was trapped."

Hilary worried her lip. "I'll go back with you. You'll hang onto my hand the whole time. Don't let go, no matter what. If I have to transport the two of us somewhere else quickly, I can do that better by holding onto you."

I couldn't help asking, even if she didn't know the answer… "Am I in big trouble?"

Hilary looked at me as if I had two heads. "Well, you're not going to be up for a commendation."

"I figured," I mumbled.

Genevieve put her arm around my shoulder. "It'll be all right. I'm sure they'll give you a chance to explain. You said there was a teacher there who was on your side, right."

"Yes, Ms. Broome. She's been pretty supportive. I think she'll understand, but she may not be able to outweigh whatever punishment Mrs. Whitehall has in mind. I expect I'll probably have to sit in solitary for a while, and think about what I did."

Genevieve winked. "Maybe I can sit with you and make it a little less solitary. You know, since I can pop in and pop out at will."

Hilary folded her arms. "Oh, no you don't! You promised not to return to Haven or interfere with the inmates there."

She smiled. "I had my fingers crossed behind my back."

Her aunt rolled her eyes. "I knew you were too agreeable when you were told to stay away, and all you said was 'okay'." Hilary leveled her gaze at Genevieve.

"You understand that crossed fingers does *not* negate a verbal contract, right?"

Genevieve smirked. "I think that's sort of the universal meaning of crossed fingers. There was no verbal contract. Just—"

"Just nothing. You promised you wouldn't interfere with anyone at Haven. So far you haven't. Jenika was already here in Summerland when you came to help her. But I'm going to insist you keep your promise. Stay out of Haven, or we will have a problem, you and I."

Genevieve put her hands in the air as if she were surrendering. "Okay, okay. I get it. Crossed fingers, not a useful loophole."

"So, that means when I go back to Haven, I won't see you again until I get out?" I asked both Genevieve and Hilary.

"Probably not." Genevieve gave me a sad smile.

"That's okay, because I only have a few weeks left and then I can visit you in Arizona or you can come to Detroit—if I'm there." Then something horrible occurred to me. "Oh! Unless they add to my time, because of this whole mess."

Genevieve grimaced. "Oh Goddess, that's right. They could add to your time. How much does one get for plunking a poltergeist into their midst?"

"I didn't do it on purpose!"

Hilary rested one hand on my shoulder and the other on Genevieve's. "Nobody thinks you did it on purpose, and I don't know if more time is going to help. You're going to need to be honest with your teacher and Mrs. Whitehall. They seem like reasonable people. I would just caution you not to lie or minimize the severity of what you've done."

"I won't. I'm shocked that it happened at all. I'd only asked to write down the spell. I didn't plan to use it until I had had time to think it over."

"And that's when he tricked you." Hilary let out a sigh. "I'm sure they'll understand that much wasn't your fault. Do you know what you would've done, if you'd had more time to think about it?"

"I don't know. I'm really not sure."

Hilary nodded. "Well, at least that's honest. And that's what you should tell them. If nothing else, I hope they'll understand that you weren't being rash. You were going to think it over." She gave me a side squeeze. "Now, let me study this spell with Genevieve in your cabin, and we'll see if we can unravel it. You wait here. I'll close the door, so we have some privacy to discuss options without being distracted. Okay?"

"Sure. Of course. Do whatever you need to do."

Genevieve and Hilary entered my cabin, closed the door, and moments later I was hurtling through space again.

I landed with a thump. Opening my eyes, I could see that I wasn't in Summerland anymore. The neutral colors were muted, and the air smelled like nothing at all. I saw four concrete walls, no windows, and a door with a peephole in it. I was guessing I must be in a Haven solitary confinement cell. But Hilary said she would hold my hand and take me herself! Was I in here with the poltergeist?

I rushed over to the peephole before realizing it was, of course, looking in at me. I couldn't look out. Yup. This must be solitary confinement. I was never bad enough to spend any time in here, but who knows, maybe I belong here now.

"Hello?" I couldn't help being nervous about the poltergeist. "Am I alone in here?"

The lock clicked, and the door opened. Ms. Broome poked her head into the cell without stepping inside. "Jenika? Are you okay?"

I jumped up and rushed toward her, then I remembered she's my teacher, not my mom and stopped short. No hugs for me. "I'm fine, I think. Can I come out? Or am I supposed to stay in here for a while."

"We need to talk. I'll join you in a minute. First, I wanted to make sure that you're okay, and alone."

"I—I think so…"

She glanced around the room, sniffed the air and said, "Yeah, you're probably safe."

With that ominous remark, she shut the door. I

guess nobody could take for granted that I'd be solo in solitary. I suppose with all the weirdness going on, it would be hard to take anything for granted. I knew they'd trapped the poltergeist in a cell. What if I'd landed inside the same cell with it? Now, that would be unfortunate. But since we were trading places, maybe he's back in Summerland. *Good riddance!*

I hoped I wasn't going to be in too much trouble. I just wanted to get back to my classes, to the awful cafeteria food, to my sparse room, and to remember to be grateful I'm alive. Not that I was dead in Summerland, but you know… I was lonely.

Ms. Broome stepped inside and closed the door behind her. There was no furniture so she pointed to the floor. "Have a seat, we need to talk."

I sat cross-legged on the floor and she joined me. That was kind of a surprise, but she didn't strike me as someone who'd put a lot of stock in the condition of her dress pants.

"I know a little bit about what happened, according to Hilary Howe. It was just lucky that Genevieve had an idea of where you might have gone and how to get there. None of us had a clue."

"It was a mistake. I didn't mean to…"

She held up one hand to stop me. "We know you were tricked. We're not holding that against you, but I need to get to the bottom of why it happened at all.

What were you doing communicating with the poltergeist?"

"I didn't know it was a poltergeist! I thought it was my Uncle Donnie."

She nodded slowly. "Okay, that makes sense. I'm sure he wouldn't say, 'Hi, I'm a poltergeist.'"

We both smiled at that.

"Seriously," I said, "If I had any idea who I was actually talking to, I would've found you and told you about it. I never would have attempted anything, if I had known."

"I wish you had talked to me first, anyway."

"I do too… now."

"Why didn't you?"

"Well, I was just going to write down the words of the spell he gave me and then think about it."

"And if you'd had the chance to think it over, would you have told me about it?"

"Um…" I knew I wouldn't have, but not because I didn't trust her. The truth is, she's one of the few people I would trust. "I'm afraid not. You'd probably talk me out of it."

She nodded. "What you don't know is how many people were worried about you. We turned this place upside down looking for you."

I hung my head. How much did I want to tell her? Did I want to let her know about the hole in the veil? Had Hilary already told her? Or had she told Mrs.

Whitehall, only? Oh well, Hilary told me to be honest, so here goes nothing…

"This is going to sound weird, but I went to Summerland. I saw you all looking for me through a hole in the veil."

Ms. Broome looked like she was about to react, but quickly schooled her features. "How did all this happen?"

"Mediumship and a spell. I don't think I died or anything. The poltergeist just said he wanted to change places temporarily, so he could do something for me. I trusted him because I thought it was my Uncle, Donnie."

"So you said. And you knew your uncle had died and you were going to Summerland?"

"Um… Yeah. He said he could arrange for me to be an emancipated minor. That he had computer skills and could hack the system, but he couldn't do it from there."

Ms. Broome shook her head slowly. "Apparently the real spirit wanted revenge on the person who took his life, but he couldn't get through our wards. We set them up the minute we knew we had an intruder. Then, he had a real fit and began breaking things and hurting guards. You aren't to blame for his viciousness, but I want you to know what happened as a result of your actions."

Tears began to well up despite my lifelong vow not to let them spill. "Is everyone…okay?" I bit my lip.

"It depends on your definition of okay. Luckily only two guards are out with minor injuries, but they'll be all right. It could have been worse. We trapped him in the cell across from this one as soon as we could contain his energy. I was worried that an exorcism might affect you, if his appearance had anything to do with your disappearance. Thank goodness the Howe witches got involved and were able to reverse the spell. With any luck, he's back where he came from."

"I'm so sorry…" I hiccupped.

She let a small smile slip. "Someday, I'd like to know more about what Summerland was like for you. And that hole in the veil! That's very interesting. I wonder if it's just because we're nearing Samhain."

I shrugged. "I was wondering that too."

After a long pause, she got back around to the thing that started it all. "I guess you're really stuck on this emancipated minor thing."

"Yes. I know it'll be hard, because there was no abuse…"

"After something like this, I'm not sure you're ready for it, even if it were possible before."

My jaw dropped. "Wait, just because I was fooled by some slick ghost you think I'm irresponsible? Anybody could have been taken in by that."

"I'm not sure anybody would have attempted something like that. Didn't it sound dangerous to you?"

"Kind of. But I didn't know what else to do. I'm fifteen, and it's going to be three years before I'm able to take care of myself, because I can't sign a contract, rent a room, or get a full-time job. I don't want to join the military or get married."

"And what about your education? Were you going to drop out of school?"

"I could always get my GED later."

Ms. Broome stared at me so long I began to feel uncomfortable. "I'm sorry you feel that way," she said. "I really am. You're bright and talented. As an empath your education is vital. You could become an incredibly valuable employee in jobs like social work. Think hard about dropping out, if you want to support yourself with something other than a dead-end job."

"Is this going to add to my time? When do you think I'll get out?"

Ms. Broome let out a sigh. "We're not adding to your time. You'll be allowed to leave in three weeks, as planned, but you're going home unless your stepdad refuses to take you. In that case, we will arrange foster care for you."

I fell backward on my elbows, as if struck in the gut. "Are you serious? A foster home? That would be worse than being with my stepfather."

"Well, those are the options. The emancipated minor business is off the table."

I wanted to cry. But I wouldn't. I wouldn't give anyone the satisfaction… I tipped my head back and took a few deep breaths just to be sure any leakage stayed in my eyes.

Her expression softened. "Someone else here was as worried about you as the staff was. Do you want to see a friend before you start your solitary confinement time?"

I wondered who that could be. Francine? I wouldn't consider her the type to be overly concerned with anyone but herself, so I was more than a little curious. "Sure. I could use a friend."

"I'll go get him. You two can visit for a few minutes with the door open. A guard will be outside. I'll come back when it's time for him to leave." She rose and walked out briskly but left the door wide open.

A few moments later a familiar face peeked around the corner. "Hey, beautiful."

"Patrick! I didn't expect you to be the one who was worried about me."

"Why wouldn't I be?" He looked nervous. "I don't want to come all the way into the room… They might slam the door and lock us both in, then throw away the magical key." He leaned against the doorjamb. "And, *of course,* I was worried about you. You're my only friend here." He grinned.

I rolled my eyes. "You still think of me as your friend?"

He shrugged. "You're the only one who stopped telling me to get lost. You didn't care for me when I first got here, but then I grew on you. Admit it."

I snorted. "Okay, I guess that makes us friends."

"So, you want to hear another joke?"

"Oh, please Goddess, no."

"Did you hear about the kidnapping?"

I bolted upright. "No. What happened?"

"It's okay. He woke up."

I groaned… loudly.

"So where were you, anyway?" he asked. "I looked everywhere inmates were allowed to go—twice!"

"I'm not sure you'd believe me, if I told you." And, to be honest, I'd decided not to tell anyone but the staff, anyway.

"Okay, if it has to be that way… But if you ever feel like talking about it, I won't tell anyone else. You can trust me."

I didn't know if I could trust him with my life, but it was nice to know he would keep his mouth shut. I know others who want to get out of here. Who knows what they'd do to me to get the secret?

"Did they add to your time?" he asked.

"No. Are you still getting out soon?"

"Yeah. As it turns out, I may not be as hopeless as

they thought. But you know this place… Nothing is guaranteed."

"Yeah. Did Francine protect you like she did me?"

He snorted. "Not really. Alien is still hoping her father's lawyers will get her out, so she's been concentrating on him."

I was glad Patrick was the one who wanted to see me, and not just because he was leaving soon. If what Ms. Broome said was true, he might be the only kid who gave a damn about me. My empathy confirmed that his concern was genuine. I guess I could give him a little information and see if it went anywhere. That way I'd know if I could trust him with more later on—if there was a later on. I really would like to talk about what happened. Genevieve couldn't be with me here and I didn't know if I could hold it in for three weeks.

One of the guards stepped up behind him and said, "Hey, kid. It's time to go."

"Okay." Patrick glanced over at me. "I'll sit with you at lunch, right?"

"Who knows? If they let me out of here, and I wind up in the cafeteria at the same time you do, maybe we'll sit at the same table." I gave him a sly smile.

He laughed. "Okay, and if I'm still in the mood for your company, maybe I'll sit with you." We both grinned.

As soon as he left, the guard closed the door but

didn't lock it. He was probably still standing on the other side.

Suddenly it hit me, they hadn't suppress my powers when I got back! I wondered if I still had them. I could try a little harmless spell as a test… If what Genevieve said was true, I didn't need to write a rhyming spell. Instead I concentrated hard on what I wanted, held out my hand, and said "Tic-tac."

The conjured mini-mint appeared, and I popped it into my mouth. I felt like rubbing my hands together and saying, "Muahahaha…"

CHAPTER 7

I DIDN'T HAVE LUNCH WITH PATRICK. INSTEAD, I received a tray in my cell. I assumed I was in here for a while. Sometimes when we messed up, they gave us a time-out to sit and think about what we did wrong, but that wasn't in a solitary cell. *All* I could think about was what I had done wrong and how I blew my chances of becoming an emancipated minor. Now I had to depend on a stepfather who'd never wanted me in the first place and *hope* he'd be willing to take me home.

Home is a relative term for me. I had lived in Nebraska and Japan for a few years with my parents, then Detroit with my grandfather and mom for five, then the suburbs with my mom and stepfather for two more, then to another suburb with my stepdad for two more, and most recently in the city when my stepfather moved us there to cut down his commute. I could change the saying "There's no place like home" to "There's no home anyplace."

I still hadn't joined the general population. Instead, I found myself sitting outside Mrs. Whitehall's office. I'd overheard the secretary talking to Mrs. Whitehall about getting my stepfather on the phone. I guessed this time they weren't going to let me talk to him. Too bad, because I was prepared to apologize and beg forgiveness.

One thing they hadn't counted on was my powers. When the secretary had her back turned, I concentrated on the phone in the administrator's office and whispered, "Listen in."

"What about foster care? Can't she go somewhere else? Maybe someplace in the suburbs?" My stepfather asked.

"Am I to assume you don't want Jenika to return to a stable home? That you'd rather she be placed with other children whose parents have problems severe enough to have lost their parental rights?"

"Well, when you put it that way…"

Oh, wow. Mrs. Whitehall was advocating for me, in spite of what I had done. And talk about a hard sell! I wondered if she had told him what had happened. Probably not. As far as I could tell he still didn't know I was a witch. My mother had made sure I understood how difficult that would be for both of us, if I had told him. The staff weren't about to let the fuggles know we even existed.

"Look, she's a strange kid. I don't even know how to handle a regular kid. I'm not exactly the TV father type."

"What do you mean by strange?"

"She always seems to know exactly what I'm thinking. Would you like someone like that around you?"

"She's very sensitive. That's not a bad thing. And as for being a TV father, don't judge yourself too harshly. Most parents aren't well prepared for the task of child rearing, and you came into it late. Whatever faults Jenika may have, I can tell you honestly, they're minor compared to what you call regular kids. She's had a lot of losses. And she's doing the best she can to cope with them."

"Then why did she electrocute a fellow student?"

Mrs. Whitehall took an audible breath. "She perceived a threat to her safety. Someone came up behind her and put his hands over her eyes. And that was shortly after the school shooting. She was the one who stopped it, you know."

"Is that what happened? Nobody told me that."

"Are you kidding? Jenika didn't tell you?"

"We don't talk much. She keeps to herself, and so do I."

Mrs. Whitehall let out a 'Hmph' sound, followed by

a long pause. At last she made a final push. "I must insist you do your duty as her guardian. Don't worry about being the perfect father. Just give her a place to call home."

He sighed. "I guess I can try, but it's for her mother. I don't know if there's an afterlife or not, but in case she's watching, I'll do what I have to do."

"Good. I'm sure Jenika will appreciate the effort, even if she doesn't say so."

"Yeah, well…"

She waited, but the conversation seemed to have ended there. They said their goodbyes and I expected I'd be called in and given the relatively 'good news' soon.

I had mixed feelings. If I went back to Detroit, I'd go back to my most recent school. He couldn't afford private school on a postal worker's salary. On the other hand, if I went to another new school, even in the burbs, I'd be an outsider again. I'd had enough trouble fitting in with the kids in my middle school. High school was even more brutal, although being here in Haven taught me a few things about survival. Maybe I'd be better prepared this time.

Nope. Two weeks later, I wasn't any better prepared for the bullying and taunting directed at a high school kid who's been to juvie. Worst of all, they were trying to implicate me in the school shooting. They thought juvie had to be for that.

When I got back, most of them steered clear of me. Just as well. My empathic abilities were hard to shut off, and I didn't like the negativity that overwhelmed me every time someone looked my way.

Nobody at Haven knew where I had been when I went to Summerland, and I didn't have to lie, because they were told not to ask. I told Patrick a little bit. I let him know there was a spell that went wrong, and that I wouldn't give it to him even under torture. He seemed to agree with my wisdom and assured me that torture wasn't worth it.

As it turned, out his sentence was almost up too, so they let him in to say goodbye to me. Our parting was way too brief. Apparently, he'd only needed to be rehabilitated for a few weeks. I had been there for a year. But the good news was that I'd be turning sixteen soon. Sixteen is closer to seventeen and seventeen is almost eighteen. I sighed. I only had to endure this for two more years. Two…more… years. That became my mantra.

My stepfather and I continued to live under the same roof, cook for ourselves, and avoid each other pretty much all the time. I spent most of my free time in my room with my familiar—my beautiful kitty Star.

Now that my fair weather friends were not friends at all I had few places to 'hang out'.

I missed Genevieve. She promised not to go to Haven, but she hadn't promised not to come to Detroit. I didn't know how to get in touch with her in Arizona, and I never told her how to find me here. She was living and working at some spa with her aunt, but she said something about being tethered to me. What that meant, I still didn't exactly know. We'd gotten distracted before she could explain it.

I guess I would have to deal with the stupid taunting from my classmates. It couldn't go on forever, right? Okay, it could go on for two years and that would feel like forever.

For some reason, the kids at school had decided that they should come up behind me and scare me. They didn't touch me, but they would yell *boo* in my ear, or *zap*…stupid stuff they hoped would set me off. Fortunately, I expected it from them. Nobody was going to catch me unaware again.

I wanted to learn more about my powers. Genevieve had hinted about our being more than we were led to believe, but I didn't have anyone to teach me. Part of me was afraid of what I could do without any supervision. Another part of me was really curious and wanted to experiment.

Unfortunately, the only spell I wanted to do right

now would be to hang my classmates upside down by their toes and keep them suspended like that until they promised to leave me alone. But, that would be wrong.

Yup, Haven had taught me a few things. Even if it was just what kind of magic was considered okay, and what wasn't. Sometimes that was valuable in itself. I didn't have a teacher like Ms. Broome looking out for me here in Detroit, but I had a guidance counselor—not that he provided much guidance. His name was Jonah La Vallee. He let us call him Jonah. Even without my empathic abilities, I could definitely tell he hated his job. He basically had the same internal mantra. *Two more years... I can retire in two more years.* I tried to talk to him about the bullying, and his idea of dealing with it was to ignore it. Even though I had been doing that without any positive results, he thought I should just keep doing that. Sure... I just hoped I didn't accidentally electrocute anyone again.

I remembered that Ms. Broome thought I'd be valuable in a job like social work. But I couldn't think of anything I would hate more. Dealing with kids who were unwanted or screwed up by dysfunctional families... I had had enough of that to last a lifetime.

So what did I want to be when I grew up? I had no idea. Maybe I would figure it out while I was in one of those dead-end jobs she talked about.

Before juvie, I had thought about becoming a cop.

Some really disturbing accusations against police offi-cers and their treatment of the black community seemed to indicate change was coming. I could be a young black woman there to protect and serve, the way a cop is supposed to… and if I were in a life and death situation, I could use my magic to protect myself. Guns jam or misfire, right? Nobody would have to know I'm a witch.

Protests all around the country made me think I could make a difference. However, if my juvie record was discovered, that would probably kill my chances.

⸺⸺⸺

I couldn't take it anymore. All I could think about was committing a victimless crime, hope I'd go back to Haven and age-out at eighteen. Before I did something stupid though, I called Ms. Broome from my front porch.

"Jenika?"

"Yes, Hi. Ms. Broome, do you have a few minutes to talk?"

"Um…sure. Just let me close my door."

A moment later she said, "What's up?"

"I—I just can't take it here anymore."

"Did something happen?"

I took a deep breath and let it out slowly. How

could I explain it? I had no idea what to say, so I just started babbling and hoped she could figure it out.

"I'm really sorry. I don't mean to bother you, but I have to talk to somebody, and nobody seems to care, except my familiar, Star, and she can't do much. It's about kids taunting and bullying me at school. My stepfather, doesn't give a damn what happens to me—you must know that. My guidance counselor doesn't want to be bothered... People I thought I could be friends with avoid me... or worse. My empathic abilities are driving me crazy. I just want to move to some small town and work as a waitress for a while. I just need a quiet life with no complications."

"Are you safe? Is anyone trying to hurt you?"

I sighed. "Not physically. The kids in school are trying to scare me and get me to react badly, and the only reaction I want to do is a bad spell. I know not to do revenge spells. Just so you know, I'm not going to. I understand that's black magic and will rebound on me three times."

"Thank the Goddess! I'm glad you don't want to do that. Did you learn that lesson from Haven or did your mother teach you that before she died?"

Oh, man. She had to bring up my mother... Now I was going to choke up. I could feel tears trying to form and my throat closing. *Get it together, you can't cry right now, Jenika. I need to show her that I'm strong enough to take care of myself.*

After my long pause, she asked, "Are you and your stepfather getting along?"

"I guess… We're pretty much ignoring each other."

"What has he said about the bullying?"

"He doesn't want to get involved. He said to tell someone at the school."

"And have you?"

"Yes, I've told my guidance counselor. He thinks I should just ignore them. I know that's not going to work. That's what I've been doing. I'm getting sick of it."

"Okay, what other choices do you have?"

I spit out the first thing that popped into my mind. "I wish I could come back to Haven. At least you cared what happened to me. Nobody else does."

"Oh, Jenika…"

I didn't need empathic abilities to hear the pity in her voice. I also didn't mind hearing it for once. It was nice to know somebody sympathized.

"It's only been a couple weeks, how am I going to endure two years of this? Seriously, I want to come back to Haven. How can I do that other than committing a new magical crime?"

"Jenika, that's not the way to handle this. For one thing, Haven East might not take you back. They may feel you're not getting what you need here, if you're still committing crimes. They might try sending you to Haven West."

"I thought Haven West was for witches west of the Mississippi River and Haven East was for witches on the east side of the Mississippi River."

"Ordinarily, it is, but not always. Listen, I can only think of one thing that hasn't happened, that should have long ago."

"What's that?"

"Family counseling. You and your stepfather need a therapist. I think it would be a good idea for each of you to have a separate appointment and then get together and all three of you discuss what's going on. I can set something up. Unless your stepfather would rather find his own…"

I laughed. "I don't think he'd be willing to go to a therapist if he were dragged to the office by wild horses."

"Well, let's hope it doesn't come to that. I could help make the appointment, if you can't. That's the one thing I would be willing to do from here."

"Could you just pop up here for a few minutes and talk to him in person?"

There was a long silence on the other end of the phone. Ultimately, I made sure she was still there. "Ms. Broome?"

"I'm here. I really don't think that's something I should do. It would be best if it comes from you first. If he won't listen to you, I can get on the phone and try talking to him, but I don't want to gang up on him."

"Okay… Is that really the only thing you can think of to help me?" I know I should've been grateful for whatever she was willing to do, but it just didn't seem like counselling would accomplish anything.

"I'm not even supposed to do that much, Jenika. I just feel that in your case, this is a piece we let slip through the cracks, so I can intervene for that reason."

I took a deep breath and let it out, trying not to sigh in defeat. "Okay, I'll try that. Thanks."

"By the way, Jenika, there's something you might like to know…"

"What's that?"

"Patrick wants to look you up. We couldn't give him your address, of course. But I think that boy is determined enough to find you on his own. I just thought I'd give you a heads-up."

That made me smile. At least someone wanted to be in my company. "Thanks for telling me. I don't suppose you could give me his address either."

"You supposed right. But if he does find you, I know it'll be nice to have a friend. My advice would be to just stay friends and try not to turn it into any more than that. You're vulnerable right now. Understand?"

I shrugged, even though she couldn't see me over the phone. "Yeah, I think so."

"Okay, I'll be interested to hear how it goes with your stepdad. Just give it your best shot before you call me back, okay?"

I was heartened to hear she wanted me to call her back. I hadn't expected that. Some part of me had thought she might not talk to me at all, because she didn't have to anymore.

"Thank you for listening and for helping me, even though I'm not living there anymore."

"You're welcome. Best of luck, Jenika."

"Thank you. You too." I don't know what I was wishing her luck for, unless it was just putting up with the rest of the Haven population. Supposedly I was one of the easy ones, but I guess we all present our own unique challenges.

⚯

"Phil, can I talk to you?" He was making a sandwich at the kitchen counter and looked up briefly. "Talk? About what?"

It was hard to explain the content without talking. I guess I'd just have to launch into it. "I'm not happy."

He shrugged. "So, what you want me to do about that?"

"I thought maybe we could go to therapy."

He laughed. "Therapy? Don't you have a guidance counselor for that?"

"Yeah, but he sucks. I think we can do better."

"What do you mean 'we'?"

"I mean you and me. Family therapy. My guidance counselor is way overworked and probably underpaid."

"Sounds like my job."

By this time his sandwich was made and he brought it over to the small dining table we had on one side of the kitchen. At least we were sitting together, even if we weren't eating together.

"I was hoping we could figure something out to make us both happier."

He squinted at me. "You keep saying 'we'. There is no 'we'. You live under my roof. I give you all kinds of freedom. What more do you want?"

Oh, I don't know... Maybe I don't want to be resented for living? Even despised at times? I could never say those things out loud, though. I just wanted to have a civil conversation. "Look, the guidance counselor has about five-hundred students he's responsible for. I think the therapist would have a lot fewer patients and could devote more time. Maybe an hour a week?"

He leaned back and folded his arms. "Yeah, right. They charge a couple hundred dollars an hour. Who's going to pay for that?"

Yup, this was going as badly as I expected.

"I called Ms. Broome at Haven. She said family therapy was about the only thing they didn't get to do while I was there."

"They wanted me to take my vacation, drive down

to Florida, and talk… Yeah, that wasn't freakin' happening."

"But now I'm here. Ms. Broome said she'd help set up the appointment, if you didn't know somebody up here who would be good."

"Well, first of all, I doubt she knows somebody up here either. And second of all, no. Just no."

It didn't seem to make any difference what I said. The money was part of it, yes, but the other part was just him being a stubborn ass. I knew he probably wouldn't open up, but I promised Ms. Broome I would try. Maybe I'd have to be my own therapist. "Why do you resent my being here so much? I don't cause any trouble."

He rolled his eyes. But he didn't say anything.

"Am I? Am I causing you trouble?"

"Now that you're out of Juvie, you mean?"

"Yeah."

He shrugged one shoulder. "Kind of…" After a long hesitation, he finally blurted out, "Look, there's a woman at work I want to date. It's the first time I've wanted a girlfriend since your mom died…but I can't because *you're* here and she lives with her mother. I mean I could take her out to dinner, but what about afterward?"

I knew what he meant. Where would they have sex? It made me a little squeamish, but I figured maybe if I didn't object, it would actually help. Maybe he would relax a little.

"I understand. And I wouldn't mind at all, if you take someone out and then come back here. I can just go up to my room and close the door. You could have the whole downstairs to yourselves."

He shook his head. "That's nice of you, but it won't work."

"Why not?"

"Just knowing you're in the house would kill the mood."

I didn't see how, unless his girlfriend was a screamer. "Look, I wouldn't listen or anything. I could put my earbuds in and listen to music, and I wouldn't hear a thing."

He was quiet for so long it became uncomfortable. At last he said, "Don't you have a friend or somebody that you could have a sleepover with?"

"No. That's part of why I'm unhappy. I have no friends anymore. Not at school. Not after school. Not anywhere."

He finished the first half of his sandwich and picked up the other half as he rose, probably deciding to finish it in front of the TV. He did that sometimes.

Before he got too far. I said, "So, will you at least think about it?"

"Think about what?"

"I don't know… Everything?"

He just shook his head and resumed walking.

I hoped Patrick would find me, but I doubted he could. My name wasn't in the phone book and his probably wasn't, either. Both of us lived with a parent, and who knows if his last name was the same as his mother's. Some women never changed their maiden names—not that I knew her first name, anyway. Even if they had the same last name, they may have an unlisted number or only a cell phone. I decided to check social media for Patrick. After all, I had nothing else to do.

I went upstairs to my room and closed the door. There was nothing on Twitter or Instagram. He probably didn't use his actual name and I didn't know his handle. I checked Facebook, and I was surprised to find more than one Patrick Hightower. I guess his name isn't as weird as I thought. But none of the pictures looked like him.

I closed my computer and went back to the library book I had been reading earlier. I flopped onto my bed and started to read the section on well-paying non-college careers. So far, nothing seemed to require less than a G.E.D. I knew I needed more education and training, but to be honest, I would take anything at this point.

Maybe that's how I could get lost. Take an after-school job and not come home until two o'clock in the morning. Yeah, right. Like they hire sixteen-year-olds to stay out that late. Still, the idea appealed to me.

Maybe with a fake ID, I could pass for eighteen? Who was I kidding? I barely looked sixteen. Maybe make-up would help. But again, no money.

Hey! I could steal some make-up and conjure a fake ID... and if I didn't get caught I'd get a job. Even if I did get caught, I'd wind up back in Haven. East or West, it had to be better than the suck-fest I had to put up with every day in my current school.

CHAPTER 8

I'd scoped out a few stores that sold high-end makeup. Hey, go big or go home, right? I figured they'd have cameras, and since I wanted to get caught and sent back to Haven, I didn't bother covering my face or wearing a hoodie. I sported my usual outer wear…my beat-up jean jacket. Underneath I wore my t-shirt that said, "Detroit High." Some of the kids thought that was hilarious… But Detroit High should help identify me.

I did a quick spell to get into the boutique. Genevieve had said that 'super witches' didn't have to rhyme, but I kind of liked to, so I composed something before I got there. Whatever happened, it would beat Patrick's lock picking lesson.

"Dear Goddess, I need to get into this store, so please help me and open the door." It was simple, but harder to misinterpret that way.

I tried the handle and it opened easily. *Halleluiah!*

I browsed the store, casually, as if shopping during the day. I picked up a few items to try on. The light sucked, so I waved my hand over a make-up mirror with side lights, and my affinity for electrical current didn't let me down. I have to admit, I was worried about a bolt of lightning setting the place on fire, if I tried to light up the whole store. I still hadn't learned what I could do or how to control it.

I figured I'd start with foundation. There were about two dozen shades for white girls, and a few for those of us with darker skin. I tried not to let that get me down. One of the bottles looked like it would be pretty close. I pumped a generous amount into my palm and applied it all over my face.

Wow! What a difference! I tucked that bottle and an extra one into my pocket. I had watched plenty of videos on how to apply eyeliner. Figuring that would make me look older, I grabbed the most expensive of the solid black options. Once I had it on, I had to fill in a few places to make the line smooth, but a thicker line made me look even older. *Great!* I picked up another one of those and, just for good measure, I took one in dark blue too. Might as well have a little fun and coordinate with my ensemble at the same time.

Okay, my pockets were getting a little full, so I walked behind the counter and grabbed one of their bags. I continued to 'shop' for sulfate-free shampoo and leave-in conditioner. I grabbed two of the latter, knowing I'd be using that daily. I also found some expensive Moroccan oil with a black woman on the box. My hair wasn't totally black. Thanks to some unknown ancestors, mine was a mousy brown. I never liked the color, but the oil would make it shiny. One last essential item I needed was a good wide-tooth comb. I found one made of olive wood and tucked that into the hip pocket of my jeans. Then it occurred to me that it might break or stab me in the butt, if I sat down, so switched it to my jacket pocket.

Okay, that was fun! I remembered Patrick's philosophy of life. I think it was something about having as much fun as possible. I might understand him a little better, now. I would like to learn how to have fun, without breaking the law, though.

On my way out, I made sure the security cameras got a good look at me from all angles. Then, I got on my bike and rode home.

I woke up, went to school as usual, and nothing happened. *Are you kidding me? I can't get arrested, even if I want to?* F.M.L.

Finally, toward the end of the day, I was called to

the office. My stepfather and two uniformed police officers were waiting for me in the principal's office.

Uh oh... Phil is furious. His neck veins are bulging. I didn't really expect him to be happy, though. The door wasn't closed yet when he lit into me.

"What the hell is wrong with you? Stealing makeup? Why?"

I shrugged.

"Oh, no. You don't get to clam up. *You're* the one who wants to talk all the time."

All the time? Was he referring to the one conversation we'd had in three weeks?

The principal was sitting behind her desk, and she finally interjected, "The reason doesn't matter right now. The thing is, Jenika, you have to go with the police."

"Am I under arrest?" I asked, hopeful.

The older looking black cop answered, "Not yet, but you probably will be, Miss Jones."

"And I'll probably have to blow my life savings bailing you out!" Phil bellowed.

"Don't bother," I said.

Phil looked like he was about to yell something else, but the cop raised his hand to stop him from speaking. "You can talk to her more when we get to the station, Mr. Ford. Are you going to come with us, willingly, Miss Jones?"

"Oh course," I said. Nobody would guess how cooperative I'd be since I was getting exactly what I wanted.

The ride to the police station was pretty quiet. Phil followed behind in his car. I don't know if he had to get out of work early or if it was his day off. Either way, he was probably mad at me for that too.

When I arrived, I was shown a picture of myself from last night's 'hidden' cameras. I was still wearing the same jacket. I had left a few unopened products in my pockets in case there was any doubt. Naturally they found those when they searched me. They also found Patrick's lock picking tools in my jean jacket pocket, which I had forgotten all about.

I was read my Miranda rights in front of Phil, and then finger printed, photographed, and booked. Instead of keeping his mouth shut, Phil immediately volunteered, "She just got out of Juvie, you know…"

"Shut up, Phil." Hey, I had to make my role look realistic, right?

"What did you say to me?" Phil puffed out his chest and began to stride toward me.

The cop stuck his arm between us and yelled, "Calm down, you two!"

Phil stopped immediately. I don't think they'd be dumb enough to call his bumping into the cop's arm, "assaulting a police officer," but these days, who knows?

I was manhandled by a female police officer. She searched me more thoroughly and stuffed me into a private cell in a separate area for juveniles. It was smaller than you'd expect, but at least I had enough room to lie down, if I were stuck here for any length of time.

Most police officers aren't privy to magical information. They don't even think magic exists. But the judge will know when he sees I've been to Haven. Judges and sometimes chiefs of police have been trusted with proprietary information. It's all kept on the down-low so the lower pay grade officers don't suddenly start blaming every friggin' mystery on magicals, allowing the real perps to get away with their crimes.

Fortunately, each cell came with walls on three sides, so I didn't have to share war stories with anyone. Privacy was also convenient for one other thing; I had a little drop-in company. *Patrick had found me.*

"Hey you," he said, as if he had just seen me in the hall at school and decided to send me a grin and a greeting.

"How did you get in here?"

"A glamour. I made myself look like a cop."

Putting his hand on the locking mechanism he turned it forty-five degrees. It clicked and he entered my cell quickly, then closed the door behind him.

"Neat trick."

He shrugged. "It was a bit of a challenge, but

nothing a magical burglar can't handle. Besides, I like a challenge."

"How did you know where to find me?"

"I hung out by your school a few times. Today, I got lucky and saw you being arrested."

I snorted. "Yeah, today was one of my finer days. Aren't you worried about the cameras?"

"Nope. I disabled them for a few seconds, and then stuck them on a magical loop. Now don't move, and when the real video comes back on, the cops won't notice the difference." He glanced at the angle of the camera, as if checking for a blind spot.

"I don't have much room to move anyway."

"That's okay. Hey, I have a good joke for you."

I smirked. "Fine. I think I could use one now."

"What did the duck say when she bought lipstick?"

"I don't know."

"Put it on my bill."

I actually chuckled that time.

He smiled that charming grin and I noticed his teeth were really white. Why didn't I notice that before? I also noticed he was a little cuter than I remembered. Maybe because he'd had a chance to come home, use his electric toothbrush, get good close shaves, wash and style his hair a little... I don't know. Something about him was different.

He tipped his head to the side, as if noticing me for the first time too.

"You look different. Older."

"Yeah, that was the goal…that and getting caught." I didn't feel like going through the whole rigmarole with him again, but I gave him the highlights. "I'm wearing makeup to look older. I want to get a job, so I can take care of myself, financially—then try for the emancipated minor thing again."

"Yeah, I'm going to have to find a different line of work too."

"Do you have any ideas?"

He shook his head. "Not really. I have a driver's license, so if my mom lets me borrow her car I could do deliveries. Sometimes people tip well. It all depends."

"Just don't tell them any jokes." Why hadn't I thought of things like deliveries? It sounded easier than waiting tables. Well…it could be because I didn't have a driver's license. Who knows if I ever would, since money seemed to be such an issue with Phil. I could just imagine how thrilled he'd be to pay for the Driver's Ed course, then the permit, then the license, not to mention increased insurance… *Yeah, no*. I didn't see that happening until I got out on my own.

"That sounds like a good plan. So, what are you doing here?" Not that I wasn't grateful for his company. It just seemed a little stalker-ish.

"I thought I'd check in on you…see how you're

doing. I'm kind of glad I did. It doesn't look like you're doing all that well."

I laughed. "It's okay. I want to go back to Haven."

"Are you kidding me?"

"Not even a little bit. Home sucks. School sucks. I can't take it anymore. Even in this jail cell, I have more peace than I've had in a long time."

"I wish I had room for you to move in with my mom and me in Ann Arbor, but we live over a garage, and it was tough enough to squeeze two-bedrooms in there. I don't think she'd let us share, but if she would, I'd totally let you." One side of his mouth tipped up in a smirk.

"Yeah, don't worry. I'll find my own way, eventually. I'm hoping Ms. Broome will help me once I get back to Haven. At least there I can talk to other magicals who understand a little better what I'm going through."

"*I* understand. I could use someone who understands me too. We should have kept in touch. Although, now it doesn't look like that's gonna happen."

"Shhh…somebody's coming." I could hear shoes clicking on the floor. "Go. You can't be seen in here with me."

He kissed me on the forehead and said, "I won't go far." And then he was gone.

I touched the spot he'd kissed, and it tingled.

My arraignment took place the following day. I was quiet throughout my whole virtual hearing. On live video, the prosecuting attorney presented the evidence, including the lock picks in my pocket. Then my 'referee'—that's what a non-attorney acting as a lawyer is called in Michigan—made a weak case for my sad circumstances, and how therapy would be the way to go. *Oh, boy... Phil would just love that.*

I was sure the judge was going to sentence me to Haven, but this was just my arraignment. Phil sat next to me, stewing. I'm pretty sure he was able to afford an attorney and they'd have made him pay for one, if I hadn't waived my right to council. So I just shut up and waited for them to finish.

"What do you have to say for yourself, young lady?" The judge asked.

I just looked at the floor and shrugged.

"Just answer one question then... Did you steal because you had no money? Or did you steal for the thrill of it, knowing there was the possibly of getting caught?"

I didn't know the correct answer that would send me to Haven, but I guessed it didn't really matter. Either way, I was going back and I couldn't wait.

"I guess it was a little bit of both," I said.

The judge looked resigned and said, "Ms. Jones,

you're probably looking at six weeks in the Detroit juvenile detention center. Bail is set at five thousand dollars due to flight risk. I will also require monthly family therapy sessions."

Phil jumped up. "Five thousand dollars?"

I bolted upright in my chair. "Detroit juvie? You can't do that. I should go to Haven in Florida."

"The judge folded his arms. "It doesn't look like they did you much good. Maybe a different facility would help. Someplace local, so your stepfather can participate in your rehabilitation."

"Shit," Phil muttered.

"No, I really need to go back to *Haven*."

The judge banged his gavel, picked up his papers, and walked away from his computer.

I whirled on the referee. "I should go back to Haven. Please! Call him and tell him."

I was even desperate enough to enlist Phil's help. "Please, Phil, ask them to send me back to Haven."

He smirked. "It seems like if you want to go to Haven so bad, you should go anywhere *but* there. Maybe you'll think twice about breaking the law again."

I caught sight of Patrick in the window. He must have been listening in. I could tell he was as surprised as I was. My empathy picked up his inner shockwaves.

"You can ask at your trial," my referee said. "But you should get a licensed lawyer."

Phil looked like a volcano about to blow his top. I knew he was seeing dollar signs.

"Can I leave now?" I asked.

"Yes," she said. "I'll escort you back to your jail cell."

Phil would never bail me out. The judge figured I'd be a flight risk, and he was correct. Even if I lost, then appealed, I would probably be sitting here until Phil found the cheapest lawyer available and then I'd be on the next transport to Juvie. *Fuggle juvie!*

"Can I go to the bathroom before you lock me up again?"

"Sure."

In the bathroom, I closed the door and went to one of the stalls. There were no windows anywhere in there. The referee was standing right outside the door and people were walking back and forth in the hallway. Disappearing would raise a lot of eyebrows, but I needed to prove that Haven was where I belonged.

I concentrated really hard and saw my bedroom back in Phil's house. I hoped I could get there magically, because I needed a few things if I were going on the run, which I would. Most definitely.

I concentrated specifically on my bed. I visualized the quilt my mother had made in every detail. I imagined its softness under my fingers, remembered the colors and patterns, and breathed in the barely-there scent of the detergent I had washed it in. It was my mother's gift to me when I was born. She had hand stitched it herself and kept enlarging it with new quilt squares as I grew.

I don't know if it was the love of that quilt or not. But when I opened my eyes I was no longer sitting on a toilet, I was actually sitting on my bed. *Yes!*

Now to get packed, quickly.

I dumped the school books out of my backpack and took a certain satisfaction in knowing I wouldn't be needing those again. Then I threw some clothes in, followed by the toiletries and makeup I had bought, excuse me, *stole*, and then I ran to the kitchen pantry and stuffed the rest of the pack as full as I could with nonperishable food. I didn't know how long I'd be gone, or even where I was going, but I figured I might be able to conjure a bus ticket, if I could see what one looked like.

I needed a different jacket since I *didn't* want to be identified now. I found the little red riding hood costume I had kept from a Halloween party at school two years ago. The wool was warm enough for late October, so I put it on, over my jean jacket. *Hey, the Superwitch finally has a cape!*

As soon as I was packed, I threw the backpack over my shoulder and concentrated on the bus station. I hadn't been there very often, but often enough to find it. The bus station was, ironically, located near the police station I had just escaped from.

I took a moment to look up the schedule and tickets

online. Then I deleted my browser history. The next bus out was going to Indianapolis, Indiana. I didn't know anyone there, so Phil wouldn't expect me to get on that bus. *Perfect.* And off to the bus station I went.

It looked like I might actually get away with it, when someone put a hand on my backpack and tugged. I grabbed the straps hard so whoever was behind me wouldn't be able to take my stuff, and when I whirled around, I saw a smirking Patrick.

"Holy… How did you find me, again? Did you put a tracker on me or something?"

"Not exactly. I just knew where you'd be going eventually. Props for getting here so fast!"

"Did you happen to see what happened back at the station?" I was hoping he could tell me what kind of confusion I had caused when I never came out of the windowless restroom.

"I was waiting with your stepdad, and by the way, he's a prince of a guy."

I rolled my eyes at the sarcasm. "Tell me about it."

"Yeah, he was bailing you out—at my insistence—when he found out you'd absconded. I wanted to cheer!"

"He was going to bail me out? With actual money?"

Patrick chuckled. "I don't think he tried to use monopoly money."

Then he must have realized it wasn't time for jokes and his expression became serious. "He wrote a check.

They didn't want to take checks, but before they could decide what to do, the referee came running toward us, asking if we knew where you were. Your step-dad shoved his wallet back in his pocket and took off."

"So, I jumped bail? Is that what you're telling me?"

"Yup, and we better get on this bus quick before they figure out where you went."

"We? Are you coming with me?"

"Of course. You need me."

I snorted. "I'm pretty sure I can pull this off without you. Besides, don't you need to stay here, finish school, get a job, and take care of your mom?"

He shrugged. "My mom can take care of herself for a while. I'll give her a call and let her know I'm fine. But right now we gotta get on that bus. It looks like the door is closing."

I ran for it. "Wait!"

The bus driver opened the door and made like it was such a huge inconvenience. I handed him my ticket and found a seat toward the back. Patrick held out his hand as if he were presenting a ticket to the bus driver. Even though he didn't have one, the driver just nodded, then tipped his head toward the back and said, "Go sit down. It's time to leave."

I couldn't agree more.

When Patrick and I were safely away, I pondered the pickle I was in. I had jumped bail. Someone would probably hire bounty hunters. This bus was nice enough to provide free WiFi, but I knew not to use my own phone in case GPS was tracking me.

"Can you look up something for me? I need to shut off my phone."

"See?" he smiled. "I told you you'd need me."

"Yeah. Maybe so, but you're going back home as soon as we get to Indy, right?"

"Sure. As long as you're safe. So what do you want me to look up?"

"Bounty Hunters."

"Shoot. I hadn't thought of that. You're right to worry about getting caught and returned to Detroit."

"Is there any chance the people who saw you back at the police station knew who you were? Did you introduce yourself to anybody? Could they track your phone to find me?"

He crossed his arms. "Who do you think you're talking to? I didn't give anyone my *real* name." Patrick pulled out his phone and Googled *Bounty Hunters.*

He read for a while and then gave me the bad news, reading quietly so as not to be overheard.

"A bounty hunter is a professional person who captures fugitives or criminals for a commission or bounty. The occupation, officially known as bail agency enforcer, bail enforcement agent, or fugitive recovery agent, has traditionally operated outside the legal constraints that govern police officers and other agents of the state. As a result, bounty hunters hired by a bail bondsman enjoy significant legal privileges, such as forcibly entering a defendant's home without probable cause or a search warrant..."

"Oh my Goddess!" I realized people were gazing over at us, so I lowered my voice to a whisper. "So, I'm a fugitive now? And they can just storm into any place to find me?"

"Yeah. Let me keep reading. Oh… Here's some good news. 'Everyday citizens approached by a bounty hunter are neither required to answer their questions nor allowed to be detained'."

"I guess that's good news for both of us."

"Yeah, and if Phil just wants you gone, he doesn't have to snitch on you either."

I wondered if he'd even want me to come back. Probably not. "So, who hires a bounty hunter, anyway?"

He read some more. "Bounty hunters are typically independent contractors paid a commission of the total bail amount that is owed by the fugitive; they only get paid if they are able to find the 'skip' and bring them in."

"Grrreat. So, they're motivated to earn their pay."

I hung my head. I could feel tears wanting to escape, and for once I didn't feel like I had to remain tough.

Patrick didn't seem like the type to hold a few tears against me, so I let them roll.

"Hey, now… It'll be okay. We have a secret weapon on our side, right?" He winked.

I knew he meant magic, but I still didn't know what my powers were. We practiced only simple, harmless spells at Haven.

"I guess so. I can harness electricity, but I don't know how to control it."

"We can practice when we get to a safe place."

If we can get to a safe place.

<hr>

I felt my shoulder being jostled. I opened my eyes and blinked a couple of times, then realized I had fallen asleep on Patrick. I bolted upright and rubbed the sleep out of my eyes. "Sorry," I mumbled.

"Don't worry about it. You must've been exhausted from your harrowing day yesterday."

"Is it tomorrow already?" I asked. The sky was dark outside and rain was whipping the windows.

He showed me his phone.

"Eleven o'clock?"

"Not exactly, tomorrow, but today's pretty much gone," he said.

"I guess I was really tired. I didn't sleep much in the jail cell last night."

"Yeah, I imagine you weren't particularly comfortable there."

I stretched and tried to get the kink out my back. Finally, something popped, and I felt better.

"So, how close are we to Indianapolis?" I asked.

"Almost there."

"Have you called your mother yet?"

"I texted her while you were asleep and said I would call when I got to my destination. However, I told her I was going to Wisconsin."

"Wisconsin? Do you know somebody there?"

"Yeah, my cousin. She probably won't call to check. Every now and then I go visit for two or three days, usually on a long weekend. He and I like camping, and she doesn't."

It must be nice to have relatives who enjoy your company...

We pulled into a bus station and it was clear we were finally at our stop. The bus driver opened the door and announced, "Everybody out."

"Well, that's one way of saying, 'You have reached your destination'. I would have preferred a nice GPS voice," Patrick said.

I stood and stretched. My body tingled as the blood returned to my legs. I wondered how long I had been leaning on Patrick's shoulder. He didn't seem to need to stretch, so I hadn't cut off his circulation.

"So, Red Riding Hood, do you think that cape is going to keep you dry in the rain?"

It was pouring out. I could see that even through the darkness. "I doubt it. When I have a chance, I'll look for some rain gear."

"Why don't I look for a store to rob and then find a place to squat?" He whispered as we reached the pavement.

"I'm sure the bus station has a restroom."

He laughed. "Yeah, you can cop a squat, if you want to. I was talking about finding an abandoned building where we could spend the night. You know... squatters."

I realized my mistake and laughed at myself. But the idea of spending the night with Patrick was a little unnerving. He seemed like a nice kid and everything, but was he really? I still didn't know him all that well. Was he acting stalker-ish? Would I be safe squatting with him in an abandoned building?

As if he could read my mind, he said, "Don't worry, I won't bother you at all during the night. We might need some sleeping bags, so I'll look for a camping store where I can get those and some rain ponchos. You can wait here if you want..."

"No thanks, I'll come with you. Just give me a minute to go to the bathroom. I'd like to learn how to magically appropriate what I need without getting caught."

His face lit up. "Appropriate! Good word. I would have said liberate, but it's all the same. And I'll be happy to show you my skills."

We didn't know the downtown area, but it didn't take long to find what we needed. There was a strip mall and some stores that you would expect to find there, and it had closed for the night. Patrick was able to scan the place and find the store he was looking for. *Camping World.*

"You be my lookout, and I'll be back in a flash with what we need." He winked.

I found it hard to believe that he could get in without being seen in such a public place, but I noticed his checking out the cameras first. He waved his hand in their directions, and then smiled at me. "There. No more cameras. Not that they would really know who we are, but it's always good to be on the safe side."

"You're able to interfere with cameras magically?"

"Yeah, it's a skill I'm proud to say I've perfected. As long as I know the camera is there, I can disable it. It's the little freaky ones like a teddy bear's eye that I can't see and could miss."

I chuckled and said, "That's right, Teddy Bear."

He smiled and didn't seem to mind his nickname anymore. Anyway, we entered the store through the back. There were restrooms back there too, and I wished I'd waited for a clean place like this instead of the bus station's restrooms, which were ewwww... I doubt I could have held it this long anyway.

"Hey, one last joke for luck…"

"A joke for luck? I've never heard of that, but okay… Do what you need to do."

"Why couldn't Cinderella play soccer?"

I just shrugged.

"She kept running away from the ball." He took off down the hall before I could laugh.

I hung out watching for security guards, not knowing what I'd say to them if they found me. Luckily, they didn't. Patrick came out quickly with a couple large plastic bags. I could see two sleeping bags, a raincoat sleeve, and a couple of other things stuffed inside."

"I didn't know your shoe size, or I would've brought you a pair of hiking boots. I guess your sneakers are comfortable though, right?"

"Yeah, they're comfortable all right. I've been breaking them in for two years," I said as we exited the store and walked around to the sidewalk.

"Two years huh? It's about time for some new ones. Let me go back in and get you some."

"No, don't bother. I'll wait until I have some honest earnings, and then I'll buy myself some nice ones the old fashioned way."

"How are you going to earn your money?"

"I can probably learn to waitress pretty fast. It doesn't seem too difficult."

"They pay crappy you know. You really have to rely on tips."

"You don't think I'll make good tips?"

"As a brand-new waitress? Probably not. Unless you told people a few jokes…"

I didn't know whether to be insulted or not. It was true that I wouldn't have the fine points down for a while, and I guess waitresses did make such poor wages that they relied on tips to pay their bills. But what else could I do? I didn't have a driver's license, so I couldn't do deliveries. There was a florist near Phil's place, and I thought I might like to do that someday, but I didn't know shit about flowers. As we walked further downtown, I checked out the various possibilities for work.

"I found them," a low voice said from behind us. I whirled around and saw two people coming toward us. One was a middle-aged man, and the other was either a tough-looking woman or a smaller guy.

I didn't know who they were, but I didn't want to hang around to find out, either. We took off down the sidewalk, toward a neighborhood. Soon we rounded a corner with the two pursuers not far behind. It was clear were going to have to use magical speed to lose these guys. I looked for a fence to hop or some other way to put a barrier between us.

The old neighborhood seemed promising. Houses were close together with fences between them. The two of us could probably hop those fences and run faster than the adults chasing us could, although, they were pretty damn fast!

"Stop!" The man called.

I just ran harder.

"Jenika!" The guy behind us called out again. "Don't you recognize your own father?"

Patrick glanced over at me with an incredulous look on his face. I was tempted to stop and talk to them, but he grabbed my hand and kept running. "No, don't stop. You can't trust anything they say, especially if you don't recognize them."

"I wouldn't recognize my father, if I tripped over him."

"We'll talk about it when we get somewhere safe," he said and vaulted over another fence, and then another one. I was surprised I had no trouble keeping up with him.

We finally lost them and once we knew we were safe, we looked around for an abandoned house. We found one with boarded up windows, and a cellar window that wasn't blocked. Patrick managed to make the glass disappear with a wave of his hand. "Ladies first."

The window was only big enough for someone my size and possibly Patrick's, but certainly the adults would never fit through it. So, I semi-dived through the window and did a tuck and roll on the concrete floor. Patrick shimmied through, right behind me, and then waved the glass back in place as soon as he landed upright.

We hid in a corner. If someone looked through the window, they wouldn't be able to see the two of us, flat against the wall, trying not to breathe hard. Although I have to admit, I needed to catch my breath big time.

Eventually, we had to come out of the corner. During our mad dash, Patrick had dropped the sleeping bags and whatever else he'd shop-lifted. I was shivering from the damp cellar and he shrugged out of his coat, then draped it around my shoulders. *Wow. An honest-to-Goddess gentleman.*

"Could that guy really have been your father? He was white."

"Yeah, so? I'm biracial."

"Oh. I guess I never really noticed, but maybe I should have. Your hair isn't black and tightly curled, as I'd expect and your skin is…"

"Lighter than dark and darker than light? Like it can't make up its mind if it's black or white?"

"Huh? No. I was going to say it's kind of café-au-lait."

"Okay. I've never been compared to French coffee with milk before, but I'll allow it."

He seemed sweet… just unsure how to state the obvious, like so many white people.

"I figure there might be a couple of bedrooms upstairs," he said.

"Are we really going to stay here?"

"For now. I can set up a few wards, so the bounty hunters won't sense us."

"Sense us?"

"I don't know how they found us. I'd guess one or both might be magicals." He started up the stairs.

The idea of a magical bounty hunter shook me to my core. I followed close behind Patrick as he ascended the stairs.

CHAPTER 9

Patrick seemed trustworthy, so far. I guess I could handle sleeping near him for warmth—and safety.

On the second floor, we found one queen sized mattress and a couple of moth-eaten blankets. I spread one blanket on top of the beaten-up mattress and lay the other over that. "If we share this bed, will you behave yourself?"

He looked offended. "Of course!" Then he winked and added, "You'd probably turn me into a toad, if I didn't."

I rolled my eyes, then sat cross-legged on the blankets and grabbed my backpack. The adrenaline was still pumping from our near capture, and I didn't think I'd be able to sleep right away. I pulled out a jar of peanut butter and a spoon.

"Oh, yum! Dinner," he said.

I stuck the spoon in it and handed it to him. "So… Tell me your story. All I know is that you're a thief who tells corny jokes and got caught on a hidden camera. How did they know it was you?"

He chuckled softly. "You eat first. I'll tell you my story and eat dinner after you've had yours."

I didn't have to be asked twice since I was starving. I took a large spoonful and stuffed it in my mouth.

"First of all, I don't usually steal from people I know, but these guys were asshats, so it fit with my Robin Hood value system. Steal from the rich and douche-baggy and give to the hardworking poor, like my mom and me. In Ann Arbor there's a hell of a lot of rich people, but we're not two of them.

"My mom cleans toilets. Okay, not just toilets but everything else too. She's a maid. We live over a garage at one of the mansions. It's not ideal, but it's the best we could do after my dad died. I don't know why he had no life insurance to help take care of us, but maybe that's because he never expected to die in his thirties." Patrick tapped his head. "Note to future self, buy a cheap whole life policy sometime between the wedding and honeymoon.

"Anyway, my mom and I found this estate where we could live over the garage, I could go to a good school, and my mom could work. If you ask me, they work her to the bone. She's always tired. She looks forward to putting her feet up at the end of every day, and if I'm around I even rub them. It's the least I can do since she's saving all her money for me to go to college. *Someday,* she hopes to be able to buy a little house and a decent car. But she's always thinking of me first."

"So. you stole to help your mom. That's sort-of nice. Did she know where the money came from?"

"Heck, no!"

"Where did she think you were working?"

"Babysitting at night. She thought I was making good money doing that. Those cheap bastards wouldn't pay me nearly enough to take care of their spoiled brats. Okay, so I sound a little jaded. Maybe I am. Thus, began my Robin Hood evening adventures."

"Tell me about the time you got caught."

He laughed. "Okay. I'd heard about this mansion that would be unoccupied for a few days. I hadn't babysat there for a while, so I had kind of forgotten the layout. So, there I was, walking out of Mrs. Asshat's giant closet, wearing her fur coat and tiara. I made sure she had plenty of other warm coats, because that's the kind of thoughtful guy I am."

"And a Tiara? What was that for? Visiting royalty?"

"Ha! I'll tell you later. Anyway, I was going to check the other rooms where valuables might be stashed. Usually, there's a safe in the master bedroom, but that wasn't the case here. In my experience, that means there's an office somewhere, and that's where the money is.

"Because I'm a witch, I can get into just about any safe. It's my gift. But even if I couldn't open them with magic, I've practiced safe-cracking the normal way, and I would say I'm pretty good at it.

"Sometimes I actually do babysit, and when the kids are asleep, I give the house a good once over. Then if the parents ask me to babysit again, I tell them I'm too busy with homework and would rather refer them to one of my friends at school. It's kind of a win-win. Some regular kid gets a babysitting job, and they get a reliable babysitter.

"And you get to case the joint."

"Yup. Anyway, back to the Asshats… I turned the doorknob and looked into a room with a crib. They must have had another sprout on the proud family tree. So out of curiosity, I walked around the room, even though there didn't seem to be anything special in there, just toys, more toys, and more-more toys. Yep, this kid was probably going to be the type that wants the best bike, the latest games, the coolest car… you name it. Sometimes I wished I had been born into a situation like that, but I'm kinda glad I wasn't. Most of those kids are spoiled rotten. Eventually, they get so used to their privileges, they see them as rights.

"Even if the kid screws up in high school, we all know parents can buy them entrance into their alma mater college. Then the kid has to go there and become a carbon copy of their parents or risk being cut off from their trust fund."

I snuggled down more comfortably under the blanket and listened as he continued.

"I hope to go to college, but it'll be one I can afford. I'm a good student. I can probably get some scholarships. A single mom who works as a maid with a kid who's bright and willing to study... I imagine we can probably swing it. And if I want to grow up to better the environment, I can. Nobody will tell me I *must* earn an MBA."

"An environmentalist? Cool. I never would've have guessed," I said.

"Yeah. Try throwing a gum wrapper on the ground in front of me. I'll read you the riot act. But seriously, I recycle a lot. Mostly at the pawn shops."

I rolled my eyes.

"I knew pawning the stuff from the lady's closet would be a little difficult, but I could always use the story about my grandma dying. So far this year, my grandma has died five times."

I couldn't help laughing. Then handed him the jar of peanut butter. He put a spoonful in his mouth and said, "Mmm..." rubbing his tummy until he swallowed.

"Anyway, again, getting back to the Asshats... Finally, I found the office downstairs—or maybe it was the library. Lots of built-in book shelves surrounded a polished dark wood desk. I just had to find the safe. They usually tuck those things inside a large cabinet or hide it behind a painting. Heck, these people might even have a secret room. With all those books, trying to find the one that would open the secret door would be a pain in the butt, except I knew one clue to look for. Which book had the least amount of dust on top? That's the one Mr. Asshat would have to pull on to open a door to a secret room.

"I scanned the books but found nothing. I peeked behind the framed artwork and signed photographs. Nothing there either. So I hoped I'd find some clue in the desk. I slid open the first two drawers easily. Nothing noteworthy there. I was beginning to lose hope of finding a safe until I tried the bottom drawer, which was locked. I found the keyhole on the left underside, next to where his leg would go, and placed my hands over the lock. I didn't even need the key, because, well…magic! I closed my eyes and pictured the sheer line falling into place, and then when I pulled the drawer, it opened!"

"Were you surprised?"

"Not really." He gave me his impish grin before he went on. "Files lined the front, but behind them I saw a strongbox—one of those little fireproof boxes with enough room for cash and passports. I pulled it out, set it on the chair ready to do my thing. This time it was a combination lock. That's a little more difficult, but not too much for a crackerjack burglar like myself.

"So humble."

"Hey, truth is humility. Anyway, I let the clickity click go until it stopped. I didn't even have to touch it. I let it do its own thing. The next row of numbers rolled the other way. Clickety click, click, and it stopped. One more row spun and clicked into place, then I opened the lid and—Score!

"Four passports, some documents, and cash. Lots and lots of wonderful cash. Also a super weird-looking ring. It was odd enough that I wouldn't be able to pawn it, because it might be traced back to them at some point. Cash is mainly what I look for. Or stuff that can be replaced. Not heirlooms. I'm not a jerk. I don't want to deprive people of their memories. Some people have legacies handed down from their ancestors. Not me, though. I have hand-me-downs from Goodwill."

I took a bottle of water out of the backpack and let him have the first long swallow, before he continued.

"Cold hard cash doesn't have any sentimental value that I know of. To us it has rent, college and maybe a new car value. Under the fur coat I wore a military jacket with a few big pockets, plus a couple on the inside. There was plenty of room to stash anything small.

"Now, it was time to blow this popsicle stand, as my dad used to say. I don't know what the heck that meant. I've never seen a popsicle stand, but the way he said it made me giggle when I was a kid."

"Cute," I said. I took the water bottle from him when he offered it, since it was my turn to wash down the sticky peanut butter.

"Checking outside to make sure everything was as I left it when I entered the property—motion sensors off, alarms off, no people or dogs in sight... I simply strolled out the side door, jogged down the driveway, got on my bike and pedaled home. If the cops stopped me and asked why I was wearing a fur coat and tiara, I'd just tell them I was on my way to a costume party. It was early for Halloween, but people in that neighborhood don't need much of an excuse for a party. They have parties for everything. I could call it 'George Washington's First Haircut Party' and no one would bat an eye.

"Seriously?"

"Well, I'd probably come up with something better than that. Anyway, until I could get to the pawnshop, I had to stash the fur coat and tiara in my usual spot— our big recycling can. My job was to take out the trash, and trash day wasn't until Tuesday. That's why I usually took Monday nights off from burglary, because Tuesday my mom might think she was doing me a big favor by bringing the bin out to the curb. If she found my stash, I could not explain that away.

"Anyway, it was the weekend. My mom was supposed to have weekends off, but no, because... parties! She worked harder on the weekends than during the week. She helped the caterers set-up, walked around with trays of food or drinks, cleaned up after people that let something spill, then cleaned the house from top to bottom until everything sparkled, just to make sure the owners didn't wake up to a total disaster. She'd usually hit the sack around two a.m.

"She wasn't just the maid. She also did the cooking, laundry, and ran errands for them. Basically, she was a paid slave. Someday, I'll make plenty of money, the honest way of course, and I'll buy a little home for her. Not one of those palatial mansions… So much space, so few people, such a waste. But a nice house in the 'burbs would make her really happy. That and time to pursue her creative hobbies."

"What hobbies does she like?"

"Making and decorating stuff. That's one good thing about living by the Great Lakes. Plenty of beaches, plenty of seagull feathers, shells, sand—all of those things she can use to make jewelry, coasters or other beachy decorations. She glues shells around mirrors, makes doorstops, wall art, wreaths… People pay good money for something glued or painted on driftwood. Whatever free time she has, she uses for making art. She says it's fulfilling.

"I'm not creative like that. I'm more gifted in problem-solving. So when I thought about the problem of getting myself home on a bike wearing a tiara and a fur coat, I already had my excuses ready. Cops don't usually stop people who look rich, unless they're doing something really dangerous. Me? I was just riding my bike, going home to our palatial mansion's address. Hey, they don't know I live over the garage…

"Unfortunately, that night I hadn't counted on the nanny cam and apparently they recognized me when I poked my head in to the kid's room, wearing Mrs. Asshat's old Miss America crown."

"And off to Juvie you went."

"Yeah. Speaking of going, I have to use the bathroom."

Before he exited the room, he turned to me and said, "Why did Tigger stick his head in the toilet?"

"Oh no. Why?"

"Because he was looking for Pooh."

⸻✴︎——✴︎⸻

While he was gone, I found myself thinking about Patrick and rooting for Robin Hood. I felt sorry about his capture.

When he returned, I asked, "You're still going home tomorrow, right?"

"Uh huh."

The way he said it didn't sound convincing at all. "Well, I appreciate all you've done for me, but I can take it from here."

"Are you sure about that?"

"Yeah, why wouldn't I be? Nobody knows me around here."

"Except one of those magical bounty hunters."

Suddenly things clicked into place. *Magical bounty hunters?* "Is that a thing? Bounty hunters using magic? Do you really think that's how they found me?"

"I wouldn't be surprised."

"Crap. That one guy said he was my father. I never knew where my magic came from, but I always wondered if it was him. I only knew my mother's side of the family and none of them seemed witchy. But considering the lecture I got from my mom the first time I revealed my powers, I figured nobody would ever use them, even if they could."

"Yeah. When I found out I could do stuff the other kids couldn't do, my mom pulled me aside and gave me that lecture. Probably all young witches get it.

'Don't tell anyone you can do special things. Someone will take advantage of you. They'll blame you for anything that goes wrong. Some bad people might even want to kidnap you and use you for their own greedy purposes, or perform experiments and try to weaponize you,' etc."

"*Weaponize?* Uh, no. That wasn't part of the lecture I got."

"Well, you know the general drill... Most of us magicals are scared to death from the moment we can feel fear, and taught NOT to use magic except in life and death emergencies."

"You got that right. I didn't mean for lightning to shoot out my fingertips. I just reacted instinctively to a perceived threat. But you've used your 'talent' a lot." I emphasized the word *talent* with a touch of sarcasm.

"And nobody saw me doing it. Without all that practice, I doubt I'd be as good as I am."

"And humble…"

He grinned. "Oh, yes. Aren't you glad you have me as your magical mentor?"

I snorted. "Magical mentor?"

"Of course. Everyone needs someone to show them the ropes. My uncle and cousin taught me some, even though my mother asked them not to."

"Nobody taught me anything until I got to Haven."

"All the more reason for me to help you. Or don't you trust me?"

As weird as that sounded, I *did* trust him. I had wondered about his familiarity with magic for a while. I'd also been wondering if he were stalking me. He seemed sweet, but you never knew… I hadn't been stalked before, so I wouldn't know what to look for. He seemed like a thrill seeker, so maybe that's what the attraction was…just the thrill of an adventure might be enough to make him want to stay with me.

Whatever it was, I trusted him enough to fall asleep that night. We woke up early to the tromping sound of heavy boots from downstairs. I bolted upright and so did he.

Had the bounty hunters found us?

We stared at each other for a moment, and then both of us looked for a place to hide. I grabbed my backpack, pointed to a closet, and we ran for it. The door didn't shut all the way, but it would have to do. We both hid in there, holding our breaths. I was terrified the magical bounty hunters had broken through Patrick's wards.

Fortunately, by listening intently we figured out the intruders were real estate flippers. And they had brought a camera crew with them for some kind of TV show.

We gazed out through the crack in the closet door, my head beneath his, and watched them amble into the room. The woman talked about how the place only needed cosmetic updates, then one of the men took out a marble from his pocket and set it on the floor. When it didn't roll, he said the upstairs seemed structurally sound and was worth taking the chance.

If it were me, I'd figure that out when four of the five crew members didn't crash through the floor. One big guy was operating a large camera, one man and one woman were in front of the camera, somebody tall with long hair was lighting the couple with something that looked like a kid-sized white trampoline, and a guy with a long-handled microphone brought up the rear. It was quite the set.

A man strolled toward the closet, and I was terrified

he was going to open the door. Patrick raised his hands on either side of my head, as if pushing with an invisible force, and the person turned around, then walked the other way and out the door. We could hear them as they all followed him out and into the next room, which was the bathroom. I couldn't wait for them to leave, because I was going to need it soon. I'm surprised I didn't wet my pants when that one guy looked like he was about to open the closet door.

As soon as we were sure they'd left, we stared at each other and laughed. It was one of those nervous, half-hysterical laughs that break the tension. Before long we were rolling on the floor, holding our sides.

When we finally got ourselves under control, he said, "House flippers... I did not see that coming."

I excused myself and made my way to the hall bathroom, which thankfully still worked. They hadn't shut off the water or anything. The whole time I had been wondering how the heck we were going to get out of this.

A few minutes later, we double checked to be sure the trucks were gone. Then we gathered up what little we had and walked downstairs. The front door was no longer boarded up.

As we tromped into the kitchen, Patrick asked, "What can you do? I mean, what are your powers?"

I shrugged. "I'm not sure. I was taught, like you said, never ever to use my powers or people would kidnap me, use me, and yada yada yada…" I set my backpack on the small kitchen table.

He smiled. "But, you must have tried them when you were alone in your room, right?"

I shook my head. Feeling a little foolish now, I admitted, "No. I'm afraid I didn't. My mom had no reason to lie, so I believed her."

"I guess the first thing we need to do is find a deserted spot, not in a populated neighborhood, where you can practice. If we know what our powers are, we can use them to protect ourselves."

My brows shot up. "What if I accidentally fry you? It could happen."

He laughed. "Not if I cast a protection spell around myself."

"If that's all it takes, why can't we do that to protect ourselves from the magical bounty hunters?"

"Because we don't know what they're capable of, and we don't know what kind of ethics they have. I know you and I were taught, *'Do no harm'* at Haven, if not before. But there are those who use magic in different ways."

"You mean black magic? Are you telling me these magical bounty hunters might actually put curses or hexes on someone?"

He shrugged. "Hey, I don't know them any better than you do. Maybe less well than you do. Is it possible that guy is your father?"

"I thought about it." I had been thinking about it nonstop, actually. "I haven't seen my father since I was about five. He was in the Air Force, stationed in Japan when my mother and I came home to the states. They got divorced later, but I don't remember seeing him after Japan. The last time I heard anything about him, was when I overheard a conversation between my mom and grandfather, saying he had gone into some sort of top-secret civilian work, and that we'd probably never hear from him again. Mom said she hoped she wouldn't, since she was engaged to my stepfather at the time."

"Weird. So he could actually be doing some sort of top-secret magical work for the government or something?"

I shrugged. "Who knows?"

Patrick took a deep breath and blew it out. He scratched his head. I couldn't read his mind, but I could certainly feel the confusion and see the wheels turning, I hoped he was coming up with some kind of plan, because I had none.

At last he stopped and looked at me. "Well, clearly we have to get out of here. Especially before the demolition crew shows up."

We both chuckled again.

"We could wait until nightfall, and that might give us some cover," I said. "But where do we go?"

"I'd like to go someplace remote where we could practice our powers, and find out what you can do."

"Aren't we kind of out in the country? Well, not Indianapolis, but the state of Indiana has tons of farmland where we could get lost in a corn maze or something," I said.

"A corn maze? I think it's the wrong time of year. The corn has probably been harvested."

Duh. City girl here... "Do you want me to practice my control, like shooting lightning around corners?"

"Yeah, or at least see what's possible. If we can find a big field, we can set up some kind of target practice. Now how do we get there?"

I had been kidding, but clearly he wasn't.

"We could hitchhike…" he murmured.

"Do you really think anyone would pick us up?"

"I can conjure an empty gas can to make it look like we ran out of gas somewhere, but that would just get us to the next gas station..." he said, frowning.

"What if you conjure a full one, and then we can get to the next abandoned car in the middle of nowhere."

"Hey, that's a good idea. See? I knew you were smart."

I had never said I wasn't, but no matter… "What if there are no abandoned cars? Can you conjure a car?"

He laughed. "If I could do that, I'd conjure a bright red roadster with a full tank of gas."

"Okay, okay. You seem to know a lot more about your powers than I do."

"No kidding. You really need to catch up. I can teach you some things, after we get to your…corn maze." His sly grin made my heart do a little flip.

I laughed to cover my reaction. "I guess we can walk until we find a Highway somewhere, then follow it outside the city to some fields. I hear there's a lot of them. But I'm pretty sure the corn will all be mowed down by now. Or, you know…harvested." Erg. Now I was babbling like an idiot.

"We'll find something…"

We walked in companionable silence until we were able to hear road noises and spot a highway close by. So with one gas can and two thumbs out, we had a ride in seconds. I don't know if Patrick used a glamour to make us look more trustworthy than we were. He probably didn't have to. A couple of kids out of gas made for a fairly sympathetic picture.

The truck driver who picked us up seemed kind enough. He wasn't creepy or anything. I guess Patrick was used to getting around that way, but I had been afraid to try it. I'm sure if he were a girl he might feel as nervous about it as I did.

As we rode along, he chatted casually with the truck

driver. After maybe fifteen minutes, he finally said, "Okay, there's a car up ahead about two miles."

I wondered how he knew that. But I was impressed by all he knew about his magic, anyway. I couldn't wait to learn more about mine. In a couple miles I saw something red by the side of the road. As we got closer I saw a little sports car, just like he had described it earlier. Could he really have conjured a car?"

The truck driver pulled over to the side and let us out. We thanked him profusely and he seemed happy to have helped.

As soon as he drove off. I looked at Patrick and said, "Really? You conjured the car after all?"

He sighed and the car disappeared.

"What the…"

"It was a glamour, just a trick to fool the eye. I would love to be able to conjure a real car someday."

"Yeah. You and me both…"

"Maybe if we keep practicing…" He cast his winning smile and my spirits lifted for no other reason than he was fun to look at.

CHAPTER 10

I GLANCED ACROSS THE FIELDS AT LONG ROWS OF STUBBY stalks. "Okay, now that we're in the middle of nowhere. What do we do?" I asked.

"Well, I could use something to eat, I don't suppose you have anything in your backpack for hungry magical teachers, do you?"

"As a matter of fact, I do."

He hugged me. "You're my hero!"

If only it were that easy to be a hero. Then I remembered the snack machine and what every seventeen-year-old boy needed. "Are you going to eat all my food? Because I didn't bring that much."

"Of course not. Besides, when we finish up here and get to a town, I'll buy you more food. Right now, I'm just glad you managed to hang onto your backpack when we ran from the bounty hunters. Did you know you could run that fast?"

"Actually, I didn't. At one point I felt like I was flying."

He grinned. "I'll bet you were. I never thought your short legs could keep up with me."

"Are you calling me short?"

He laughed. "Not while you're holding food hostage. Let's have some nourishment and then try it."

My eyebrows shot up. "Try what? Flying?"

He spread his arms and walked backwards. "Why not? What's the worst thing that can happen?"

He had a point. If all I managed to do was run fast, that wouldn't hurt anything. I suppose I could trip and get a face full of dirt. But right now I was hungry too and could use some fortification, especially if flying burned a lot of calories.

"So where are we going to have our brunch?"

He looked around and pointed toward some trees off in the distance. "It looks like there's some shade over there. Plus we might be spotted here in the open. Let's get off the road a bit." He picked up the gas container.

"What are you going to do with that?"

He shrugged. "It's a nice brand-new plastic jug. Maybe we can find some fresh water somewhere."

I thought he was being pretty optimistic. But, filling up the can with water sounded pretty smart. I only had one more twelve ounce bottle of water with me. "Okay, so what are we going to do? Run really fast and try to fly over to those trees?"

He smiled. "Sounds good to me. I'll race you."

We took off and I kept up with him, even though he had longer legs than mine. I was pretty impressed with my speed, if I say so myself. Suddenly my feet left the ground, but I kept going. Just for the heck of it I spread my arms out wide and lifted my feet higher off the ground behind me, as if I were flying. The row of what use to be corn stalks was straight, flat, and made for a pretty good runway.

The bizarre thing is, I didn't fall flat on my face. I didn't even slow down. I *was* flying!

I looked over at Patrick and his eyes grew huge when he gazed back at me. He hadn't left the ground yet, but he was keeping up with me by running as hard as he could.

When we neared the woods, I wasn't sure how to slow down. I didn't want to end up looking like one of those Halloween witch decorations—the kind fuggles attached to a tree trunk to look like a stereotypical witch and her broom had smashed into it. It's supposed to be funny, but to me it just looked painful.

I tried to turn, but nothing happened. *Oh Goddess!* What if I really did smash into a tree trunk? I pictured myself riding on a broom. Maybe that's how I could steer? I wasn't as good at conjuring as Patrick was, but I tried… and failed. No broom appeared.

At the last minute, I just pretended I was an airplane and banked to the left. Soon I was flying *alongside* the trees and not into them, *thank the Goddess!* But how was I supposed to stop?

Patrick was jumping up and down and applauding me, but I wasn't sure if I deserved any applause, yet. I had to figure out a way to slow down and stop. I just kept banking left and flying around him in circles. "How do I stop this crazy ride?" I shouted.

He quit jumping and clapping, and just stood there with his mouth open. Eventually he cried out, "You can't stop?"

"I don't think so." Talk about feeling stupid.

"Try picturing yourself slowing down," he shouted. "Use your mind and strong visualization. Maybe imagine an anvil tied to your leg."

"I'm afraid if I close my eyes, I won't be able to steer. Maybe I'd even land on you!"

"Go ahead, I'll catch you."

I was tempted to laugh, picturing myself dragging Patrick along as he tried to hang onto my legs, but I had no better ideas and decided he was probably right. I had to visualize myself slowing and lowering myself to the ground, simultaneously.

Closing my eyes against reality, I visualized slowing down and gradually moving toward the ground. Then I slowed some more and actually touched the ground and ran in circles. I must have looked like a little kid pretending to be an airplane.

Finally I dropped my arms and my feet stopped moving. Panting, I fell over backwards, landing on my ass, then flopped flat on my backpack. We were in an area between the woods and corn stalks or what was left of them. I sucked in deep breaths until I was able to relax and breathe normally.

Patrick blocked the sun as he loomed over me, grinning. "Color me impressed!" Eventually he reached down and grasped my hand so he could help me up. "You are one f'ing powerful witch!"

Once I was on my feet, we both laughed.

"That must have been your first time flying. It looked like you had no idea what you were doing and no control whatsoever."

"You're right. It was my first time flying, without a plane." Thank goodness I could laugh about it. If I'd wound up wrapped around a tree I wouldn't find it amusing.

"Well, now that we've made it to the woods, let's go see if there's a rock to sit on or something. I'm starving."

We found an interesting spot several yards into the woods. A large cleared area with a few logs had been set in a circle. It looked as if the logs had surrounded a small bonfire at one time.

"This reminds me of a place behind my cousin's house where we used to camp out."

"Is that the cousin you're supposed to be staying with now?"

"Yeah. I should call my mom and let her know I'm okay, but I'll wait until after lunch. Priorities, you know?"

We found a fallen log that was longer than the others and both of us plopped down on it. I swung my backpack to the ground and rummaged around until I pulled out a box of crackers and some cheese slices.

"Cool! Cheese and crackers. One of my favorite snacks."

"Are you kidding?" I thought he was being facetious, but he just tore into the crackers and stuffed a few into his mouth. He closed his eyes, and rubbing his tummy, his face relaxed like he was in ecstasy.

"I guess you weren't kidding." I grabbed a cracker and shoved it into my mouth before he could eat the whole box. Then I opened the package of cheese and made a couple of crackers into a sandwich.

"Don't worry," he said, spitting cracker crumbs. "I'll buy you more food. I'm sure we can find a store at some point. This land is so flat, you can see everything off the highway on both sides."

I would've asked how we would get to a store, but knowing he had all kinds of tricks up his sleeve for getting around, I figured I'd find out soon enough.

We enjoyed our cheese and cracker sandwiches until our stomachs were no longer making hungry growling noises. Then I put the rest away and watched as he sat on the ground and lay back, using the log like a pillow under his head. He folded his hands over his stomach and closed his eyes. I don't think I'd ever seen anyone relish a simple snack more.

Something I was discovering about Patrick... He knew how to live life to the fullest. That's just one thing I wished I could learn from him.

Opening his eyes and giving me a half smile, he said, "Well, that was fun... Watching you fly, I mean."

"It was an experience, all right."

He laughed as he levered himself to a standing position, then reached down, grabbed my hand, and yanked me to my feet.

"So what do we do now? You said you can shoot lightning out your fingertips, right?"

"I did it once, and it was totally by accident. I don't know if I can do it on purpose, or not. Maybe I should try that?"

"Yeah," Patrick said. "Try it."

I didn't want to set anything on fire, so I decided to aim at the sky. I remembered how guilty I felt when I whirled around and electrocuted that poor senior. But this time I wasn't reacting to any real threat, so I didn't even know if it would work.

I closed my eyes and pictured lightning, then thrust my hands at the sky.

I didn't feel anything. Before, when it happened my hands vibrated wildly. Opening my eyes, I didn't see anything that looked like lightning. Glancing over at Patrick I asked, "Did you see anything?"

"Nope. Try again."

I did the exact same thing and got the exact same result. "Maybe it was a one-time deal. I thought I was being attacked and my instinct kicked in to knock the problem away from me. Right now I have no threats, and don't come up behind me and say boo!"

He smirked. "I wouldn't do that. You'd know it was me. Besides, I'm not a self-destructive idiot."

Well, at least he believed me. That's more than I could say for the students and faculty at my former school. "So, what should I do? Just keep trying?"

He shrugged. "Why not? Third times a charm, right? But this time, add some emotion."

Why not, indeed. I lifted my face, focused all my energy on the sky, infused my anger at life into my body and let loose. Streaks of lightning shot out of my vibrating fingertips and into the sky, shocking both of us, but in a good way.

"Holy crap," Patrick said, beaming excitement.

"I know! Oh, my Goddess!" I checked my fingertips to see if they were smoking.

"That's awesome! See if you can direct it around the trees."

"I don't think that's a good idea. What if I set them on fire?"

He rubbed his chin and looked thoughtful. "Right. That wouldn't be good. Well, see if you can move your hands around, and if the lightning moves with them, but up in the sky."

I channeled all my anger and rage, confusion and hurt, and blasted lightning right out of my palms this time. I moved my quivering hands back and forth and the lightning crackled throughout the sky. I was getting lightheaded, but so excited that I didn't want to stop. I swiveled and made a wide arc that the streaks of lightning followed. Then I separated my hands and made two currents, holding them until I almost passed out.

"Shit!" Patrick yelled.

I looked to where he was pointing. I'd hit one of the treetops and it caught fire.

"Oh, no! What do I do now?"

"Can you make it rain?" Patrick asked.

"I don't know. I've never tried."

"Now would be a good time to try it."

I aimed my mind at the sky above the trees and commanded, "Rain!" Beautiful blue skies mocked me. There was no rain in sight. Meanwhile, the top of the tree was starting to burn lower. "It's not working. Can you try?"

"Let's both try…and come up with a rhyme if you can."

"Goddess help us put out this fire! To make it rain is our desire!"

Patrick and I both raised our hands to the sky over the burning tree and kept repeating the words, "Goddess, help us put out this fire! To make it rain is our desire!"

I felt the first drop of water on my face. *Oh, Lord and Lady, I hope that's not just my imagination.* I opened my eyes just as a larger drop splashed my nose and another one wet my cheek. Finally, the rain came pouring down, soaking not only the trees, but the cornfield too. I checked the road, which was miraculously still dry. I don't know if the Goddess picked the spots that needed it or if we somehow controlled what wound up wet and dry.

"Thank you, Goddess!" I backed slowly toward the road as did Patrick. When it abruptly stopped raining the top of the tree smoked a little bit, but the fire was out.

"We should stay here long enough to be sure it doesn't catch again," I said. I remembered why Francine Costa, aka Alien, was sent to Juvie. She'd practiced controlling the weather until she'd flooded most of the Midwest.

"Wow. You're one impressive witch," Patrick said,

"How did you not know you had all these powers before this?"

I shrugged. I had already admitted I had just never tried. If you're told over and over *never* to use those powers for any reason, well…

Patrick shook his head, as if amazed. "I'm pretty sure we both have powers we don't know about, and right now I kind of want to try one of my own."

"What would that be?"

He grinned and jogged to the side of the road. "Come on," he called over his shoulder. Following him, I hoped he didn't want to try flying anymore. I was too tired. This magic stuff had taken a lot out of me.

"You go ahead. I'm gonna walk. See if you can do whatever it is without me."

He didn't even glance back at me as he called out, "Suit yourself."

Soon I knew what he was going to try to do. That little red car he had conjured before reappeared, gleaming in the sun. I wondered if this one would actually work and would take us wherever we wanted to go.

Patrick was grinning like the cat who ate the canary. But when he tried to open the door for me, the car faded and disappeared.

"Damn. I thought I had it."

"Maybe you could try to conjure something smaller."

"That was pretty small, but yeah… I'll try it."

He closed his eyes, looked like he was in deep concentration, and then a motorcycle appeared.

I applauded. "Great job. Do you know how to drive one of these things?"

He shrugged. "Nope. But how hard can it be?"

"Uh… I'm not sure I want to get on the back of that thing, if you don't know how to drive it."

He threw his leg over, as if he were going to sit on the motorcycle, but it vanished, and he fell on his ass.

I pressed my hands over my mouth to keep myself from laughing out loud.

"Maybe the Goddess won't let me drive something I'm not familiar with," he said, as he rose, rubbing his butt.

Every morning I asked the Goddess to keep me safe, so this may have been her doing just that.

"Let me try one more thing—something simpler."

I was impressed with his persistence. In a split second, he was holding the handle bars of a tandem bicycle. His eyes widened as he rolled the bike back and forth, and when it didn't disappear a big grin lit his face. "Now this, I know how to drive."

I laughed and was relieved there was nothing electronic to go wrong with our ride. All we needed was pedal power. "Do you think it will disappear underneath us?"

He picked it up by the handlebars a little bit and

dropped it. "It feels pretty solid to me." He sat on the front seat and smiled. "Hop on."

I wiggled on the back seat to position myself comfortably with my backpack balancing my weight. He walked a few paces with me on there and smiled. "So far so good, right?"

"Yup."

He hopped on and we both began to peddle while he steered the front wheel. I was still a bit tired, so I was happy I wasn't peddling alone. I had to admit I was almost as impressed by his ability to conjure things as he was with my ability to fly.

Eventually, we hit a good stride, but there was only one problem…

"So, where are we going?" I asked.

Patrick turned around and grinned at me. "I have no idea, but we're making excellent time."

I couldn't help laughing. He was cute and funny. He seemed to really come alive with freedom. I tried to lose my cares, close my eyes, and feel the wind in my hair. I felt the softest breeze stroke my cheeks and fore-head before it feathered through my hair. Like the Goddess was smoothing my hair out of my face. I hadn't felt like this, maybe ever. At least not since I was a really little kid.

I'm happy that my juvenile delinquent friend is someone who could bring me this feeling again. I caught myself. I almost called him my boyfriend in my head. *That was in my head, right?* He didn't turn around so, I guess it was. *Whew.*

At some point we would have to figure out a destination, but for now it was all about the joy of the journey.

⊱ ⊰

As much as I hated to break the carefree mood, I had to bring up a sore subject. "Patrick, how are you going to explain your absence to your mother?"

He heaved a big sigh, then stopped the bike and turned around. "I'm going to text her. But I guess we should make a plan."

That seemed reasonable. "Good. What kind of plan?"

"I think we should turn around and go back to the Indianapolis bus station. We don't know this part of the country and could wind up stranded in the middle of nowhere. We'll grab another bus there and see if we can find a safe place to go. I know you don't want to go back to Detroit, and I'm not asking you to. But I think you should spend the time it takes to peddle back to the bus station to come up with an actual destination, and someone on the other side to greet you."

Yeah, wouldn't that be nice? As much as it sounded like a great idea, I couldn't think of many people who would be open to a runaway witch.

I wish I could go back to Haven, but I didn't dare say that out loud. Ms. Broome was the only one who would probably welcome me, there. Other than Genevieve in Arizona, and Ms. Broome was in Florida I couldn't think of a safe place to hide, and there was no way I could get to either one of them very quickly.

"So, back to Indianapolis…" I sighed and let him turn the bike around and then helped him peddle in the direction from which we came.

I really had no good ideas. Even when we got to the bus station all I knew was I didn't want to stay there very long, knowing that there were magical bounty hunters still looking for me. Or maybe they had given up. *Yeah, right!*

As we wandered through the bus station, checking the schedule, I picked up a strong vibe and knew some-body was watching us. I turned in the direction of the emotions I felt and spotted the bounty hunter who claimed to be my father. As he began walking toward me, I grabbed Patrick's arm and hissed, "We have to go. Now!"

We ran out the out of the station and headed toward the lines of buses. We slipped around the nearest bus and saw another one that was boarding. All the people looked like senior citizens with gray and white hair, but they were laughing and smiling and one of them yelled out "Vegas baby!"

Patrick grabbed my other hand. "What did you see?"

"One of those bounty hunters. The one who said he was my dad. He must have been watching for me."

Patrick looked at the people boarding the bus, looked back at me, and a sly smile grew across his face. "I have an idea. Do you trust me?"

I rolled my eyes. "I think by now I should. What did you have in mind?"

"I'm going to put a glamour over us to make us look like an old couple and then we're going to get on that bus right there. He pointed to the Vegas bound bus with the octogenarian gamblers.

"Seriously?"

"Yeah, he won't look for us on that bus, for sure."

He had a point. And there's no way he'd recognize us in our eighties. I knew if Patrick was able to use a glamour to make everyone see a little red sports car that wasn't there, he could probably age two teenagers.

"Okay, go for it."

Next thing I knew I was looking at a very old, wrinkly Patrick. He was a little stooped over with his pants hitched up way too high around his waist and belted over his tucked in shirt.

Then he said, "How do I look?"

I giggled. "Hideous. You look like you need a few years more sleep."

"Perfect! By the way, so do you."

I glanced down at our linked veiny hands and gnarled fingers. "Holy moly. I look...old!"

He grinned. "See, we'll blend right in. Let's go get on that bus."

The bus driver was busy loading luggage into the compartment underneath, so we simply joined the line and were able to sneak in while he had his back turned. We walked about halfway down the aisle and slipped into a row that was unoccupied. With empty seats in front, behind, and beside us, I just hoped nobody would sit nearby and want to strike up a conversation.

When the bus was finally loaded, most of the empty seats were gone. Patrick slipped his arm around me, as if we were at the movies. And to tell you the truth, it felt so good, I just cuddled into the crook of his arm. Finally, the bus pulled out of the station and I felt a huge sigh of relief...except for the part where we were on our way to Las Vegas.

But you know what? That was a whole lot closer to Arizona, so that meant maybe I could get to Genevieve, her twin sister, and their aunt. There was a lot to be said for that destination. But in the meantime, this was going to be one long bus trip.

The driver seemed cheerful as he announced we were rolling onto Highway I 70. A major east-west thoroughfare. I wondered about stops and where we might get caught and thrown off the bus... Or if we were going to overnight anywhere. I turned around and saw a restroom. Knowing that a lot of these folks would need to use that, I figured I would go now and not have to wait in line. It had been a while anyway. I tapped Patrick's leg and he looked over at me with his bushy white eyebrows raised. I almost laughed.

"What is it?"

"I'm going to the bathroom. I think a lot of old people have small bladders, and I don't want to wait."

He laughed and lifted his arm so I snuck out under it. On my way I heard some guy yell out, "Vegas Baby!" and after the laughter died down someone corrected him and said, "We're going to Reno." Then the guy yelled out, "Reno, baby!" And more laughter followed. Oh yeah. We've got a live one. Okay, well Reno's in Nevada too. How much further can it be from Arizona?

I did my business and then on my way back to my seat I heard someone else say the trip was thirty hours. Thirty hours! I slipped in next to Patrick and whispered, "This trip must be nonstop and it's going to take thirty hours."

Patrick looked at me for a second and then barked out a laugh.

"What?"

"I just texted my mother to tell her that I was going camping with my cousin Chuck, and if she didn't hear from me not to worry, because my battery was low and I didn't know if there would be any electricity where we were going. As lies go, I thought that was a good one."

He would buy some time with that, but thirty hours? And then thirty back? That's sixty hours. That's… How many times does twenty-four go into sixty? Wait… and then there are meal stops.

He could see the worry on my face, I'm sure. He just put his arm around me again and jostled me a bit.

"Don't worry. It'll be okay."

"Are you kidding me? We're on a seniors gambling trip to Reno, Nevada, and all you can say is, it's going to be okay?"

He shrugged. "What else can I say? It's *not* gonna be okay? We're going to get caught? We're going to get thrown off the bus? It doesn't much matter, does it? Here we are. We might as well make the best of it."

"How do you do that?"

"Do what?" He was rubbing my shoulder now. It felt nice and soothing, but I was still freaked out.

"How do you just take everything in stride? Aren't you worried about anything?"

He shrugged. "And where would that get me?"

I had no answer for that. I guess it would just get us to wherever we were going, plus worrying about it the whole way. I sighed. "Okay, we're on our way toward Reno, but we don't have to go the whole way. Right?"

"Where did you want to get off?"

"I don't know. I'm not familiar with this part of the country, at all."

Patrick leaned across me and asked the couple on

the other side, "Do you know where we're stopping first?"

The guy laughed. "Why? You need to stop already? The restroom is behind you."

"No, I'm just hungry. My wife didn't pack much for snacks. And I forgot to eat lunch."

"Well, I hear were going to have dinner in Kansas City. Mmm mmm. I can smell the steaks already!"

"Oh, right. Thanks."

Patrick leaned back and looked at me. "Kansas City. I don't know if that's in Missouri or Kansas. I think there's one of each."

I let out a long sigh. I didn't know what to say. Should I just tell him to get off the bus in Kansas City and go home, and then I would stay on and go to Arizona? That would be a little suspicious. Would these folks believe we broke up? Maybe we could pick a fight…

"Patrick, why don't we stage some kind of big fight and you say to the bus driver you're not going on to Reno, and then you can turn around and go back to Detroit. I'll get back on the bus and act all broken-hearted but determined to go to Reno and spend our last dime."

He leaned back and stared at me like I had sprouted another head. "I'm not going to leave you. I can't do that."

"Why not? I don't understand why you're even here with me now. You don't have to do this."

He adjusted in his seat to face me more straight on, then took his arm from around me and held both my hands. He looked into my eyes and I saw only sincerity there. "Jenika, you need me. I don't want to lie to you. I'd feel like the biggest heel on earth if I just dumped a sixteen-year-old girl in the middle of the country and said, *'Good luck, kiddo'!* I'm sorry. You're stuck with me."

Part of me wanted to melt. That was maybe the nicest thing anybody's ever done for me. Usually people either ignore me or avoid me. Maybe I was giving off *leave me alone* vibes and didn't realize it. I kind of expected people to reject me anyway, because that had been happening my whole life. 'Oh, you must be the new kid, huh?' Unlike in teen movies, nobody walks up to you and becomes your best friend right away... and if you're not particularly outgoing, it doesn't happen at all.

I was holding Patrick's warm hands in mine and contemplating all these feelings going through me. I looked up and suddenly his lips landed on mine. He was kissing me! I know, that sounds kind of weird, but that's pretty much how it was. I just looked up and his lips collided with me. I have to say it felt really nice. Reeeeeaaaally nice. I didn't pull away. In fact, I let my hand snake around his neck and may have pulled him a little closer. In the background, I vaguely heard some of the seniors mentioning how we must be newlyweds or something. I didn't care. I don't think Patrick did either. We just kept making out and let the rest of the bus worry about themselves.

At least I wasn't thinking about bounty hunters anymore.

CHAPTER 11

Say what you want about old people. One thing they all have in common is that they know stuff, and they seem happy to show off their knowledge. That was handy once Patrick and I were able to peal ourselves off of each other. He hadn't shaved in a couple of days, and even though his stubble was incredibly sexy, I was getting beard burn. So we had to cool it. Besides we had been getting teased about our hormones, needing a room, etc. The old guys even wanted to know what meds we were on.

We discovered that a couple of former lawyers were on the bus and that helped us in a couple of ways. I made up a fake granddaughter who was in trouble with the law and tried to figure out what bounty hunters were all about.

One of the guys mentioned that bounty hunting was illegal in some states. He didn't know exactly which ones since new ones were coming on board from time to time. He knew they were outlawed in Maine and Illinois, but that wouldn't have helped me anyway. We were heading west.

Once Patrick and I figured out what we needed to know, we realized we'd have to find a way to look things up without leaving a trail of breadcrumbs.

"I don't want to use your phone any more than I want to use mine. By now the bounty hunters have seen you with me twice. I'm sure they're smart enough to figure out we're traveling together."

"If they even know who I am."

"I don't want to take any chances. What if they were able to get a picture of us? Or can magically zoom in on your energy now?"

I was learning that witches came with different gifts. And those powers were sometimes stronger if you could team up with someone else. Couples could fill in powers the other lacked, and voila, you'd have the original 'power couple'. Maybe that's why we had two bounty hunters on us. Maybe one of them was really good at tracking and the other one...I don't know... Magical restraining? Freezing? Transporting? I didn't want to think about it.

When we made a meal stop in Wyoming, we decided to sit at a table away from the other bus's occupants. Patrick's glamor was starting to fade and he didn't know how much longer he could keep it up.

"So, while we're in the state, we might as well visit Yellowstone Park." I was trying to embrace a more 'Patrick' attitude. Live for the moment. Less worry; more fun.

"Do you want to see geysers like Old Faithful instead of geezers?" he asked.

I laughed. "Yeah."

Patrick nodded, "We can."

I enjoyed cuddling up to him and he seemed to enjoy indulging me. I don't know why I didn't see this mutual attraction before. I should have. I guess it says something about low self-esteem because I didn't think a cute guy like Patrick would be interested in someone like me. Not that there was anything all that wrong with me. I was just shy and awkward and a couple years younger than him.

I kind of hated the idea of leaving the bus, and I didn't think we could ride bikes all the way to Yellow-stone, but now that we knew how to copy a bus ticket or hitchhike, we could find our own way. I know, I know… Hitchhiking is bad. But with the two of us and our magical abilities, I'm pretty sure we could take care of ourselves.

While we were stopped for lunch in Laramie, Wyoming, Patrick and I staged a huge fight. It was over something stupid, but realistic—how much money we were willing to lose in Reno. He picked a high number and I picked a low number. That's pretty much the way it would probably go in real life.

As soon as we had told the bus driver we wouldn't be going on to Reno after all, we borrowed the waitress's cell phone to look up Yellowstone and decided to start our Wyoming adventure there. The other couples just shook their heads and one of the lawyers mumbled something like, "All that passion. It's a damn shame…"

Little did we know that Laramie was a long way from Yellowstone, but once Patrick decided something sounded like fun, he figured out a way to make it happen. When the bus rolled away, we left the restaurant. Patrick led me around the back where we couldn't be seen from the parking lot, then our disguises rippled away.

Suddenly we were young and in need of a ride again, although he didn't take me all the way back to my teenage appearance. We realized that my youth might trigger an Amber alert, so he made me look like I was in my twenties or early thirties. He conjured a mirror and I was shocked when I saw myself just a few years older.

I looked hawt! He even found a way to give my hair some glossy dark twists instead of my natural curly brown or the short white fuzz I'd sported as an elderly woman. I even felt more confident—a confidence I desperately needed. I hoped that when I got to be this age, I would actually *be* that confident.

We trekked to the highway closest to us and planned to hitchhike from there.

"First we need to do a spell for protection," I said sagely.

"Yeah. Good idea. Maybe the Goddess can help us catch a good ride too!"

"What kind of spell would that be?"

"How about a success spell?"

"That might work. Okay, do you have the words?"

"Hey, that's your department."

I sighed. "Yeah, with your terrible rhyming, I'd better handle it."

He just grinned, letting me know he wasn't offended at all.

"Dear Goddess, we ask you today to guide our way. Give us protection and choose our direction. If it harms none, so mote it be done." We stuck our thumbs out.

"Let's hold hands while were hitchhiking," Patrick said. "I think people would be more likely to pick up a young couple, don't you?"

"I think you just want to hold my hand."

He grinned. "Busted. Look, can I help it if I can't keep my hands to myself? I really like you, Jenika."

"I really like you too." We smiled at each other, both unwilling to take that next step into any kind of mushy commitment. That was okay. I had no idea what was going to happen from here. Maybe we would just have this great adventure and then find we had nothing in common. Or maybe I'd make it to Arizona, get a job, but find out Patrick couldn't take the Arizona heat. Or maybe he'd realize he *should* get his butt back home before his mother wondered what had happened to him. I imagined all kinds of things.

We made it to Yellowstone with one ride from a truck driver. He must've really wanted to chat, so we listened and asked questions. I imagine it must have been pretty lonely on the road for long periods of time. He told us all about Yellowstone National Park which he had visited numerous times with his family. Apparently he made this trip on a regular basis. He said he and his kids were really into camping.

I hoped Patrick or I could conjure some kind of tent and sleeping bags when we got there. I didn't have great faith in our coming up with a trailer, especially if it was made with an engine. Clearly the Goddess didn't trust our driving skills.

Our truck driver commented on a lack of camping gear and asked if we'd be renting a cabin. I gave Patrick a barely perceptible shrug, meaning, *Okay, let's go with that.* It was dark by the time we got there, so a cabin would be the best option anyway.

We were fortunate enough to get into the park with the driver's annual pass, then he let us off just inside. He said the cabins weren't far, but he didn't want to turn his big rig around on the narrow winding unpaved road.

"No problem, Bro," Patrick said. "We can take it from here." The guy probably wasn't used to being called 'bro', but his face lit up and he saluted as he drove off. We both called out, "Thank you," then hiked into the park.

Someone had left a tent next to a trash can, so we scooped it up. We could conjure a missing part if that were the problem, but it seemed as if whoever tossed it had just decided they'd had enough of camping for one lifetime.

We found a picturesque spot and pitched it. The canvas was old and worn, but as long as it didn't rain we'd probably be okay. We each conjured our own air mattresses and sleeping bags. Why didn't we do that in the abandoned Indianapolis house? Simple. We didn't think of it. Patrick was learning more about what he could do on this trip too.

He had the brilliant idea that we could zip the sleeping bags together and use our body warmth for even greater comfort. I didn't doubt he'd behave himself, if I asked. so I didn't ask. We were so bone-tired by then, a few kisses was all we could manage, anyway.

We spent the next day visiting places on the park map. Patrick practiced transporting us short distances when nobody was around. We saw bison, elk, and a moose. The map said the park's ecosystem also contained wolves, wolverines, and bears, including grizzly bears. They were harder to spot, because they avoided humans, fortunately.

We hiked something called the Fairy Falls to get to some geysers and a beautiful lake. Transporting wasn't even necessary since it was an easy hike once we made it to the trailhead.

"Now I can tell my mother I went camping and it won't be a lie," Patrick exclaimed.

"Yeah, but I'm not your cousin."

"Thank the Goddess," he said, then swooped in for a long, toe-curling kiss.

As we were lip-locked something whizzed by my ear. I jumped away from Patrick and spotted someone hiding behind a tree with what looked like the barrel of a shotgun pointed right at us. I think it was the female bounty hunter. She was squinting, as if aiming for a second round.

I grabbed Patrick's hand and yelled 'Let's go. Quick! We're being shot at!"

He held on tight and we ran into the woods. "Where do we go now? Our little trash tent won't protect us from bullets any more than we were protected from bears."

"Just run!"

The guy who said he was my father wasn't with her, at least not that I could see. He hadn't been armed in

Indianapolis, but he was fast. Maybe the bounty hunters had been working independently.

"Shoot, I mean… Don't shoot! Crap. Do you think we can outrun her?"

"I don't know."

Suddenly a male voice called out, "Jenika! Patrick! Stop!"

"Damn!" Over my other shoulder I spotted the male of the two. He seemed to be closing in.

"Oh, no. It's both of them. We've got to do something, quick." I squeezed his hand as he ran right beside me. I wanted to see his face one last time, if I died.

"Look. There's an open field to our right," he said. "Do you think you can fly?"

"I don't know, but I can try."

"Good. Go! You're the one they want. I can hold them off, you just need to fly and get away."

"No way." I let go of his hand just long enough to clamp my fingers around his wrist. "I'm not going without you. Maybe we can Peter Pan this thing."

He glanced over at me. "I don't think you can lift me since you're just a little bit of a thing."

"Watch me!" I broke into the open field and stepped on the gas, running as fast as I could. Patrick kept up with me and my feet left the ground. Holding his wrist hard, I could see he was trying to let go.

"No, dammit. Hold on!"

"I'll just hold you back. Go without me. I'll meet you back in Laramie."

"Let me try first. Please, hold on!"

I tightened my hold on his wrist and flew higher, lifting him off the ground and soaring into the air.

He muttered something that I'm pretty sure was a swear, but in a good way. The wind helped lift us up over the trees on the other side of the meadow. Just for the heck of it, I turned and looked over my shoulder to see both bounty hunters standing in the field with their mouths agape. I guess neither one of them had the power to fly, and I was very grateful for that.

Patrick was now holding onto me with both hands and we were soaring over the woods. I looked down and saw two bears.

"Grizzlies!" Patrick yelled. "Don't land."

I wasn't about to. I didn't want anyone to see us flying, except maybe the elk and bears, so I stayed over the thick trees. I figured they would give us enough cover and most people didn't look up anyway.

I didn't know in which direction we were flying, but as soon as we were well out of the range of the bounty hunters I found another field and lowered us down to it.

Patrick laughed as we landed, then bent over and put his hands on his knees. He laughed harder than I had ever seen him laugh before.

When he straightened up, he said, "Holy heck,

Jenika! That was un-freakin-believable! Now that we've lost them, where are we and where do we go from here?"

"I was wondering about that too. Let's go to a library. Maybe we can map out a route to Arizona that avoids states which allow bounty hunters."

"That sounds like a good idea. Maybe we could throw them off by heading south, since we're going to go that way to get to Arizona anyway. I'm pretty sure we've been flying north up until now."

"Yeah. Maybe we can go back to Laramie, or to Cheyenne. I know those are two large cities in Wyoming, and they're sure to have a library. I assume, since they know your name, you won't want to use your phone anymore."

"Probably not. Do they know you might be going to Arizona?"

"I doubt it. I never told anyone but you."

"Good. We can certainly hitch a ride on a highway. That's a good idea about going south again. As far as they know we're going north and west."

"Let's go south and east. That will certainly throw them off. Or we could continue South and West. We can skip Nevada and go through Colorado. I think it borders Arizona," he said.

"Sounds good to me. I saw a highway while I was up in the air. It was that way." I pointed toward the setting sun.

"Okay, let's go that way. Do you remember how far it was?"

"I'm not good at judging distances, but I'd guess it's a couple miles. Something we can easily hike."

"Meanwhile, maybe I can teach you some major protection magic."

We started walking in the direction I had pointed. "Protection spells? Really? And yet you got caught."

"I'm pretty good at disabling cameras, as long as I know about them. I didn't know about that nanny cam. And it was stupid of me to rob the house of somebody that knew me. So, yeah, I didn't use my head that time."

I tried to think of some double entendre joke, but nothing occurred to me. Just as well. We walked in silence for a while, and then he started telling me about ways to cast a protective bubble around myself. Supposedly, nothing could enter that bubble. I didn't know if he could cast a double bubble. That sounded funny to my own ears, so I had to say it.

"I don't think I can cast a bubble, can you cast a double bubble? Would that be too much trouble?"

He groaned. "You had that one in the chamber, didn't you?"

"I don't know if that's a metaphor I'd want to use right now. I wonder what kind of amo the female bounty Hunter was shooting at us. Do you think she was using regular bullets or maybe just a tranquilizer dart or something?"

"I couldn't tell you from looking at the barrel of a gun. But I doubt they'd put a 'dead or alive' bounty on a kid."

"It sure looked like a shotgun to me." I pondered for a while, then did some more thinking out loud. "If that guy really is my father, he wouldn't let her kill me, would he?"

"I don't think so," Patrick said. "But I don't know the guy."

"I don't either."

We walked in silence for a while. Eventually we got to the highway, and Patrick used the same glamour spell to make us look a little older. *No Amber alerts, please...*

A trucker stopped to pick us up and fortunately this guy was going to Cheyenne. I heaved my backpack onto the wide, bench-seat and followed it into the cab. Patrick hopped up and sat next to me.

"You're lucky I'm taking you as far as Cheyenne. It'll be dark by the time we get there. Do you have a place to stay?"

"Not really," I said, meaning not at all.

"There's a motel off the interstate. I can drop you there. I sleep in my rig at a truck stop, but I don't have room for both of you."

"A motel would be fantastic," Patrick said.

I wasn't really sure it would be 'fantastic' since I didn't have a credit card, but maybe he did or knew how to conjure one. We had been lucky so far. He seemed to be able to fool people into taking invisible money or just giving us what we needed. Why not an invisible credit card to rent a room… or two. We hadn't quite discussed that yet, but maybe it was best to wait until we got there. I really liked him, a lot. But was I ready for all of it? According to a certain vending machine, he was more than ready.

We had to get to the motel first, or it would be a moot point.

I glanced out the window at the passing traffic, wondering how the bounty hunters were getting around. They probably had a car. I hoped they didn't see us hitchhiking and getting picked up. I doubted they could have followed us if they couldn't fly. I just didn't want to jinx it by assuming we were in the clear.

"Is there any possibility you know where a library is in Cheyanne?" Patrick asked.

The truck driver laughed. "You're in luck. Sometimes I stop at a library for books on CD." He tapped a CD player on his dashboard. "Books keep me company on a long haul, and the librarian knows I'm coming back around since I have a regular route. If I'm a couple days late, I pay the fee without complaining. The librarian is kind of cute too."

Have you ever seen a really big man blush? It's kind of adorable. Even though the sun was setting, I didn't think it was just the oranges and pinks coming through the window that tinted his skin.

Patrick tossed his arm around me and grinned. "Did you hear that? We can go to the library tomorrow. It'll probably be closed by the time we get there tonight."

"Is it close to the motel?" I asked.

The truck driver shrugged. "It's pretty close. You're young and able to walk a fair distance, right?"

"Yeah, we've been walking a lot."

"Then you shouldn't have any trouble walking a few miles, especially if you've had a good night sleep and a chance to rest."

"Sounds like we have a plan," Patrick said.

I relaxed. Although having a plan and having it happen were two completely different things.

⸻ ⸻

I woke up the next morning and for a moment, I didn't know where I was. I rolled over and bumped into… Oh, yeah. *Patrick.* We were both so tired, we just about passed out last night.

His eyes fluttered open. No boy should have long, dark eyelashes like that. It's true. I had eyelash envy.

"G'morning," he said with a lopsided smile.

"Sheesh, you even wake up cheerful."

"Why not start the day off right?"

I heaved myself out of bed, still wearing most of my

clothes. I sniffed under my armpit. "Ewww… I need to shower."

"Might as well make the most of it while we have one," he said.

My body felt like an old person. Aches and pains everywhere, especially my right arm and legs.

"Do you want company in the shower?" he asked, and raised his eyebrows twice in rapid succession.

I just groaned and trudged off to the bathroom.

"Kidding," he called after me. "I'll go get breakfast."

"Good." If he thought he was going to intrude on my hot water and soap, he had another thing coming.

Once out of the shower, I felt brand new. Even my body aches felt better. I had forgotten to bring clothes in with me, but the towel covered everything important.

"Patrick?" No answer. Relief flooded me as I rushed to my backpack and dug out a change of underwear, clean jeans, and a new shirt.

I didn't want to put on my gross jacket again, so I found the sweater I had packed at the bottom. Once I had everything and was on my way back to the bathroom, a click warned me that the room door was opening. I rushed past and lost my towel as I was closing the bathroom door.

I heard him chuckle, so he'd probably caught a view of my backside. *Whatever.* I was rapidly losing my inhibitions as I learned to 'make do,' or as he would call it, 'making the most of the situation'.

I smelled something delicious, so I dressed quickly and came out to see what Patrick had brought for breakfast.

He was unloading Styrofoam containers, some wrapped baked goods, and a couple bottles of orange juice. "We need sustenance! The library is about five miles from here according to the desk clerk."

"Thank you! Do I dare ask how you paid for this?"

He shrugged. "Do you really want to know?"

I thought about it for one second. Grabbing the juice, I shook my head. "Nope. I guess I really don't."

The orange smell reminded me of Haven East, hidden in an old orange grove in Florida. The scent was almost nostalgic. How many kids remember juvie fondly? Probably only me.

After eating, checking out, and walking to the library, we discovered what we needed to know. Several states had banned the practice of bounty hunting within their borders, such as Illinois, Kentucky, Oregon and Wisconsin, and more recently Nebraska and Maine abolished it. It wasn't lost on me that we'd blown our chances of reaching three or four of those states, depending on our initial direction.

Nebraska was the closest possibility now. "We could probably make it back to Nebraska before we're discovered. What do you think?" I asked.

"It's your adventure. What do you want to do?"

"I want to get my emancipation papers—legally— and find a room over a store or restaurant where I can work and continue school online."

Patrick scratched his head. "That's a big ask. I can forge something for you, but being strictly legal isn't my forte."

I laughed. "I know. Do you think you'll ever change?"

"Sure I will. As soon as I get home I'll call the community college and ask if I can start in January. I was supposed to be there now, but, you know… juvie. I don't want to interrupt my mother's dream twice."

"When do you turn eighteen?"

He grinned. "Yesterday."

"What? You had a birthday and didn't tell me?"

"Hey, you didn't tell me about yours either."

"Oh, right. But I had just gotten home and didn't even know where you were."

"I know. So, did you have a cake and gifts and stuff?"

I snorted. "No. My stepfather didn't even remember."

"I did," a low male voice said from a few feet away. He came around the nearest rack of books. "You were born on November sixth, in Omaha, Nebraska."

I gasped and froze.

Patrick grabbed my hand. "That's a matter of public record," he ground out between clenched teeth.

"What isn't in any record is how I loved you from the minute I first held you. And how heartbroken I was when your mother took you away from me. She drained our savings account, snuck out in the middle of the night, boarded a plane in Kawasaki, and flew back to the states."

"You could have researched that," Patrick said.

"Do you still have that scar on your backside?"

I sucked in a big breath. How could he know about that? Patrick's eyebrows shot up. Obviously he'd gotten a peek at it too.

"You sat on some shards of glass when you were four. They went in deep and had to be extracted at the base hospital and then you were stitched up. Your mom had thrown a glass at me. You tried to stop her from throwing a plate too and fell backward onto the glass."

Tears sprang to my eyes. "Dad? Daddy?"

"Yes, baby. It's me."

"But you're a bounty hunter, chasing me."

"No. I teamed up with a bounty hunter to find you. She had connections, access to databases, cameras... things like that."

I glanced around the library, afraid she'd point her shotgun at us any second. "Where is she now?"

"I sent her on an errand. She's researching something at the state house, and I said I'd try my luck at the library. Now that I've found you, I'll avoid her, completely."

"But how did you know where to look?"

"Did your mother ever tell you where your magic came from?"

"No. She just told me never to use it. Did it come from you?"

"Yes. She hated it. She said it made us unequal, but the truth is she was afraid. I agreed not to use it."

"But you're using it now?"

"To find you, yes. I only learned about your mother's and grandfather's deaths a little while ago. You must have been devastated."

The tears threatening my composure began to run down my cheeks. All I could do was nod.

Patrick put a protective arm around my shoulder. I could tell he was still suspicious, but I wanted to explore this more. Some facial features matched the faded memories of my father that I'd stored away.

"Have you eaten?" he asked.

"Yeah. We had a big breakfast," Patrick said.

"Can I interest you in some ice cream? Do you still like strawberry?"

Now I knew he had to be my father. How would he know my favorite flavor had always been strawberry? Anyone who was just guessing would probably say chocolate."

I put my hand on Patrick's arm. "It's him, and the empath in me says he's sincere."

"Are you sure it isn't just wishful thinking?"

"I'm ninety-nine percent sure."

Patrick nodded and a smile crept across his face. "Let's get some ice cream, then."

As we left the library, I kept glancing over at the father I never really knew. He glanced back and smiled. A feeling of relief and safety washed over me.

"So where is this ice cream place?" Patrick asked.

My dad didn't get a chance to answer. A dart went whizzing by my head. He stepped in front of me, shielding me while he shouted at the female bounty hunter.

"Stop! I have her. You don't have to tranq her!"

Patrick was livid. "I knew it! I knew you couldn't be trusted!" He tried to grab my hand but I yanked it away before he could.

"He can! I know it! Look, he's protecting…"

Suddenly I felt a sharp pain and I became a little woozy. I didn't have a chance to finish my sentence before I passed out.

CHAPTER 12

I came to, jiggling in the back of a van. I wasn't tied up. It didn't look like there were any guards on me, so what happened?

The guy who said he was my father—still might be—was driving. I didn't see anyone in the passenger seat. I scooted up closer to him and looked out the windshield to see if I could get an idea of where we were.

"Ah! You're awake."

"Where are you taking me?"

"Where do you want to go?"

Was this some kind of test? What should I tell him? I doubted I was on my way to Genevieve's aunt's place in Arizona. I didn't see Patrick, but he could have been questioned, and then what… dropped off by the side of the road?

"Where's Patrick?"

"He's fine."

He might have told them about Haven East but he didn't know where in Arizona we were hoping to go. Could we be driving all the way to Florida?

"Just tell me where we're going. And where Patrick is. And while we're at it, why don't you tell me about that bitch who tranquilized me."

He sighed. "I didn't lie to you about teaming up with the bounty hunter. She's not in the picture anymore. I managed to get you away from her and she doesn't have my powers to track us. I'm pretty sure she has no idea where we're going."

"Well then, she and I have something in common."

"Look, I'm sorry, but I know a little bit about you from the research I did before I left Michigan. I understand you and your stepfather don't get along."

I snorted. "You could say that, yeah. What does he have to do with this? You're not taking me back to Detroit, are you?"

"Well, you jumped bail. Fortunately I was able to speak to him and the judge. He doesn't want guardianship, and because I'm your real father you are now under my care. I paid Phil back the money he spent to bail you out, and he was satisfied."

"Okay, so now what?"

"You were arraigned but never made it to your sentencing, so the bounty hunter was supposed to bring you back for that. I was able to intervene and had your trial held remotely."

"Sheesh! How long have I been out?"

"Not that long. I'm able to manipulate time a bit."

"A bit? Sounds like an understatement."

He shrugged, looking secretly proud. "Anyway, you were sentenced to six weeks."

"You're taking me to Juvie?" I bolted upright.

"Not just any Juvie, Haven West."

I relaxed, a little bit. At least I was going to a Haven and not regular Juvie. He must've explained to the judge why I had been at Haven East. My stepfather had no clue.

"But, I wanted to go to Haven East. There's a teacher there who was trying to help me."

He glanced over his shoulder at me. "What was she trying to do to help?"

Should I tell him? I guess it wouldn't matter now. She had already told me she wasn't gonna help me become emancipated anymore. "It sounded at first like she was going to help me with the emancipation process. I really wanted to become an emancipated minor and take care of myself. I know I can. And I would get out of my stepfather's hair at the same time."

"That's interesting," he said.

"That's all you have to say about it? Interesting?"

"What would you call it? Shocking? Alarming? To me, it seems understandable. If your stepfather was not a good parent, and you could be a better parent to yourself, it makes perfect sense."

I hoped he was telling the truth, but how would I know since he was taking me somewhere in a van? How did I know he meant it when he said he was taking me to Haven? He also said he was taking me for ice cream. I didn't have any ice cream.

I glanced at the clock on the dashboard and at the position of the sun. It looked like it was about noon, so I couldn't tell in what direction we were going. I didn't see a directional setting on the van's dashboard, so I looked for signs on the highway. Finally I saw one that said we were heading south. That would make sense if we were going to Haven West, which I had heard was in Colorado. I'm not sure *where* in Colorado, but I think someone said it was up in the mountains. It would be cold there now.

"So, you said you're taking me to Haven West. Where is it?"

"It used to be a ranch, just outside of Divide."

"Divide? Where is that?"

"It's a small town up in the mountains right on the Continental Divide. That's how it got its name. And the ranch, like I said, is near that town. But the important thing is that it's for magicals, like you."

I had to think about that for a bit. He obviously knew I was magical. That must've been kind of hard to miss when I flew off with Patrick. Again, I wondered where Patrick was.

"Where's my friend? What did you do with Patrick?"

"Your friend is fine. He's on his way back to Michigan. His mother knows about his involvement, and he won't be charged with your kidnapping."

"Kidnapping! He didn't kidnap me. I was on my own, and he insisted on accompanying me to protect me."

"I know. He explained that. And I thanked him for it. You would've been much more vulnerable as a young woman alone."

He called me a young woman. Not a girl. I suddenly realized I felt more like a woman than a girl now. Maybe it was time to act like one and get some burning questions answered.

"So what happened to you after mom and I left Japan?"

He was silent for a while. At last he said, "I'm not completely proud of my past. I can tell you I had an honorable discharge from the Air Force, and then I went into a civilian outfit that employed ex-military trained operatives."

"Operatives? That sounds like… What, mercenaries?"

"Basically, yes. I saw parts of the world most people don't get to see… and don't want to, for that matter. One thing you might like to know is that I *wasn't* on the wrong side of the law. I spent most of my time righting wrongs, like young women being kidnapped and trafficked. My job and that of my unit was to find them and return them to safety."

I had to think about that for a while. If he was telling the truth, then he was a hero. I'd to look into it when I could, although I'm not sure his clandestine work would be well documented. I could check on the honorable discharge though.

"So, that's why you just disappeared?"

He nodded. "That and your mother didn't want anything to do with me. Things were not going well between us, but you probably know that now. We hid our fighting from you as much as we could. I wanted to stay in touch with you, but she promised to make it as difficult as possible. I could've had her jailed for not allowing visitation, but then you wouldn't have your mom. And she was a good mom."

I looked down at my lap. "Yes, she *was* a good mom."

"I told her I wouldn't get a hardship discharge, and if she took you back to the United States, she'd be severing our relationship... yours and mine. She was fine with that."

"Did you even try to work it out?"

"Yes, we did. However, she would never have felt differently about my magic."

"So, where did you go after that? After you got out? Why didn't you come back to Detroit?"

He took a deep breath and sighed. "As I said, I'm not

proud of certain decisions I've made. She didn't want me, and I figured she'd just poison you against me, so you wouldn't want me, either. I should have fought for you. That's probably my biggest regret.

Instead, I took a job where I was wanted and needed, working with this civilian outfit. If I couldn't help my own daughter, I figured maybe I could help the daughters of countless others. I'm afraid I can't tell you much more than that. It's all top secret."

"Okay, but you can tell me where you spent your time, can't you?"

"A little bit in Thailand, we had just one job there and I can't tell you about it, so don't even ask. And then we were in the Philippines for a while. Again, don't ask. And then Africa. I spent the rest of my time there. I'm out of that line of work now though. I'm happy to say I'm in a serious relationship with a wonderful woman in Ghana."

My eyebrows shot up. "Ghana? As in Africa? Is that where you live now?"

He nodded. "It is. I don't expect you to come back to Africa with me, but if you want to the invitation is open..."

"Oh, no, thanks. I mean, that's not a terrible place, from what I've heard. I'm just pretty happy here. Ghana is fairly tame as a country, I think, right?"

"Tame? Do you mean they have a stable government?"

"Yes. I mean, some places in Africa are a mess. They have corrupt governments and martial law and stuff."

"That's true, but Ghana is not one of them. It's actually one of the most stable countries on the continent. Because it's small and they cherish their democracy, they're making advances all the time. My girlfriend works with this wonderful organization called Empowered to Educate. They work with African girls and are mostly STEM education focused. But my girlfriend is into the arts. She's interested in teaching business to artists, so they're not taken advantage of."

I knew STEM stood for science, technology, engineering, and math. Definitely not my strengths. I had to admire his girlfriend though. It sounded like she was doing something worthwhile too. In my opinion, that's when you know a place is worth living in. When arts flourish, making the whole place more beautiful.

"So, what's your girlfriend's name?"

"Aaliyah, but everyone just calls her Lia. I would like you to meet her, sometime. But you'll be busy for a while."

"Yes, apparently. I'll be in Haven West."

He nodded again, keeping his eyes on the road. "Are you hungry?"

My stomach growled. "Yeah, I'm starving."

"There's a cooler back there with some sandwiches and bottles of water. Help yourself."

"I guess you don't trust me to stop at a restaurant. I won't take off, you know."

"I didn't think you would, but I promised to get you to Haven West as soon as possible. They're holding a spot for you, but the admin said it might be filled if we don't get there by tomorrow."

That made me wonder where we'd be staying that night. Or maybe he was just going to drive straight through. He seemed pretty tough. I wouldn't put it past him.

Divide was one of those towns where people say, "Don't blink or you'll miss it." I think we went through the whole town in less than five minutes.

"So where is this ranch?" I asked.

Earlier, my dad had taken some directions over the phone because his GPS might not work up here. He read a little about the town before leaving Colorado Springs and told me its population was less than 150 people, and its elevation was over nine thousand feet. I was feeling a little lightheaded, but he assured me that the altitude was something I'd get used to.

My sentence was six weeks—not very long since all I did was a little shoplifting. Since I was so close to Arizona, relatively speaking, I might work on my dad in the meantime to see if I could get released to

Genevieve's Aunt Hilary when my time was up. After all, she was already raising and educating Genevieve and her twin sister Tawania. What's one more witch? I couldn't wait to see her again. All of them, actually.

They were all very magical, and I guess I was too. I'd heard that Genevieve's aunt had some sway with the spa they all worked at. She got the girls part-time jobs and she was homeschooling them the rest of the time. I didn't know what she might be able to do for me, but it wouldn't hurt to ask. If nothing else, I'd still love to go for a visit.

Speaking of visits… "Are you going to be visiting me here, or are you going back to Africa right away?" I hadn't decided yet whether to call my biological father Dad or William yet, so I just left off his moniker altogether.

"I told the principal I'd be staying down in Colorado Springs. It's close enough to drive up here, while big enough to have a choice of hotels—not that I wouldn't feel perfectly comfortable camping alongside the trail." He winked at me.

"I don't know about that. It's pretty cold up here."

"True." After a long pause, he said, "I probably don't have to emphasize this, but… don't screw up while you're here. Six weeks isn't that long."

"Yeah, that escape from Haven East was an accident, did anyone explain that to you?"

"Yes, I spoke to the administrator down in Florida

before talking to the judge. She seemed happy to know I was back in the picture. Was your stepfather really that awful?"

"He didn't abuse me or anything. It was just neglect, I guess."

"So, you didn't have money to buy those things you took?"

I laughed. "I never had any money. If I asked for any, he thought I was just going to use it for drugs. Eventually I stopped asking. Maybe that's what he did when he was my age, but that's definitely not my thing."

My father smiled and nodded. "Your teachers said you're a smart kid. You just needed some guidance. They knew your stepfather wasn't giving you any and hoped that I would."

"I kind of wanted to know that too."

He glanced over at me. "I'm willing if you are. Just know I'll need to return to Ghana."

I was open to anything at this point. I didn't have a lot of options. At least not good ones.

"Sure. That sounds reasonable."

"Can I count on you to stay out of trouble for six weeks?"

"I won't cause any trouble, unless it looks like someone is gonna cause *me* trouble. Then I'll look out for myself. Does that make sense?"

"That makes perfect sense. Don't let anyone put you

in a bad position. Watch your back. I'm sure you'll be okay. From what I understand this place is smaller than Haven East. You'll probably be watched a lot closer."

Delightful.

When we finally arrived at the ranch, I saw what he meant. We were already going down the other side of the mountain, but not that far down. We were probably still at 8,000 feet. I felt a little wobbly as I got out of the car, but that may have just been from riding for so long.

The place was very different from Haven East. Instead of a cinderblock structure, it was built log-cabin style, but larger. Instead of orange groves, it was tucked among tall ponderosa pines. I don't actually know one pine tree from another, but that seemed like a good name for these towering trees.

I also didn't know what kind of ranch it was. I didn't see any prairie or anything for cows to hang out on. It all seemed to be pretty mountainous. As I was stretching my legs someone on horseback clomped up to me and gave me a once over, from the top of my head to the tips of my feet. *Sheesh, I'm glad I took a shower before I was kidnapped.*

"And who might you be little lady?"

Wow, an honest-to-Goddess cowboy. "My name is Jenika Jones," I said. "Is this Haven West?"

"Well, if it isn't, then I'm in the wrong place." He laughed at his own lame joke. He jumped off the horse and took off his cowboy hat, then brushed his hair back with his fingers. "I'm the administrator here, Mr. Stetson. Welcome, Jenika Jones. One of our staff will show you around after we get you situated. For now, why don't you and your Padre come with me?" He nodded to my father, acknowledging him for the first time. It's odd to talk to the kid first, isn't it? Maybe he was making me feel welcome, which was a good sign. Right?

He led his horse to the railing beside the wide steps leading up to a wooden front porch, then wrapped the reins around that railing. I noticed there were no rocking chairs on the porch. I guess this was kind of like Haven East in that they didn't want things that could be easily picked up and thrown. Delinquents will be delinquents.

I looked over at my father and he just shrugged. That made me smile, and strangely enough I wanted to reach for his hand. Nothing like going to a new Juvie to make one feel insecure. But I still hardly knew this father, so holding his hand would've been weird.

Once inside I could see this might have been a very nice ranch at one time. There was a giant fireplace with large rocks making up an entire wall. No roaring fire at the moment. That was no surprise since nobody was there to tend it. Well, no visible body, at least. I had to remember this place was magical. Who knows what might lurk in the shadows? Oh, there goes my imagination again...

A couple of large couches and a few big easy chairs were placed on either side of the fireplace, like a conversation area. Maybe this is where they had assemblies. It looked so comfortable though, I'll bet it was reserved for the well behaved inmates to socialize. There must be a cafeteria somewhere. That's probably where everyone gathered.

A curved counter that looked like a hotel lobby check-in desk was set off to one side. The principal led us past that and around the corner of a wide corridor. I now realized the building was a lot bigger inside than it looked from the outside, because...magic. He stopped at the first door on the right and opened it for us. "Step into my office," he said.

He took the swivel chair behind the large desk and my father and I sat in wooden chairs that had been made out of half logs. I wondered who did all this wood chopping. Hopefully, it wouldn't be me.

"Now, as you may have gathered, this here place is very different from Haven East. And I'm not just talking about the weather. We only have eight to ten young witches at a time out here."

I wondered if the witches west of the Mississippi were better behaved than the ones on the east side, or if there were just fewer magicals out here. I was guessing it might be a bit of both.

"Most of the kids are in classes right now, but every afternoon we have work details. I believe Haven East didn't have a lot of work for students."

As I thought about it I realized they did have a landscape company mow the grass. There wasn't a lot of interior maintenance to do except washing the floors and they had a janitor for that. They sent the laundry out… So, yeah, I guess we inmates were probably the workers here at Haven West. Unless someone from Divide came down to do that stuff.

"What kind of work do you have the students doing?" my father asked.

"We have a few horses that need tending to, but that's a gig they all want and it has to be earned. There's also dishwashing, snow shoveling, laundry…"

"Snow shoveling?" I asked, looking at my medium weight sweater.

"We get a lot of snow up here and new student inmates do the shoveling."

I grimaced. My father caught my worry. Maybe he's an empath too?

"I'll have to come back with a heavy jacket and some warmer clothes for her. I think the jacket she has with her has seen better days, and I don't think it's that warm either."

Okay. He was officially my hero and deserved a title. "Thanks, Dad. That would be nice."

"Yep," the cowboy principal said. "She'll need that

here, but we might have a few things in lost and found for her. She looks about the size of a couple of our charges who left things behind."

Who would leave a warm jacket behind? Someone who left in a hurry?

My dad nodded. "Okay. That might do, for now. I'll come back at the next visiting hours and bring her some things. Can I have her make a list for me?"

"Of course." The principal, Mr. Stetson, handed me a pen and a pad of paper. I jotted down my sizes first and then asked for seven pairs of underwear, four bras, two pairs of thicker jeans and three long sleeve jerseys. I handed the list to my father and said, "Is that too much?"

He glanced at it. "Is that enough?"

The principal said, "May I see that list?"

My dad handed it over and Mr. Stetson nodded. "She might need some boots and ski pants too—something waterproof."

"Oh, yeah. For when I'm shoveling snow, right?" It was all I could do not to roll my eyes.

"Yes, that would be what you used them for. You guys don't go skiing." He laughed again, like he was hilarious—which he wasn't. Then he cleared his throat. "It gets pretty cold at night. You might like some long johns too."

I had to remember that November in Colorado might differ from November in Detroit. Lake effect snow made our winters almost unbearable, but mountains probably made it worse. "I don't see much snow around—yet."

"We're so close to the sun that it can snow three feet overnight and a few days later it's nearly gone. Snow is late this season. Blizzards can happen way up into late spring too. But in the middle of winter you'll find us buried in snow all the time."

Six weeks brings us to late December. Aaagh...

Haven West was very different from Haven East. There must've been thirty-five or forty staff members between teachers, guards, and cooks at Haven East, but there were only a handful of guards and teachers at Haven West. So far I'd only counted two guards per shift, and it seemed that there were more chores and fewer classes.

The classes weren't nearly as fun, either. Just straight up math, English and American history—all the boring stuff. I wasn't happy, but I wasn't miserable either. Well, not yet.

Last night, just as Mr. Steadman had promised, it snowed like it was trying to bury us alive. This morning we woke up to at least three feet of fresh powder. I had already been told that I'd be on shoveling duty and the driveway was going to be a bear. It was steep and long and turned into a giant circle at the back where the stables and parking lot were located.

In front of the ranch, the road twisted down the mountain. We didn't have to do the road, of course. A separate plow sat next to the stables and looked as if it could be affixed to a four-wheel drive truck. I guess if anybody wanted deliveries before the town got around to plowing, it could come in handy. I was told we might be completely snowed in for a day or two.

I put on my borrowed ski pants, which were too long, and borrowed ski parka, also too big, but at least the hat and gloves fit. Three of us were escorted to the porch where three shovels were waiting for us. They were made of lightweight aluminum, but sturdy enough for the job. My breaths came out in steamy puffs and the cold stung my exposed skin.

I gazed out over the unspoiled landscape. The view was nearly worth bundling up and coming out here for. The snow sparkled where the sun hit it. The wind had created some dips along with mounds, which made the landscape more varied and interesting. I wasn't looking forward to shoveling and spoiling that beautiful tableau, but it had to be done, and apparently three of us kids had to do it. The guard stayed on the porch and leaned against the railing.

"Do all of you know what to do?"

I shrugged. The other two rolled their eyes. Jimmy, whose name I had just learned, was about seventeen and especially sullen. "I think I know how to shovel snow," he grumbled.

The girl, Belinda, who seemed a bit younger and was extremely pretty, just grabbed a shovel and started pushing snow off the edge of the porch onto the steps below like she was used to it.

"I just assume we shovel snow here like we would anywhere else, right?"

The kids laughed. The guard smirked. "No, kid. This is Colorado snow. I don't know where you're from, but Colorado snow is different than any other snow."

Was he kidding me? Being sarcastic? I didn't want to embarrass myself. So I just ignored him and started clearing off the other side of the stairs. Jimmy tromped down the steps between Belinda and me and said, "I'll start clearing the driveway."

I noticed he kept glancing up at the guard from time to time. The guard was holding his cell phone, but it looked like he was playing a game. He wasn't talking to anyone or even pausing as if texting.

Belinda accidentally on purpose bumped me as we were clearing the lower stairs. Did I get too close? I thought I was doing one half and she was doing the other. We had gotten almost to the bottom step when she cleared her throat and whispered, "Did Jimmy tell you the plan?"

Plan? "What you mean?"

Belinda looked over at Jimmy who was looking at the two of us. "Jimmy and I have it all worked out. We need you to be on board."

Oh, no. I know how this goes. Whatever it is they need me to do, I'll probably get in trouble for it. But if I do anything else, they'll make life miserable for me when it fails. Shoot. This is one of those things my dad was talking about when he said 'Don't let anyone put you in a bad position.'

I tried to ignore her and shovel the front walk a little faster. She was right behind me and caught up easily, shoveling the same way we had done the stairs. Splitting it side to side, and the path was cleared before I knew it. When we got to the driveway Jimmy whispered, "Did you tell her?"

"Not yet. She's running away from me."

I stood my ground. "Look, I don't know what you're up to, but I don't want anything to do with it. I just got here. I don't need to lengthen my sentence."

"That's why you're the perfect patsy," Jimmy said.

I wasn't quite sure what he meant, but rather than be blind-sided I asked, "What are you planning?"

"We're escaping. Look, there are three of us and one of him." Jimmy pointed his chin at the guard on the porch. "Inside there's only one other guard. If we take off in three different directions, he can only follow one of us. Even if he takes the time to go back in to get the other guard, then two out of the three of us will probably get away. Your job is to distract them and with your short legs, you're the one they'll probably catch, but we all have to go in different directions in order for it to work."

There were so many problems with this plan, I couldn't begin to formulate questions and I guessed they didn't want to spend too long figuring out the details. As we three shoveled next to each other going down the driveway, Jimmy whispered, "I'll take the road going up and into town. You take the woods, Belly, and you, Jenny or Jennifer or whatever your name is, you go downhill."

"I told you I hate that nickname," Belinda groused.

Jimmy just grinned. Not the good-natured grin Patrick used. You could tell this guy enjoyed being mean. "Get as far away as you can as fast as you can. I hope you'll be able to outrun them more easily since you're heading down the mountain," he said to me. "I'll be running uphill and if Stetson decides to follow on his horse, he might try going through the woods, so chances are he'll come after you, Belly." Then he turned to me again. "You've got to go downhill as far as fast as you can, and then cut into the woods in case they try to use a truck or hook up the plow to use on the road. Don't let them catch you easily. Is everybody clear?"

I groaned.

"Do you have a problem with that, new kid?" he asked me.

I stopped shoveling and leaned on the handle, "Why should I help you?"

The guard looked up at me and yelled, "Hey you, get moving. No breaks until you're done."

Jimmy smirked. "Does that help answer your question?"

Belinda chimed in. "You haven't been here long enough to know what jerks these guys are. Trust me, you *don't* want to be here."

I realized I didn't have time to get the whole story, but maybe I could at least get enough to help me decide whether or not I should do anything. "Have they hurt you?"

"By working us to death, yes. I burned my fingers unloading the dishwasher and they didn't even care. One of them leers at me all the time. Makes me want to hurl. When I told him to stop, he just laughed. And when I threatened to report him, he laughed harder. Said nobody would believe me. He goes into one of the girl's rooms all the time. She just pouts and won't talk to anyone. I think I'm next."

"The other one likes boys," Jimmy said. "I can't get out of here fast enough."

Shoot. I didn't know if this were true or not, but if it was, then yeah. Not only did I not want to be here, but *nobody* should be here. If they knew where they were going, then that might be helpful, but I sure didn't know where to go from here.

"What are you going to do when you get away? Do you have a car waiting somewhere? You can't just run around the mountains in the snow."

Jimmy snickered. "That's why I'm the one going to town. I know how to hotwire a car."

I wanted to say, *oh yeah, well, I can fly*. But I didn't know if I could anymore. Of course they gave me the spiel about my powers being suppressed. I didn't want to test it in front of anybody, and so far I hadn't been alone at all. We had roommates here and I was rooming with a girl who was even quieter and shyer than me. I didn't even know her name.

"When we get to the other side of the driveway, we break. I go up the road you go down the road and Betty goes into the woods. Got it?"

"My name isn't Betty, either."

He sneered at her. "Do you want me to pick you up or not?"

She rolled her eyes.

I shrugged. "Okay, I got it." I honestly didn't expect this to work. There were horses and four-wheel-drives that could easily outrun us in this snow. I didn't know how many staff members lived on the premises, but I'd seen a long outbuilding, which could house more people. We'd probably be picked up in seconds.

"Belinda, you start shoveling the other way, toward the woods. I'll pretend I'm helping the new girl do the driveway toward the road."

At last we reached the end of the driveway, and Jimmy yelled, "Now!"

Belinda took off into the woods, Jimmy ran up the road toward the town of Divide, and I, being the dutiful little patsy, plowed my body through the snow down the hill toward who knows where. I hadn't been here before. So for all I knew this road dead ended.

I supposed since I was on a mountain, all I had to do was keep moving down and eventually I would come to the bottom. There was civilization down there. I didn't know how long it would take me, but I remembered hearing it was about twenty miles from Divide to Colorado Springs. I hoped to find some cabin or town sooner than that. I'd probably find the tail-end of a four-wheel-drive and wind up sitting in it, handcuffed.

All of that was flashing through my mind as I was running, stumbling, trying to wade through or jump over huge piles of snow. This was the stupidest getaway plan I had ever heard of. Either the kids were dumber than rocks or they were desperate. If what little they said was true, I guess desperation might fit.

So, off I ran into the woods, continuing a downward dissent as soon as I had left enough tracks for anyone with coke bottle glasses to follow. I didn't know if the juvie had called out some kind of helicopter rescue and retrieval team or what, but I expected it wouldn't be long before all three of us were caught. This must have happened before.

Surprisingly, it took a while before I heard panicked voices coming from higher up the mountain. I could no longer see the ranch, so I didn't know if the guard had run inside and found backup, or if it was just him yelling at the other kids. All I knew was that I was running, wading, jumping, and sliding downhill through pine woods, hoping I didn't twist my ankle on something I couldn't see beneath the snow. That's all I would need. Freezing my ass off out here in the middle of nowhere. I was already thinking of my capture as a rescue mission.

CHAPTER 13

Suddenly a shot rang out. It didn't sound close, but I halted anyway. Looking over both of my shoulders, I saw nothing but trees with small chunks of snow falling to join the piles below, so I don't think they were shooting at me. However, it gave me the motivation I needed, and I charged down the hill.

As I ran, I thought I heard a bear growl. *Perfect. There are bears up here.* I hadn't even thought of that. I wished I could call on my ability to fly, in case I needed to get up higher in these trees than bears can climb. *Can bears climb trees?* Oh, yes. They sure can. *Great.*

I continued my inner conversation while I charged further and further down the mountain, until another shot rang out. This time the growl stopped mid-noise. If I were guessing correctly, I'd guess somebody shot the bear. I waited and listened for any further sound.

Something like a whimper came from above me. I

slowly glanced up into the trees and saw a tiny bear cub. *Oh, no.* "I hope that wasn't your mama."

The cub started climbing down.

"Oh, shoot. No, that isn't what I meant. I'm not your mama. No! Don't follow me!" I took off down the hill again. When I felt I was far enough away, I glanced over my shoulder and to my horror, the cute little bear cub was lumbering after me. Sometimes scampering on all fours and sometimes rolling ass over teakettle down the hill. At one point, it rolled into a tree and stopped short. Snow fell down on him. He shook his little head. *So darn cute!* Then he picked himself up and came toddling after me again.

"Please don't follow me. Please don't. I don't know how to take care of a bear cub. I can barely take care of myself out here. Just go do whatever bears do."

The cub kept scooting along following my very well marked trail through the snow. There was no way I was going to lose him unless I could fly and without getting enough traction, I doubted I could do it. I'd only flown after running my very hardest on a flat dry surface. Just for the heck of it, I thought I would give it a try. So, I put my arms in front of me and jumped. Nothing. I felt stupid, but figured I should try again, just in case.

I jumped again! Nothing. I stayed right in that spot, so flying was not an option today. What other protective measures could I use? Patrick had taught me to cast a protective bubble around myself. I guess I could try that, if the bear cub got too close, but right now it would just zap my energy for no reason. The cute little critter was still about twenty feet behind me and doing his best to run and scamper on four legs, but he wasn't very good at it yet. Especially not in deep snow.

He was so darn adorable, but I still didn't want him around. It was bad enough that I knew somebody out there had a gun. If I made it to the bottom of this mountain and civilization, I don't know what the poor bear would do.

For that matter, I didn't know what I should do. Find my father? I don't remember where he said he was staying. Colorado Springs is a pretty big city, so trying to call all the hotels would take a while—and a phone, which I didn't have. And then I'd have to hope they'd tell me if they had a guest by the name William Jones. And well... Who knows if someone using an alias might not pick that name? The names William and Jones aren't exactly unusual. I could wind up with several of them.

I guess I could try to get to Arizona. It sounded like it might be my best bet anyway. If I could just get to Genevieve and her very magical aunt, maybe I could find a way to not get locked up again.

That's really all I wanted. A simple life, where I didn't have to worry about other people's motivations and moods. I'd be happy, if I could just make a living and support myself until I could find some interesting new field of study. I didn't know what it would be yet, but at least I would have a chance to look into it. Think about it, study the options, I could find a fulfilling profession, I was sure.

Ms. Broome was very insistent that I had the brains to go to college and definitely should finish school, but these were trying times. I had always known my step-father's help was out. He would never pay for college. In fact, he had probably been counting the days until I turned eighteen and he could change the locks.

I seriously didn't know anything about my father yet. I didn't know if I could trust him to help or not. He lived in Africa, for heaven sake. It was more than nice of him to stay here until I got through juvie and help me get situated in some kind of safe situation, but after that? Was he going to hang around and find a place where I could live with him as my Guardian? He'd already said he was going to go back to Ghana. Or did he believe I could handle being an emancipated minor while I was a student? Probably not. Now that I was sixteen, I could get a full-time job. That was something at least. I could worry about the GED, or whatever else I could do, later.

I glanced behind me and sure enough that darn little cub was gaining on me. "Stop following me. Seriously, I don't want you around. Go do bear stuff. I don't know what to do with you." The little critter found some red berries on a bush and stopped to eat him. Just then my stomach growled.

Oh, right. Food. It was well past lunchtime and I had been exercising heavily. There's no way I wasn't going to starve if I didn't reach a restaurant eventually or find someone willing to offer me a free meal. Maybe if I saw some more of those berries later on, I could pick some, provided the bear cub didn't keel over.

In the meantime I resumed my walk. Although it was less of a run now, my progress was casual but steady. I saw some more berries—white ones this time—and stopped to grab a couple of handfuls. The little bear came running up and batted them out of my hand. I thought he was mad that I was taking all the berries, but he didn't pick them up or take any off the bush.

He seemed to be trying to communicate with me. These weren't the same berries. Did he know that? They weren't the red berries like the ones he'd eaten. Did he just not like white berries or were the white berries poisonous? I don't know what his problem was, but he seemed very upset. He was jumping around as if he knew something bad was going on with those berries.

"Are you trying to tell me these berries are poisonous?"

The little bear nodded. Nodded! How the heck could he communicate with a human? He could barely communicate with another bear. Well, *if* that's what he was doing. I guess I wouldn't know just yet. If I were starving to death, maybe I would eat them, but so far I was just normally hungry not starving, so I continued on, hoping to find some of the berries that the cub had eaten earlier.

I slogged through the snow. By this time my toes were numb and so were my fingers. I didn't think I was getting frostbite since I had boots and gloves on, but I was certainly cold all the way through. Arizona sounded even nicer right now. I doubted they had several feet of snow. Unless... I don't really know much about Arizona. I guess they do have some mountainous areas, but where my friends are or what kind of weather conditions they have, I wasn't sure yet. I thought it was mostly desert. Anyway, it was still November, and if I made it to Arizona, I'm sure it would be better than this!

The little bear cub was staying close to me. I was kind of at a loss as to know what to do about it, though. I figured it wouldn't hurt as long as he didn't try to attack me. If he wanted to show me which berries were not poisonous, I guess he might even be useful. So I just kind of ignored him for a while. Eventually I came across more of those red berries. I stopped and glanced over at him as I picked a handful. The cub didn't shake his head *no*, so I went to put one in my mouth and he just stood there. "Is it okay? Can I eat these?" I asked.

Suddenly the bear cub started growling, then laughing? A moment later he shimmered into an eighteen-year-old boy, rolling in the snow, laughing hysterically.

"Patrick! What the heck?"

He just continued laughing and holding his sides as he rolled back and forth. He was wearing a brown fur coat and brown corduroy pants. When he pulled himself together, he cleared his throat, rose and said, "You just asked a bear if you could eat berries or not. And you expected him to nod or something didn't you?"

I felt stupid, but what could I say? It was true.

"You must've known it was me."

"I *didn't* know that! My father said you went home to Detroit. *And you should have.* What are you doing here?"

"I had a talk with my mom. I told her everything. She agreed that you shouldn't be on your own, trying to get to Arizona by yourself or with a man who might or might or might not be a good guy—close relation or not. Even though you have magic, you have no idea how to use it yet. You still need me."

I huffed. Part of me was happy to see him, and another part of me was angry that he didn't believe in me enough to take care of myself. "I'm glad you were honest with your mother, at last."

"She understands. She even likes that about me, I think."

"Likes what about you?"

"That I won't leave a friend in need. That instead, I'll be a friend, in deed. See? I'm even rhyming better now."

He tipped his head and gave me that silly grin that I had come to know. Patrick was literally the only person I could guarantee was on my side right now. Well, I'm sure Genevieve would be too, if I could just get to her. And now here's Patrick telling me he's willing to help me do that.

"I don't know whether to be mad at you or to hug you."

He strode to me and rested his hands on my shoulders. "I vote for the hug."

I leaned in and wrapped my arms around his back. He embraced me in his furry arms. It just felt good to stand there in the cold with his warm body enfolding mine. I felt a little safer... still pretty screwed up, but safer. As soon as I leaned back and looked up at him. He leaned down for a kiss.

I pulled away. "Before we get distracted with all that, I need to know how you intend to help me. Are you going to try and take me back to Haven West?"

"Only if you want to go there."

"If what I've heard is true then, no. Not on your life. The kids I escaped with sure don't want to go back there. I'm aware that my father is probably most definitely my father. It would be nice to get in touch with him again, as long as he doesn't try to get me back into that van and juvie. He might even help me with the idea of emancipation."

"Do you really think he can?"

"I don't know, but there's one way to find out. I need to ask him."

"Do you know where he is?"

"Uh… no."

"Okay. There are a few steps to take before you can ask him anything."

"Yeah, like getting down this mountain. Can you help with that? Magically?"

"Don't you remember how to transport from one place to another quickly? Like when we were at Yellowstone?"

"Not really. You did all that, didn't you?"

"Did I? I thought I was just transporting myself, and you were hanging on to me so we'd go to the same place at the same time."

I cocked my head. "Nope. I don't think so. I just held your hand and let you do all the magical work. I don't suppose you know how to get in touch with my father, do you?"

"As a matter of fact, he gave me his contact info while you were out cold. He also gave me money for a plane ticket back to Detroit and a little more so I could Uber or take a taxi to Ann Arbor. He seems like a good guy, Jenika."

"Yeah, I think so too. So why didn't you go back to

Detroit?"

"I was worried about you. Like I said, I told my mother everything and she agreed it wouldn't be right to leave you in the lurch. In fact, I was just coming to check on you at Haven West when all hell broke loose. I must've just missed you."

"So how did you know where to find me?"

He laughed and pointed to the well-marked trail I left in the snow. "Anybody could have found you. The guard pointed me in the right direction and said they went after the other two kids. They must have done worse stuff than you did, because they seemed determined to get them first. Anyway, now that I found you, we can get you to Stapleton Airport in Denver and then to Haven East. You have to go back to juvie, babe. I'm afraid nobody could get you out of that, but I called and talked to Mrs. Whitehall. She said they would accept you, if your father or I could get you back there."

I threw my arms around Patrick's neck and hugged him...and not because he called me babe. I almost cried, because he cared at all. I wasn't used to people caring about me since my mom and grandpa died. It felt really, *really* good.

"Whoa, I never expected you to be so happy about going back to juvie," he said.

"The juvie you know is better than the juvie you don't know."

"But you weren't there very long."

"Less than twenty-four hours. That was enough."

"Wow. That must have been one bad first impression."

"Yeah. I want nothing to do with them—ever. I think I'll let my father explain where I'm going, but only after I get on the plane." I couldn't help smiling at the thought of taking off and being in the sky, out of their reach. If I went to another juvie voluntarily, there wasn't much they could do—or would want to do.

"Let's get down this mountain. Hold my hand."

"Gladly." We smiled at each other and clasped our gloved hands. A few minutes later we appeared at a place about a mile further down the mountain.

"That's a neat trick," I said. "I know we were bopping around Yellowstone a bit, but I wasn't doing it. It must've been all you. I tried flying today, but I can't take off without a runway. Can you teach me how to do that long hop? I've only done it once, and I projected myself right to my own bedroom—a place I knew. I don't know how to travel blindly, and I don't want to wind up in a tree or something."

He grinned. "Why, I'd love to, my dear."

He was so cute, and such a sight for sore eyes. I couldn't help wondering if things would work out. We were really young, and it was ridiculously soon to even think about it, but my mind went there. I wouldn't be writing *Jenika Hightower* in my spiral notebook, but a girl could fantasize.

"It's like astral projection," he said, interrupting my thoughts, "but instead of just your mind going to another place, take our bodies with you."

"I'm not sure what you mean, but I'll give it a try. Oh, wait… How do I know I'm not going to crash us into a tree or something?"

He chuckled. "Astral project first. Find a safe spot mentally, and then bring our bodies to it. It takes practice, but I'm sure you can do it. Give it a try."

I closed my eyes and pictured myself floating out of my body, soaring over the treetops to a spot a few yards down the mountain…maybe fifty or so. Might as well start small just in case I screwed up. I picked a clearing, and then holding onto Patrick's hand, I willed his body and mine to join my vision of that spot.

Upon opening my eyes I saw that we'd arrived at the landscape I had pictured in my mind. Trees had changed a little bit—I think, but who could tell? Trees are trees to me. The scene was pretty similar with one exception. Some tall blue spruce shot up toward the sky, towering over the pine trees. So, I guess we went someplace new!

"You did it!" Patrick squeezed my hand. "But why did you stop here?"

"I just wanted to test it first. Now that I know I can do it, and take you with me, I can go further down. I think you and I were going about a mile at a time in Yellowstone, right?"

"Hey, I have a joke for you."

"Oh, no. What is it?"

"Never criticize someone until you walk a mile in their shoes. That way, when you criticize them, you'll be a mile away and you'll have their shoes."

I groaned and he grinned.

"So… In your mind, project one mile," he said, as if he hadn't just disrupted my train of thought. "That will help move us out of harm's way, at least. They won't expect you to have gone that far on foot."

I had almost forgotten that I was still an escaped inmate at large. They may have caught the other two by now, so I could have a lot of pursuers. Grabbing onto Patrick's arm, I said, "Are you ready to walk a mile in my shoes?"

"As long as I don't have to spend any time in your head, I'm game."

"Yeah. I'm pretty sure that would freak you right out."

He burst out laughing.

"So, let's just keep this physical and leave our minds out of it."

"I like the sound of that." He raised his eyebrows twice in rapid succession.

I snorted.

We both closed our eyes. I projected what I thought might be a mile, found a spot, and almost like a slingshot, my body sailed through the rift I'd created and joined my astral projection. Opening my eyes, I was happy to see I was still holding onto Patrick and not some random tree trunk.

"Whew! That was a rush."

"You got the hang of it, quickly. Good for you! Are you getting tired or can you go again?"

"I think I can go another mile. It's not as exhausting as flying."

"Yeah, but it's not nearly as cool, either."

We took turns mile by mile down the mountain. When we finally reached the end of the descent and the beginnings of civilization, we decided it was better to walk the rest of the way. Disappearing in front of people would violate our policy as witches. Unless it were a life or death situation, we still needed to keep our powers under wraps.

"Do you know where my father is staying?"

"He said he was going to find a hotel near the road up to Pikes Peak, so it can't be too far from here. Let me give him a call—if you want me too."

"I think I should at least let him know I'm okay. The juvie probably contacted him and told him I'm missing."

"True. You're a smart and considerate girl. More considerate than I am."

"Are you kidding? You're here, aren't you? I'd say you're pretty smart and considerate too. That is if you really did tell your mother everything and she's as cool as you said she is."

"I did, and she is."

"Okay, then. Let's see how cool my dad is with all this."

———✁———✁———

"Are you ready?"

"Yes. Thanks, Dad. I couldn't get to Florida without your help."

My father straightened the collar on my jacket and smiled. "You won't need this after you get there. But I'm glad you had something warm to wear on your escape down the mountain."

Patrick was standing nearby with his hands in his pockets, probably not wanting to intrude on the tender moment. If you could call it that... Yeah, let's call it that.

"I'll put money in the canteen for you after I know you're there," my father continued. "You'll ask them to call me right away and let me know you arrived safely, right?"

I said I would and just to make sure we could keep in touch when he went back to Ghana, he presented me with a piece of paper on which he'd handwritten his name, phone number and address in Africa. I didn't know what good contact information in Ghana would do, but at least he was willing to offer it.

We had had a good conversation that evening over dinner. He'd told me he had done some things as a mercenary that he wasn't proud of, and he was trying to make up for it in other ways. I think I understood what he meant. I may not be able to return the makeup I stole, but I would someday actually pay for it.

My father gave me a hug and I hugged him back. Then he shook Patrick's hand and clasped him on the shoulder. "Thank you for looking after my daughter."

Patrick shrugged. "Don't worry. Nothing bad will happen to her when I'm around."

My father smiled and seemed satisfied. He stepped away and we entered the security line at Stapleton Airport in Denver. It had been about an hour-long drive and most of that was spent in silence, each one of us entertaining our own thoughts. I hadn't picked up any emotional stuff with my empathic abilities, so I wasn't worried as we all enjoyed the scenery and each other's companionable silence.

I couldn't help drawing parallels between my fathers. Anytime I had to spend more than five minutes in the car with Phil, my stepfather, it was nerve wracking. Now it sounded as if we could wash our hands of each other. Halleluiah.

When I get out of Haven East the only thing is, I'll have to go to Ghana for my real father to be my true guardian. We decided that was the best mutually acceptable solution, and we would write letters in the meantime. I was just happy he was cool with letting Patrick escort me to Haven East.

Finally, with very little in the way of luggage, Patrick and I had made our way through security and boarded the plane. My carryon consisted of a large bag from a clothing store with the underwear and other items my dad had purchased for me minus what he'd have to return, like the long johns, boots, Parka and ski pants. I wouldn't need those in Florida. I settled into our coach seat and let out a long sigh of relief.

Patrick dropped down in the seat next to me. "Did you think you might be yanked out of line and dragged back up Pike's Peak before you got on the plane?"

I chuckled. "Something like that."

He put his arm around my shoulder. "Can you stand another joke?"

I smirked. "Sure, why not?"

"Did you know we're time travelers?"

"Um… No?"

"It's true. We're all traveling into the future at exactly sixty minutes per hour."

I couldn't help smiling. Patrick always found a way to make me laugh. I needed that more than I realized. The flight was long but uneventful and we were both so tired that we fell asleep for most of it.

When we finally arrived in Florida, in the wee hours of the morning, I doubted it was a good time to show up at Haven, but we hadn't made any arrangements to stay anywhere. Patrick called them on his phone and surprisingly someone answered. "Haven East, can I help you?"

He handed me the phone and I was temporarily speechless.

"Hello? Is somebody there?"

"Um, yes. This is Jenika Jones. I'm expected, but not until tomorrow. I don't have any place to stay and I'm in the Orlando airport. Should I just wait here or could I come in early?"

There was a long hesitation on the other end of the line, and I wondered if the person had hung up.

"Well... If you want to come now, you probably wouldn't have anyone to process you. I'd suggest you call back around eight AM and talk to the secretary or administrator."

"Oh.... Okay. I'll do that. Thanks, answering service."

She chuckled. "You're welcome."

"She said nobody's gonna be there to take me in until eight or so. How would you feel about stretching out on a couple of these chairs until seven, and then taking an Uber to Haven?" Then I realized, he'd have a plane to catch too. "Actually, you know what? You don't have to wait with me at all... You can go on to Ann

Arbor. I know your mom's got to be anxious for you to get home."

"Not on your life," Patrick said. "I'm going to see this all the way through, like I promised your dad I would."

I leaned back and squinted like I was studying him. "You really are a nice guy, aren't you?"

He smiled but also seemed a little sad. "Was that ever in question? I mean, I know I was a thief and everything, but those days really are behind me."

"Well, I didn't know you at first, but yeah, you struck me as a real troublemaker."

He laughed out loud. "Now that you know me better, what do you think?"

I tipped my head back and forth as if I were really puzzling out the question. "I think I like you. No, I really like you." I leaned my head on his shoulder and he wrapped his arm around me.

He kissed the top of my head and said, "You know, if you really want to become emancipated, and nobody in your family objects, I could marry you."

I sat up so fast, it must have looked like I had a spring built into my cheek. "You what?"

"It's okay. I wouldn't mind. I mean…I'd like that. If you want to, of course."

So romantic.

"Sorry. I'm not ready for marriage, and I wouldn't want to use you that way."

"Okay," he said matter-of-factly, as if I'd just turned down the last bite of his candy bar but nothing more essential.

I had been about to settle in for a short nap, but now my mind was swirling. It was really nice of him to offer, but... Oh well. It was just nice to know somebody wanted me. That didn't mean I should dive into the pool before checking to see if there's water in it.

What seemed like a short time later, the alarm on his phone sounded. The two of us opened our eyes, stretched and yawned. "Wow, is it that time already?"

"Yeah." He looked at me with a rare serious expression on his face. "I'm going to miss our adventures, or maybe I should say your misadventures."

Again, he made me smile. Our romp across the country was something I would never forget. I didn't think he would either. Goddess knows the elderly gamblers on the Reno bus wouldn't forget us.

The Uber driver arrived in no more than five minutes. He must have been waiting at the airport somewhere. We piled into the back of the car.

"So where are you kids off to?" the driver asked.

"We're on our way to Juvie," Patrick said, cheerfully.

The guy laughed.

"No, really. We're going to Haven East, Juvenile Detention Center," I said.

He glanced over his shoulder at us, then shrugged. "Okay. I'm just here to drive, not to judge."

We both giggled like, well, teenagers, which we were. Patrick put his arm around my shoulder. It felt good to cuddle again. I would certainly miss his physical affection as well as his big smile, the way his eyes crinkled at the corners, and even his stupid jokes, no matter how bad they were.

I had been told that I would be going straight into seclusion until some details got ironed out. I wouldn't be able to mix with the general population right away. I guess it doesn't look good when an inmate goes home and like a boomerang comes right back, and then maybe gets tossed out again. But whatever they had to do was okay with me, as long as I felt safe, and I did at Haven East. So, I'd told my father, "They can go ahead and stick me in solitary for the whole six weeks, if they want to. I'll do my time without complaining and get out."

At Haven the driver let us off at the gate. A guard was standing there and opened it, probably recognizing us—or he was told to expect us. He looked familiar to me, so he had probably been there before. I hadn't paid much attention to the guards. I just kept my head down and walked past them as fast as I could.

I had to say goodbye to Patrick right there, because the guard wouldn't let him in. Apparently, he had his orders to allow entrance to one Jenika Jones, a young lady of color, and no one else.

Patrick shrugged and said, "That's okay. I can kiss

you goodbye here." I reached up to clasp him around his neck and he dipped me! Actually bent me over backward and kissed me long and deep, cradling my head in his hand, and bracing my lower back on his arm. When I finally came up for air Mrs. Whitehall was walking toward us.

She sighed. "That was quite the show you put on, Mr. Hightower."

He grinned. "I like grand gestures."

She just shook her head as if giving up on ever reforming him. I wouldn't want him to change anyway.

"Come with me, Miss Jones."

I reluctantly left the warmth of Patrick's arms. She looked over her shoulder at him as we walked away. "Nice to see you, Patrick. I hope you're behaving yourself out there."

"Yeah. I have to stay out of trouble, so I can start college in January, and then visit Jenika wherever she is next summer."

I was surprised to feel tears burning the back of my eyes as I turned to wave goodbye to Patrick.

"Hey, Jenika!" He called out.

"Yeah?"

"If you have ten oranges in one hand and ten apples in another, what do you have?"

"Big hands!" I yelled and we both burst out laughing. I guess I had finally figured out his stupid sense of humor...and I loved it.

"Come on, Miss Jones," Mrs. Whitehall said. "Hopefully you'll both stay out of trouble so you can see each other later on."

As she opened the door for me, I looked up at her. "Don't you have some kind of rule about inmates not seeing each other after juvie?"

She laughed. "Oh, yeah. That. I have the feeling we won't be able to enforce it with you two. I'm just glad you made it back safely." At last she gave me the hint of a smile.

I walked in front of her and didn't even question where I was going. I took the corridor to the right, knowing that's where solitary was. Hopefully, Ms. Broome would say hello before they locked me up and threw away the key.

CHAPTER 14

I had been pacing in solitary for four hours. A guard had brought in lunch on a tray for me, but other than that I hadn't seen anyone. That seemed strange since they already had a lot of information on me. I would've thought maybe I would have to go to the nurse to get checked out or something…but no. Instead, I've just waited in here, going crazy bored.

I wished someone would at least tell me how long I would be in here. Maybe my incarceration paperwork was being filled out by email with my father. Maybe he had to prove he *was* my father and had to dig up my birth certificate. I guess I couldn't sign any legal contracts. Still a minor. Still unemancipated.

I thought about Patrick's pathetic marriage proposal and almost laughed aloud, but laughing to myself in solitary confinement might seem a bit odd. I don't want anyone to think I'm hearing voices.

Although I would enjoy hearing Patrick's voice telling me some corny joke right about now.

Sadness suddenly swamped me. If I were going to have a pity party, this would be the perfect place for it. Some part of me knew I had a good, well-earned cry coming to me. So, I just let the sadness wash over me.

When the tears came, they rolled down my cheeks, silently. It occurred to me that I had been crying silently for years. Crying on the inside, but still... It's a wonder nobody saw it until now, including me.

How do you *not* cry when nobody wants you? Or if the only person who seems to want you is someone you've just gotten to know. Suppose after he got to know me better, he didn't want me either?

Now my pity party was well under way with only one guest attending. Me. I braced myself against the wall and slid down. Knees up, arms around them, I burrowed my face in my jeans.

Tears continued to roll and I didn't stop except now and then when I had to sniff, or I'd be wearing snot on my clothes. Finally, after sobbing my heart out, I leaned back, rested my head on the padded wall, and sucked in air through my mouth until I could breathe normally again.

Suddenly, and I mean *suddenly*, I wasn't alone. A kid with long dark hair and blue eyes stared at me from across the room. My empathy didn't pick up any vibes of recognition on her part. I blinked a few times, pushed myself up to a standing position and took in a deep breath. *Yup. She's still there.* "Genevieve?"

She shook her head. "No, I'm Tawania, Genevieve's twin."

"Oh! You look so much like her!"

She tipped her head. "Nah… I'm the prettier one."

When she grinned I was reminded of Patrick's brazen sense of humor. We walked toward each other. Meeting in the middle, we hugged—even though I didn't know her. She must have known I needed a hug, badly.

"Why didn't Genevieve come?" I would have thought if anybody wanted to help, it would be her.

"She sent me, because she's not allowed to come back here. She promised. And Aunt Hilary wouldn't let her break that promise, even though she said her fingers were crossed behind her back when she made it."

I laughed. "That sounds like Genevieve." I couldn't help wondering what her twin was doing here, though.

As if she'd read my mind, Tawania said, "She sent me to remind you of something. She attached a tether to you and knows if anything is so bad that you need her. She felt you crying and said she'd never seen or heard you cry before. She knew something had to be drastically wrong, and the tether pulled her here. But she promised not to come back here, so, she sent me to see if I could help. Or, if I can't, maybe Aunt Hilary can. Tell me what's going on,"

I leaned against the wall with my legs crossed at the ankle and folded my arms. "I don't know if anyone can help me. People are trying, but maybe I'm just not meant to be on my own."

Tawania just stared at me like she didn't understand. She probably didn't.

"Look, I wanted to become an emancipated minor. I just wanted to get a job and live my own life. Just a nice quiet life. It didn't seem like too much to ask, but apparently it is. I've screwed up all along the way, and yet it's still what I want. It just keeps looking like I can't have it."

Tawania looked thoughtful. Then she stunned me by saying, "Maybe you're meant for something bigger than that. I don't know you, but Genevieve has told me about you. It sounds like you're smart and capable of doing any number of great things. It seems like you'd be settling for some low-paying job, if you went out on your own now without a high school diploma. You only have a couple years left, right? I'm trying to make up for several years without any schooling. I was on my own after my adopted parents died, but that's a whole different story. Right now we're talking about you."

Something she said struck a chord with me. *Maybe I'm meant for something bigger.* Even if my empathic abilities were a pain in the ass, I might be able to use them to do something necessary and fulfilling. That probably meant I'd have to get a better education.

"So, when do you get out of here? Genevieve told me to ask."

"I don't know. I have six weeks as long as I don't screw up."

"Is that how long your sentence is? Six weeks?"

"As long as I don't screw up...again."

Tawania chuckled. I didn't know what she found funny, but I guess she'd have to be in here to understand how easy it is to screw up and how screwing up can really affect one's time. Me, all I knew to do was to keep my head down and go through whatever presented itself. Life had always been happening *to* me instead of my living the life of *my* choosing. I wanted to turn that around so badly. I wanted to choose. I wanted *my* goals to work toward, not to just take whatever might come along.

"I have an idea, but I'd have to ask Aunt Hilary first."

"What kind of idea?"

"I'm wondering if you can come live with us in Arizona. I mean...if you want to."

"Seriously? I was trying to get to Arizona to all of you when my plans were altered by bounty hunters. Before that I had hoped your aunt might help me find a job and a place to live."

"Genevieve and I are both home schooled, and then

we hope to attend college online. Aunt Hilary has us both working part-time jobs at the spa to pay for tuition. It's nothing glamorous like her massage therapy and acupuncture. We just work in the laundry, washing the towels and stuff."

"To tell you the truth, home schooling and working part-time, even just doing laundry, sounds like heaven to me. And to be with you and Genevieve and Hilary… That would be the best thing ever!"

"Then I'll ask her about it. I mean, would you like me to do that?"

I nodded my head so fast she probably thought I was joking around. But I wasn't. "I would like that very much. Thank you. Oh, there's one other thing, if you can manage it."

"Sure. What's that?"

"I really want to talk to a teacher here named Ms. Broome."

"I can't walk through the halls to look for her or they'll think Genevieve has broken her promise."

"That's true."

"Do you know her first name? Maybe I can look her up."

"No, I don't think I ever heard it."

"Okay, well Broome sounds like a pretty unusual name. Do you know what town she lives in?"

The air went out of my lungs. "No. I don't know her name, or where she lives, or even if she's listed in the phone book, so I guess I don't know her that well after all."

I was starting to get down when Tawania smiled and said, "Don't worry, I'll find her." And with that she disappeared.

***

Eventually, Ms. Broome entered my cell. She closed the door and leaned against it with her arms crossed. The non-smile on her face told me she wasn't exactly happy to see me back again. There went my last hope.

"Well, Jenika. You gave us all a fright. And now you've given us quite a challenge."

"A challenge? How?"

She sighed, pushed off the door, and came over to sit opposite me on the floor. "We've been on the phone most of the day, talking to your father and the Howes in Arizona and even the other Howes in Africa."

"Genevieve's parents?"

Ms. Broome nodded. "It's a happy coincidence that both your father and the Howes live in Ghana. And apparently Mr. and Mrs. Howe are both teachers. Your father is involved with a business woman who would be happy to help you with your schooling too."

I almost couldn't believe what I was hearing. *Africa?* "Am I going to Africa after this?"

"Maybe soon. That's what we're exploring at the

moment. It may take a day or two, and we'd rather not introduce you back into the population here if you're not going to be staying, so you might be in this cell a little longer."

"I'm not being sentenced here? Or anywhere? I thought I had a six-week sentence for stealing."

Ms. Broome sighed and leaned back, her hands outstretched behind her. "Like I said, it's complicated and challenging, but were hoping to find the best situation for you. It's not just a matter of juvie being a punishment. We're trying to reeducate and empower our students to be responsible and make better choices. We think with your father as your magical guide, and his girlfriend willing to help you learn business practices, and with the Howes, who are experienced teachers, we might be able to cobble together a curriculum.

"Your father is willing and anxious to accept responsibility for you. Does that sound like something you could agree to? By the way, emancipated minor is off the table. Maybe forever. I'd like to see you give this a good try and then later when you have an education and training you can get a good job, an apartment, and do whatever you want…but not now."

A lot of thoughts swirled around in my mind at once. Africa. My father wanted me and would be my magical teacher. People I didn't know were willing to take over other parts of my education… "Would I get a high school diploma that way?"

"That detail is still in limbo. A homeschooling option has to be set-up and approved, At any rate, you'd be able to take a test for your GED. Or maybe you could return to high school and graduate with your class. We haven't been able to reach your stepfather yet."

My eyebrows shot up. "I don't want to go back to my stepfather. Send me to Africa. I'll happily learn whatever they can teach me and study the rest on my own. I'm sure I could pass a test in a couple years and get my GED."

She smiled for the first time. "I'm sure you could too. This is a fantastic opportunity. I think you'd be getting a terrific experience along with an education, if you were willing to finish it up under the guardianship of your father in Ghana."

I almost giggled. Part of me was tickled pink that my father actually wanted me and that I'd be visiting someplace as exotic as Africa, but another part of me was a little nervous about the drastic changes. To be honest though, the excitement was overtaking the nerves.

"So what's the next step? Do I wait until you talk to my stepfather or do you need his permission to do this?"

"We do need to take care of some legal logistics that include documentation transferring your guardianship, school records, medical records... We're hoping that won't take too long since your father has already agreed to be your new legal guardian and started the ball rolling. He also paid for the items you stole from the shop in Detroit, and they agreed to drop the charges. Since it's too late to get in touch with the courthouse now, it looks like you'll be here at least until tomorrow."

"I could be going as soon as tomorrow? That would be awesome, but isn't it a little fast to get all that done? I usually expect red tape to take forever." Plus there were still a few things I wanted to do, like visit Genevieve and her family in Arizona.

We can help with the red tape. Not only do we have connections at the courthouse, but we can use certain…skills to move things along."

Meaning magic. I nodded. "Do I have to stay here? I mean, is my father still around and would he be willing to make a little side trip to Arizona with me? I really want to see Genevieve and her sister and aunt before I leave for Africa."

Ms. Broome rolled her eyes and let out a long resigned sigh. "Of course you have your own ideas, and making plans is a good thing, but forgive me for saying so, sometimes your plans aren't terribly realistic." She lifted one eyebrow. "Do you know what I mean?"

I hung my head. "It means I can't go to Arizona and visit my friends before I go to Africa."

"I didn't say that. It's possible, but only if your father

agrees and wants to take you. He might need time to set up things in Ghana for you. Perhaps that time can be passed with a brief visit with your friends in Arizona before you leave, but I don't want to speak for him. I'll mention it to all concerned and see what people think. We will need to know exactly where you are at all times. You'll be on probation."

"Great!" Then I remembered that the Howe's kids could probably come to visit me—even in Africa. I knew Hilary was some kind of super-powerful which, and Genevieve hinted at our being able to do things most witches couldn't. If she found me in Summerland, I'll bet she could find me in Ghana.

Plus, there was that other thing… the tether. I guess if I could figure out how to yank on it, one of the Howes might come. I just couldn't be here in Haven when I did it, so Genevieve wouldn't break her promise.

"Okay, I just wanted you to know what was going on and why it will likely take a while," Ms. Broome said. "We'll be moving in a bed for you and a small table for a couple of meals. I hope you only need to sleep here for one night. As I said before, we'd rather not introduce you into the population for just a day."

I nodded. "I understand. That's fine. I'll stay here for a week, if I need to. I'm just really glad that you guys are figuring out something that makes sense. I know it's a lot of work, but it's really nice of you to do this for me."

She smiled thoughtfully and said, "You warrant a little extra effort. I don't want you to forget that."

I smiled and looked forward to the future for the first time in a long time.

⸺ ✶ ⸻ ✶ ⸺

Later that evening the door opened and a guard came in. "Time to go."

"Go where?"

"Mrs. Whitehall wants to see you in her office."

Going to the principal's office had always been bad news, but I had reason to hope for good news this time. Anxiety fluttered around in my body until I was able to walk into her office and see her smiling face. She gestured to the chair on the opposite side of her desk from where she was sitting.

"Sit down, Jenika. How are you doing?"

"I'm… hopeful?"

She chuckled. "Well, I would say there is hope, but first I'd like to give you a chance to wrap things up with your stepfather. Is there any need for you to go back to Detroit at this point?" She added before I had a chance to respond, "Let me put him on speaker." Mrs. Whitehall pushed a button on her phone and said, "Philip? Can you hear us?"

"I can hear you, is Jenika there?"

"Yes, I'm here, Phil. How are you?" I figured I might as well be polite since I needed his cooperation and it sounded like we were parting ways.

He hesitated, then said, "I'm fine. Are you?"

"Yes, I'm all right."

We just sat there in silence, until finally Mrs. Whitehall cleared her throat. "I just want the two of you to make sure this new plan is mutually acceptable. The new plan being that Jenika's father, William Jones, will be taking over as her legal guardian and will be taking her out of the country to Ghana, in Africa."

"Is that what you want, Jenika?" Phil asked.

"Yes. I'd really like that. It seems like a good opportunity, and I won't waste it."

Phil laughed. "Yeah, I'll believe that when I see it."

Mrs. Whitehall frowned. "The deal is you *won't* see it. She'll be no responsibility of yours from now on. You do understand that, correct?"

"Yeah, I get it. That's great. And if she wants to go to Africa, let her. Just one thing, Jenika…"

"What's that?" I asked.

"Take your damn cat with you. All right?"

I almost laughed. Star never liked Phil much, either. I was probably lucky he fed her and changed her litter when I couldn't be there. "I definitely will. I'll be happy to take her with me. So, I guess I'll be coming to Detroit to pack up a few things. Do you still have the cat carrier? Last time I saw it, it was in the basement."

"Yeah, I'll dig it up for you."

It's sad that this was the most we had spoken to each other in a long time without some kind of hostility creeping in. But there was no need for that now. We were each getting what we wanted—our freedom from each other.

I felt like I should thank him for giving me food and shelter for the last couple years, but did I really want to do that? That was kind of the job he signed up for when he married my mom. I was about to let it go, then realized I could be the better person, starting now.

"Thanks for giving Star and me food and shelter, and not shipping me off to a foster home. I know you could have. But you didn't."

My empathic abilities picked up almost palpable shock waves on his side of the line. After a long pause he said, "Sure. Okay."

I guess it's hard to say 'You're welcome' when the other person wasn't really welcome at all.

"So I guess I'll see you when I come to pack my stuff. I don't know when that will be. Are you going to be around?"

"If you get here before Saturday. I might be at work. This is my weekend off."

I looked at Mrs. Whitehall.

She nodded. "Your father said he can take you any time."

"Well, okay then. I guess I'll go now."

Mrs. Whitehall smiled and said, "Ah, Jenika, we'll have to arrange a flight, and that will take a little while. Why don't you plan on tomorrow sometime in the late afternoon or evening?"

Oh, yeah. He didn't need to know that I could probably get a lift on Mrs. Broome's broom. "Sure. That sounds good to me, if it's okay with you Phil?"

"Sure is. I'll be here to let you in, and I'll stay out of your way. I'll put the cat's carrier in your room."

"Thanks." That was all I could say for now.

He just said, "Sure."

Mrs. Whitehall thanked him and wished us both luck. When she hung up, I felt like jumping for joy.

"So this is really going to happen?"

She nodded and rose from her seat. Coming around from her desk she extended her hand and shook mine. "Take care of yourself, Jenika. Your father is with Ms. Broome. I'll call them down now. Just have a seat in the reception area. They might need a minute to arrange your plane tickets."

I happily sat in the outer office on the chairs that we usually thought of as a waiting area for the gallows. But not now. It was a waiting area to the rest of my life, and I was anxious to get started on it.

It was an awkward goodbye.

Phil and I gave each other a hug as we stood in my bedroom. It was probably the most awkward hug of all time, but it was a hug. I felt good having at least attempted a decent farewell. Bygones can be bygones, water under the bridge… All that stuff.

Star leaped up onto my bed and next to her cat carrier as if she knew exactly what was happening.

My father leaned over and extended his hand to pat her. Star came right up to him, took a sniff, and rubbed up against his hand. She was a long-haired all white kitty with beautiful sapphire blue eyes.

"Oh, what a gorgeous cat," my dad said.

I sat down on my bed. "She is, isn't she?"

"She'll have to be quarantined for a short time in Ghana, but I'll make sure she's all set before I come back to get you."

Phil's eyebrows shot up. "Get her? I thought you already had her! Aren't you taking her with you?"

William rose slowly. "Don't worry, Phil. Jenika won't be in your hair. She's going to stay with friends while I get her all set up in Ghana."

"Oh." Then Phil left the room. I heard his footsteps go downstairs.

My father and I looked at each other. I shrugged. "That was Phil."

He shook his head, probably having seen all he'd wanted to of him. "Well, let's get you packed. I'll take most of your stuff in my big duffel bag, and you can put whatever clothes and toiletries you need for the next week in your backpack."

I dropped to my knees and reached under the bed, "Fortunately, I have another backpack that should hold almost everything." I grinned as I pulled the huge backpack with several compartments and attached pockets out from under my bed. "It was a gift from Patrick, in case I ever wanted to run away from home again."

He laughed. "Okay, great. Maybe you can get *all* your clothes and toiletries in there and I'll take your keepsakes and anything else you want."

In the space of two hours, we managed to pack absolutely everything I owned in those two bags. I also put a few things into the trash bag that Phil had offered me to 'pack my things' in. I couldn't help being happy to get rid of certain bad memories, like my school notebooks, and take only the memories of my mom and grandfather. I had even found a little necklace that my Uncle Donnie had given me when I was little. It was awfully small now, but it fit around my ankle perfectly.

When I was all packed we tromped downstairs, me bent over with my heavy backpack and my dad with his huge army duffel bag over one shoulder, acting like it weighed nothing, plus Star in her carrier. He stopped at the kitchen to shake hands with Phil and thank him for taking care of me. Phil just nodded, shook his hand and went back to making his sandwich.

I didn't bother giving him a second hug. The one upstairs was awkward enough. So the two of us, my dad and me, walked out the front door and closed it behind us. I let out a deep breath and couldn't help feeling ten pounds lighter, despite the load I was carrying.

"I arranged our tickets when I was at Haven. I'll get you to the airport in plenty of time, then while you're waiting I'll take all this stuff and Star to Africa. I'll be back in minutes, and then we'll go to Arizona together. He leaned toward me and whispered conspiratorially, "Don't ask me how I'm getting to Africa and back so fast. Okay?"

I smirked. "I'm pretty sure the answer, is…magic?"

He put an arm around me said, "You know it, baby. Now let's get you to Arizona."

Apparently he didn't need to call a cab, because one pulled up to the house at that moment. I just glanced up at him and smiled. "Perfect timing, huh?"

He just grinned and said, "Let's go."

CHAPTER 15

WE ARRIVED AT THE AIRPORT IN PLENTY OF TIME FOR our flight. He bought me a nice lunch and I explained that even though we'd be apart for a week, I couldn't wait to get to Arizona. He understood. He had friends in Ghana and said he would miss them, if he had to leave for a long time.

Before checking my backpack and going through security he suggested I use the bathroom while he watched star and my stuff. I excused myself to go to the ladies room. As soon as I got back, he swung the duffle bag over his shoulder and picked up Star's carrier. "I'll drop this stuff off and be back in a few minutes."

As soon as he'd disappeared into the men's room door, a woman plunked down in the seat next to me.

"Sorry, that seat is taken," I said.

I got this creepy feeling. I leaned away and took a

good look at the oddly familiar woman as she twirled a pair of handcuffs.

"It's about time I caught up with you. My skips aren't usually so hard to find."

Damn. The bounty hunter.

My heart began to pound, "Hey, you've got it all wrong. The charges have been dropped."

"Well, my contract wasn't cancelled, so you're coming with me."

I froze. What could I do with all of these people around? It wasn't like I could throw a bolt of lightning at her in a crowded airport. *Stall.* That's all I could think of. My father would be back before we got far.

"I can't just leave all my stuff…"

"You can, and you will. Now, are you coming with me quietly, or do I have to get Mr. Handcuffs and Mr. Gun involved?"

I felt something poke my into side. Glancing down, I saw what looked like the barrel of a gun protruding from under her coat.

"Okay, okay…" I rose and glanced at the men's room, hoping my dad would come out at that moment.

"Walk." she demanded.

I tried to slow my pace but she poked me in my back with her gun.

"Hurry up."

Can I find a place without witnesses in a crowded airport and get myself out of this?

As she nudged me toward the revolving door, I thought maybe I could trap myself in one of the glass sections and call for help. Then she pushed herself right in behind me and the two of us, sharing a section, started to go around together. *Damn, damn, damn!*

I did an about face and braced my foot against the glass, forcing the rotation to stop.

She glared at me. "What do you think you're doing?"

"Stopping you before you're guilty of kidnapping."

She laughed. "Do you think you're the first kid who's thought of that threat?"

"Look, lady. I don't know why you weren't called off, but you should have been. I'm not skipping out on a court date and I'm not going with you."

She tried to kick my foot off the glass. By now a few people were watching from both sides of the glass doors. I didn't dare leave the airport with her. If my father was now in Africa, by the time he got back I'd be long gone.

I gave her my best glare. "I don't want to hurt you."

She laughed. "A little squirt like you is going to hurt me? That's hilarious."

That did it. What I intended to do and what actually happened were a little bit different, but, oh well…

I grabbed the barrel of her gun, intending to rip it out of her hand, then use the handle to break the glass. I could blame my superhuman strength on adrenaline.

Instead, I grabbed the barrel of her gun and she didn't let go. In fact, her hand closed around it harder. It was too late to change my plan, so I wound up flipping the bounty hunter, gun and all, over my head, her boots smashing through the thick glass.

The deafening shatter sent people running in opposite directions. She came down hard, hitting her head with such force, she was knocked out. I carefully stepped over the large pieces of glass and the unconscious bounty hunter, then hurried to the first security guard I saw.

"Jenika!" My father's voice, crying out to me was like music to my ears.

"Dad!" I yelled and ran to him.

The security guard saw that I was with a parent and forgot all about me. Instead he leaned over the unconscious bounty hunter, and using his foot, knocked the gun out of her reach. I glanced over my shoulder and saw him radio for an ambulance. By the time they arrived we'd be through the security line.

William probably could have 'poofed' us to Arizona as fast as he went to Africa and back, but we enjoyed some time chatting on the plane, before I fell asleep for the rest of the ride.

All this magical strength was exhausting me!

He'd filled me in on more of his missions, what little he could tell me, and how magic could be hidden when used. He was proud of the way I had handled the bounty hunter, especially that I had the adrenaline excuse ready, if anyone had asked.

I told him more about Haven East. I really didn't get to see much of Haven West and was happy to keep it that way. I also confessed that I was keeping Arizona as a backup plan in case Africa didn't work out.

He just nodded and said he understood perfectly. I had the feeling I wouldn't need that Plan B though. He seemed to be genuinely interested in my happiness and well-being. That was a refreshing change from Phil's non-interest.

It was late when we arrived in Arizona. Before we woke everyone up at the spa to say we had landed, we thought it might be fun to take a short detour. Since our arrival time was flexible he gave me a choice. We could either wake up Hilary and tell her we were on our way now, or we could stay overnight in Phoenix, then drive to the Grand Canyon, and then to the spa.

I had never been to the Grand Canyon or anywhere else in Arizona for that matter, and it sounded like a place I wouldn't want to miss. Especially if Africa *did* work out and I stayed there for two years, at least. I didn't expect to be there permanently, but who knew... Stranger things had happened to me.

My dad had promised to keep up my magical

lessons. Not only would we explore my powers and how to use them, but he promised Ms. Broome to teach me the responsible use of those powers. He also said he'd teach me how to heal and to recover from using my magic faster. He'd worked out my magical curriculum at Haven before we left, and that made a big difference gaining their cooperation with this whole new plan.

"So, what will it be? Grand Canyon or straight to your friends' spa?"

I hated to ask him to spend more money, but I figured it was now or never. "Would you mind if we spent the night in a hotel and saw the Grand Canyon first? I hate for you to keep spending your money though. You've already spent a ton on airfare and hotels plus restaurants, clothing, all kinds of things for me."

He laid his hand on my shoulder and said, "I have a lot to make up for. This is nothing. I should've been there for you long ago."

On our way to the Grand Canyon, I asked, "So why were you out of my life for so long?"

"Your mother insisted I stay away. She wanted you to have a normal childhood.

I agreed to wait until you were eighteen and then I would let you decide for yourself."

"Why would she do that?"

"She was afraid of me when she saw what I could do

—even though I used my powers to save your life once. She was certainly grateful I had done that, but I guess it scared her to death to watch me pass through a moving car."

"You walked through a car?"

"Well, it was more like a car ran through me, as strange as it sounds. That was the first time your mother saw me use my magic. You had run into the street, just as I saw this car speeding toward you, not even slowing down. The driver finally slammed on his brakes, but I was already out in the street running for you. I picked you up and hoisted you over my head, and the car actually slid through me. When they got on the other side of us and the breaks stopped screeching, they looked in their rearview mirror, then sped off."

I gasped. "You saved me from a hit-and-run?"

"I guess it would be called a hit-and-run except nobody was hit. I'd pulled you into my arms and they could see that there was no blood, no broken bones… you weren't even crying. Nobody was laying on the on the road, so they just took off. I got the license number but never knew what I would tell the police.

"Your mother was standing on the front lawn, screaming. By the time I got her to calm down some neighbors had come out, wanting to know what had happened. I just told them that everything was okay. That you ran into the street and I grabbed you seconds before a car would have hit you. They could see that you were fine, so they went back inside their homes.

"I escorted your mother into the house and had to tell her everything. She was shaking so hard I gave her a glass of whiskey. I don't know if that was enough. I probably should've given her the whole bottle. Anyway, it was after that we started having problems."

My breath caught. "So it was *my* fault?"

"What? No!"

"But if I hadn't run into the street…"

"Then it would have been something else. I would have had to tell her eventually. I never expected her to be so freaked out about it, especially since I thought of magic as a good thing."

"Yeah. I guess so…"

We were quiet on the rest of our drive to the Grand Canyon, but when we got there all thoughts of 'what if's' vanished. I was absolutely stunned gazing at the mind-boggling beauty and supernatural-looking color-banded cliffs and rivers way down below. It was almost as if we were looking at some magical creation.

"This is incredible. Thank you for taking me here."

He put his arm around me and said, "I'm glad I could. This is my first time seeing it too."

We walked along some of the trails and eventually I sat on a stone wall for a few minutes to rest, still gazing at the incredible scenery. A raven swooped down and sat next to me. I looked up at my dad and he shrugged. "Don't look at me…"

I glanced at the Raven and asked, "Patrick?"

The Raven just cocked his head at me. Then it flew away.

"Now I feel stupid."

My dad chuckled. "Hey, you told me he turned up as a bear cub, then dropped the glamor and became a boy again, so why not a raven?"

"I don't think he can fly—well, not without my help, anyway. Does this happen to you? Do you wonder if some things are real or magical?"

He sat next to me. "Not usually. I've learned to tell the difference. There's a kind of frequency magicals can tune into. Some feel it as a tingle and others describe it as a hum. I can teach you more about that too. I certainly understand why you would want to know."

"So, as far as you could tell that was just a brazen bird. Not a bad omen or anything?"

"Just a bird. I don't believe in omens. The wildlife around here may have learned to trust people if tourists have fed them."

"Ah, you're right. It was really cool though!"

"Absolutely. Want to walk some more?"

"Sure. This is so incredible, I want to take in as much as I can, while I can."

"There are some very pretty places in Africa too. I hope to give you an opportunity to see some of those."

"I can't be expected to study all of the time, right?" I smiled up at him. I enjoyed how easy and natural our conversations were.

He chuckled. "Don't worry. You'll have weekends off like you would here. Lia teaches her business courses Monday through Friday."

"Is that what she does through *Empowered to Educate?*"

"Yes. We spoke briefly with the Genevieve's parents, the Howes, about what kind of education you would need to pass a GED in the states. Lia can teach you even more useful skills. If you want to support yourself when you turn eighteen, you should be able to."

I was thrilled to hear that. We wandered through the park checking out the view from all different angles, until we decided it was time to go. When we returned to the car, my father presented me with a wrapped gift.

"What's this?"

"Open it."

As I pulled off the ribbon and peeled back the paper he said. "It's a satellite phone. You can reach me easily, even where there are no cell towers, and you can talk to your friends from anywhere in the world."

"Wow. This is incredible. Thank you!" I threw my arms around his neck and he lifted me off the ground as he hugged me. I realized there was a disparity in our height, but I was still growing. Now that I knew my dad was around six feet or so, I could probably look forward to growing a few inches taller.

I was anxious to see Genevieve and wanted them to know that we were on our way, so I asked, "Can I call locally on this? Can I call Genevieve at the spa?"

He laughed. "Yes. You can call anyone anywhere on earth. I have Hilary's phone number right here." He pulled a piece of paper out of his pocket, then said, "Wait a minute. Let me make a copy." He took that piece of paper, folded it in half, and suddenly the phone number appeared on both halves. He tore it into two pieces and handed one to me, then put the other one back into his pocket.

"Wow! That looked like some kind of David Blaine trick. Do you know who I mean?"

"Yeah, those illusionists are pretty good, but real magic is no illusion. Go ahead, give Hilary a call and let her know we're coming."

"When should I say we'll be there?"

He glanced around and seeing no one, he said, "Ask her how far it is from here."

"Are we going to drive or…"

He laughed. "I can take you and your backpack the express route, if we can find a group of trees big enough to hide behind, and then I'll come back for the car and drive to the airport. We can say our

Goodbyes as soon as I get you to the spa. How does that sound?"

"That sounds awesome. Let's call her and ask if she's ready for me."

* * *

"She's here! She's here!"

Genevieve's boyfriend, Logan, spotted me first as I hiked down the slope leading to the employees cabins. Genevieve looked up from a vegetable garden she had been weeding. As soon as she saw me she leaped to her feet, shouted "Jenika!" and ran toward me.

I ran to meet her halfway. I was able to hug her easily, but she had to contend with my huge backpack. That didn't stop her. She did her best to incorporate it into our long awaited hug.

When we released each other, Logan, who was filthy and smelled like horse dung, came up to us and said, "I'd hug you too, but I was mucking out the horse stalls to bring my girl some manure for her garden." He gave Genevieve a careful peck on the lips. "I'm actually the spa's pool boy, so this…" He swept his hand down the front of his t-shirt, "is unusual."

Genevieve grabbed my hand and said, "Let's go see my aunt and sister."

She led me to a nearby cabin and opened the door wide. It looked a lot bigger on the inside than it did from the outside. I felt the tingle of magic—whether from the building or its occupants, I couldn't tell. I dumped my heavy backpack next to the door.

As Hilary and Tawania were getting to their feet, a cute little black and white kitty came over and sniffed me. I crouched down to pat the cat.

"Oreo? That's the name of your familiar, right Genevieve?"

"Absolutely, and yours is Star, right?"

"Yes. She's with my dad and has to go through some kind of quarantine before they allow her to stay in Ghana. But I know she's healthy and will be fine. I've missed her a lot though. And she probably misses me. I've been all over the place."

"I know what you mean," Genevieve said.

By then Hilary and Tawania were waiting to give me hugs. I felt so much warmth and care enveloping me already.

After I was thoroughly squeezed, Hilary stood back, still gripping my upper arms. "Welcome, Jenika. We're so happy you're able to visit us here." Then she kissed me on both cheeks.

"You and me both," I said, and chuckled, remembering what it took to get here.

"I'm afraid were going to have to find another place for you to sleep, because this cabin is crowded already. I have a friend who's willing to take you in and if you two hit it off and you decide to stay, she'll let you have her spare room for part of the rent."

I grinned. "Thank you. I can't tell you how much that means to me, but I'll be going to Africa with my dad. He's setting up everything for my schooling now."

Hilary chuckled. "That's great! Just know that while you're here, you will be earning your own way along with the girls. That's how we do things. You either pay or work off room and board."

"Don't worry," Genevieve said. "The work is easy."

"How long have you been out of Haven?" Hilary asked.

"It's only been a few days, but it seems longer. I went home and told my stepfather I would be leaving permanently. Packed all my things. And my father and I made plans for Africa even before then. Even your brother and sister-in-law are involved, Hilary! They're going to put together some type of curriculum so I can graduate, and then get a business education after that. I'm really looking forward to it."

At that point Tawania stepped in and said, "Is my aunt the only one who gets a hug from you?"

"Oh! Of course not. You were kind enough to visit me in solitary, even though we'd never met. I'm happy to see you too!" Tawania copied the long warm hug that Hilary had given me.

Genevieve slapped herself upside the head. "I'm so

sorry, I should've introduced you. I guess I was distracted and forgot you two had only met briefly."

I giggled. "It's okay. I figured out who she was as soon as I saw her."

Logan put his arm around Genevieve and said, "Yeah, now that Tawania has packed on a few pounds and almost weighs the same as Genevieve, I have to be careful and make sure I'm dating the right twin."

Genevieve elbowed him in the ribs, and he laughed.

"I can't wait to show you around," she said to me. "This place is awesome. The guests get all the good stuff first, of course, but we have our fun too — like swimming in the moonlight. After everyone is asleep Logan lets us into the pool after hours because he gets up early and cleans it, so he has the key."

"Or if it's raining and guests don't want to get wet..." he added, rolling his eyes. "Go figure."

"By the way, how's Alien doing?" Genevieve asked.

I groaned. "She's getting in trouble more often than not. I hate to say it, but I don't think she's going to make it out of Haven until she ages out. She doesn't seem to be learning her lessons at all, and her father has given up trying to get her out."

I told them about the vodka fountain and how she stuck her whole face in there and drank as much as possible, before the teachers discovered and got rid of it.

"Oh my Goddess..." Genevieve laughed. "I can just

picture Francine's perfectly styled blonde hair dripping with vodka."

"Well, it's awfully dark at the roots now. It's hard to keep up a drastic dye job in juvie."

"So, what do you do here?" I asked

"Tawania and I work part time in the laundry, but other than that we're students. I'm learning massage, and I give massages to the other employees. Everybody's happy to let me practice on them. The rest of the time I study anatomy and physiology online from a local college. I can go down to the campus and take tests when I need to. Between that and home schooling I'm getting all A's!"

"That sounds like fun," I said.

"It is. Maybe when you graduate, you can do that with me and attend the same college. Aunt Hilary is getting more into acupuncture, so they could use another massage therapist."

I glanced at Tawania. "Wouldn't your sister rather do something like massage with you?"

Tawania wrinkled her nose. "No. I don't want to work with the guests directly. Besides, I have a much longer way to go to get my diploma. Right now I'm helping in the laundry too. People mistake us for each other often enough that I can take a shift for Genevieve and nobody notices, but eventually I'd like to become a chef."

"Oh! That sounds like fun too." I remembered then

that Genevieve had told me about Tawania living alone in caves and hunting or fishing for food, after her adoptive parents died. The twins hadn't even known about each other for years. According to Genevieve, she had already come a long way. From the smile on Tawania's face, and the peace in her heart, I could tell that was true.

Hilary said, "Let me take you to my friend's cabin and introduce you to her, Jenika. That way you can drop off your backpack or suitcases or whatever you came with."

"Everything I have is right here in my backpack." I heaved it on, then swiveled to show the large hiker's pack full to bursting. "It was a gift from my boyfriend, in case I wanted to run away."

"Boyfriend?" Genevieve exclaimed. "Do tell…"

"First, let me take her to Gwen's place, so she can take that huge load off her shoulders. It looks pretty heavy." Hilary opened the door and left with me.

Gwen, the woman who was letting me crash with her, was sweet and held my hand with both of hers. I'm afraid my cabin is pretty small, but my couch opens out into a bed, and you're welcome to it for as long as you want."

"That's really kind of you. But I'll only be staying for a few days to a week. I'm just excited that I get the chance to visit with the Howes for a while before I leave for Africa."

Gwen's eyebrows shot up. "Africa? How exciting!"

I chuckled. "Yeah, I can't wait. I think it's going to be pretty awesome."

After I stowed my backpack beside the couch and said goodbye to Gwen, I traipsed back to Hilary's cabin. When we opened the door, Genevieve and Logan were kissing. They jumped away from each other.

"That happens a lot around here." Hilary said. "You'll get used to it."

Genevieve grinned. "Yeah, when your boyfriend smells like horse-shit and you still can't keep your hands off of him, it must be love."

Everyone laughed. Logan swept a few strands of Genevieve's hair behind her ear. "You know I was thinking…"

"Oh no, that can't be good," Genevieve teased.

He laughed again. "No, it's fine. I was thinking about the future. You and me and living here. It seems like taking classes online and going down to the school for the tests is working out pretty well for you. I was thinking about doing the same thing."

Genevieve looked shocked.

He quickly added, "I mean… I don't want to intrude if you're just waiting for me to get out of your hair."

She laughed. "I love you in my hair, and in my house, and in my life. Are you sure that's enough for you? You won't miss campus shenanigans and all that?"

He chuckled. "No, I won't miss all that. I think a lot of college kids are just getting drunk and acting like idiots. I'd rather spend my time actually learning something."

They whispered a few things to each other and shared a little private joke, then laughed. Something about studying library science and how nobody could get in trouble in a library…

I was just so happy to see her wide smile. She was obviously giddy in love, and it seemed like the feeling was mutual.

I was a little nervous that I might be intruding. Logan excused himself to go take a shower and Genevieve held her nose and waved her hand in front of it, saying nasally, "Oh, yeah. That's a great idea."

He didn't seem offended. He just grinned at her over his shoulder. "It's good to see you again, Jenika. I look forward to hearing more about what's happening at Haven."

"Are you sure I'm not intruding?" I asked Genevieve after the screen door banged shut.

"Not at all. I'm happy you're here! It's a nice surprise. I didn't always have good surprises, but now most of them are great. Like you calling a couple days ago to ask if you could come for a visit. I feel very blessed. Aunt Hilary is still helping me gain control over my powers and I haven't messed up in weeks!"

"How is she doing with her powers? I thought she screwed up a joy spell."

"Oh, yeah. That was an anomaly. I haven't seen her make a mistake like that before or since. It's good to know she's human though."

We hugged again, and I was happier than I had been in a long, long time. I felt safe, wanted, and loved. What more could I ask for?

The answer is nothing. Not a darn thing. Not emancipation, not hanging my classmates upside down by their toes. Nothing. I had everything I ever wanted, plus a lot more to look forward to.

"HE'S NOT COMING…" I PLOPPED DOWN ON ONE END OF Lia's outdoor picnic table, ready to pout.

My dad squeezed my shoulder. "He's coming. He said he would."

"Don't worry, Jen," Genevieve said. "He'll be here. He wouldn't miss this for the world."

"I can't help worrying that something must have happened to him. Patrick is always so reliable. If he said he would be here and isn't…"

"Sorry I'm late!" Patrick called out, as he jogged down the dirt driveway and met us in the back yard.

I jumped up. "What happened?"

He gave me a kiss on the cheek and grinned. "Do you know how far it is from the United States to the West Coast of Africa?"

"Yeah. It's a little over six thousand miles. Was your plane delayed?"

"What plane? I traveled here via witchy airlines. I was exhausted and had to take a break in the Azores."

My jaw dropped. "You tried to transport here? By yourself?"

He gave me an embarrassed grin. "I may have bitten off more than I could chew. Hey, speaking of which… What do you call cheese that isn't yours?"

"Oh no… Go ahead, tell me."

"Nacho cheese."

Everyone around the table groaned. And by everyone I mean, my father and his girlfriend Lia, Genevieve and her twin Tawania, Hilary Howe and Genevieve's boyfriend, Logan.

Logan said, "Well, now that the entertainment is here, it's finally time for your party."

"Something smells delicious! What are we having?" Patrick asked.

"We're having a multicultural cookout. With both American and African foods," I said. "You're probably smelling the barbequed chicken."

Lia held her hand out to my dad and said, "Can you help me bring out the fufu and kontomire soup?"

Hilary jumped up and said, "I'll help."

"Thank you," Lia said. "You were already a big help making the fufu."

"No worries. It was fun-fun."

Lia giggled as she disappeared into the house. She had a cute laugh.

"What's kontomire soup?" Logan asked.

"It's a delicious Ghanaian soup made from cocoyam leaves, smoked fish, mushrooms and snails," I said with authority, since I cooked it.

"Snails, huh?" I think Genevieve was about to wrinkle her nose but caught herself. She just lifted her eyebrows and said, "Mmmm…"

"Hey, why do the French eat snails?" Patrick asked.

"I don't know," Tawania answered, not realizing another joke was coming.

"Because they don't like fast food."

I laughed and elbowed him in the ribs. "Enough jokes for now, okay?"

"Okay." He grinned and took my hand, then kissed my knuckles. Whenever he touched me I melted a little bit, and it wasn't because of the African heat.

Hilary brought out some vegetarian dish she had made. It looked like hamburgers, but was made with beans. She had decided she was going to try to be a vegetarian for a while, or maybe forever…she hadn't made up her mind yet.

Patrick pulled something out of his pants pocket. It was a small wrapped package and he set it in front of me. "Don't get too excited. I made it myself."

"Well, because you made it yourself, I'm even more excited." I tore off the ribbon and paper.

"I knew you had a little girl's necklace that you

wore as an anklet, so I brought you a charm to hang from it."

In my hand, I found a little gold heart.

"You made this?"

"Okay, I may have exaggerated a bit. I bought the charm, but look, I put our initials on it."

I turned the little heart over and sure enough there was PH plus JJ. "I love it. Thank you." I leaned over and gave him a proper kiss.

"I'm sorry it's not a big expensive bracelet or something, but it's all this poor college student could afford."

My dad came out with the rest of the meal on a large tray. "And what are you studying, Patrick?"

"Environmental Science."

"Sounds great," Dad said.

"It is. I'm really hoping to use my degree for the good of all."

With the food on the table. We began passing plates and silverware, platters and bowls.

"So, how are your studies going?" Hilary asked me.

I grinned at Lia across the table and said, "I graduated! I've taken a lot of business courses and now I'm taking a few college courses and majoring in business management. I hope to learn about imports and exports."

"Interesting," Hilary said. "What do you plan to do with all that knowledge?"

"I want to bring the beauty of African culture to

America. I love my heritage, and I'm excited to share it. What I would ideally like to do someday is to open a gallery. Someplace where I can sell African artists' works and make sure they get a fair, no…a *generous* wage for their hard work."

"That's awesome," Patrick said. "Maybe I could help."

"That's sweet, but you're not exactly 'on brand'. This idea was supposed to empower African women."

"Don't feel bad, Patrick. I'm not on brand either," Dad said. "About your gallery, Jen, That all sounds great, but where would you open it? Someplace like New York would be very expensive."

"But Detroit wouldn't be," I said. I let that thought settle in while I took a bite of my veggie burger. To my relief, it wasn't bad at all…

Patrick gave me a smile and bumped my shoulder accidentally on purpose. "That would mean you could live close to me and my mom."

My father was sitting across from me next to Lia. "I'm proud of you, honey. You've really found your direction. I'll do whatever I can to help."

"You've already done more than I could have asked, by teaching me to use my powers properly."

"That reminds me," Tawania said, "I think Genevieve and I have mastered our powers too." She looked to Hilary for confirmation. Hilary had just taken a big bite of chicken, but nodded enthusiastically.

"I thought you were vegetarian," I said.

"Maybe tomorrow. This is so good!"

Genevieve glanced around and whispered to me, "Everyone here is aware of magic? Right?"

She didn't know Lia, so she probably had to double check. "Yeah, you're safe," I said.

Genevieve grinned and said, "Watch this…"

She held her hands over a blank spot in the middle of the table and with one quick clap she created a birthday cake.

"Hey!" Tawania said. "I was going to bake the cake."

"Oh, sorry," Genevieve shrugged. "But you're a chef and you do this every day. I thought you might like a break."

"Okay, I guess I forgive you." Tawania said to her twin. "But I get to give her our present."

"Present? You guys didn't need to get me gifts. Just coming here and being with me is a huge gift."

"It's kind of a serious and silly gift at the same time. I hope you won't take offense. Genevieve said you wouldn't."

"Okay, let's see then." I held out my hand and waited for something to appear. Knowing these girls they were ready to magically pop it into my possession.

Sure enough, a scroll appeared in my hand. I removed the string holding it closed and unrolled it. "An emancipation document! Are you kidding me? I'm 18 now. I'm automatically an adult."

The girls tittered. "We thought it might be fun just to tease you a bit," Genevieve said.

Tawania quickly added, "Are you offended?"

"Not in the least. In fact, it is kind of funny. I have to say, my teacher, Ms. Broome, was right. I wasn't ready for this at 15. But I think I am now." I glanced over at my dad.

He swallowed his bite of fufu and said, "As someone who witnessed your actual birth eighteen years ago today, I officially pronounce you an adult. As your dad, I'm delighted to call you an independent, responsible, wonderful daughter."

Everyone laughed.

"Does this mean I have to start paying rent?" I teased.

"Only if you open a shop or gallery in the states," he said. "You'll have to pay rent on the space."

"I'd like that. I can start off small with online sales only. Then work up to a shop. Whatever I make, I want to give a percentage to *Empowered to Educate.*"

Lia clapped her hands and looked pleased. "That would be wonderful. We could definitely use the money to fund more fellowships and educate more girls."

"I can't thank you enough for the education you offered me," I said. Looking at the others, I added, "She taught me so much. She put me right in her classes with the other girls. Now, we all know our worth and won't be taken advantage of."

Patrick bumped my shoulder and said, "Look at that. It's all coming together, nicely. So where are you going to live when you're back in Michigan?"

I shrugged. "I don't know yet. I'll find a place."

"You could live with us in Ann Arbor. Now that my mother and I bought a house, there's plenty of room for you too."

I remembered how he'd said he wished their little two-bedroom apartment over the garage was big enough to let me stay there. I was happy when I heard they'd bought a four bedroom house with an attached garage in Ann Arbor.

"Hey, I made a webpage for my mom to sell her artsy stuff online. Let me show you." He whipped out his phone, looked at the screen and said, "This isn't big enough. I want you to see a good example." He stretched the phone until it became an iPad.

We all laughed. Then he brought up a page with his mother's beachy crafts. Everybody ooed and ahhed as they passed the iPad around.

"Those are beautiful photos," my dad said. "Jenika, I think you could let him help behind the scenes, couldn't you?"

"I think I could make an exception." I bumped Patrick with my shoulder and we grinned at each other. "I just want to say one thing." I figured this little speech of mine would require standing to give it the gravitas it deserved, so I pulled myself up from the picnic bench and walked around to the head of it.

"I just want to say I love you all. Every single person around this table has added to my life in incredible, unbelievable ways. I can't thank you enough. All I can do is continue to make you proud."

"We love you too, honey." My dad said.

He put us arm me and Lia swooped in on my other side, putting her arm around my waist. "Yes, we do," she said.

I reflected on what a different stepmother I had now, versus the stepfather I used to have. Lia was loving, caring, smart and giving. *Empowered to Educate* was making good use of her teaching gifts... and so was I. Ms. Broome would be delighted to hear about my bright future.

The end

A NOTE FROM E.B. LOROW

Everything else in this book is made up, but Empowered to Educate is real! It's headquartered in Boston and I'm pleased to brag that my cousin Constance Kane is the founder and CEO of this incredible organization. It's all about women helping each other to succeed. If you'd like to learn more about it, here's their website. https://www.empoweredtoeducate.org/